THE
MALEVOLENT
ISLE

Murder, Magic and Mystery:
Yorkshire 1660

A LUKE TREMAYNE ADVENTURE

THE MALEVOLENT ISLE

Murder, Magic and Mystery:
Yorkshire 1660

GEOFF QUAIFE

ARPress
ILLUMINATING IDEAS.
EMPOWERING VOICES

ARPress
45 Dan Road Suite 5
Canton, MA 02021

Hotline: 1(888) 821-0229
Fax: 1(508) 545-7580

Ordering Information:

Quantity sales. Special discounts are available on quantity purchases by corporations, associations, and others. For details, contact the publisher at the address above.

Printed in the United States of America.

ISBN-13:   Softcover   979-8-89389-313-7
                eBook   979-8-89389-312-0

Library of Congress Control Number: 2024916231

The Luke Tremayne Adventures

(In chronological order of the events portrayed)

1648-9	The Irish Fiasco
1650	Chesapeake Chaos
1651	The Black Thistle
1652	The Angelic Assassin
1653	The Frown of Fortune
1654-5	The Spanish Relation
1656	The Dark Corners
1657	The Garden of Deceit
1657	Lady Mary's Revenge
1657-8	Murder in the Maghreb
1658	A Queen Besieged
1659	The Dale of Despair
1660	The Malevolent Isle

Characters

Luke's Men

Sir Luke Tremayne — Special agent for the incoming King
Sir Mark Cowper (Lt. Col.) — His deputy, former Royalist courtier
Sir Evan Williams — Governor of York Castle
Peter Hutton (Captain) — Commander of frigate, *Deadly Arrow*
Philip Bates (Lieutenant) — His deputy

The Islanders

Felix Bohm, Marquess of Nith — Astrologer, magician, cleric and physician
Jane Bohm, Marchioness of Nith — His second wife
Michael, Baron Bohm — Felix's eldest son and heir
Alice, Baroness Bohm — Michael's wife
Ralph Bohm esquire — Felix's youngest son, a lawyer
Felicity Bohm — Ralph's wife, widow of a French count
Margaret Bohm — Widow of Harry Bohm
William Perry — the Baron's secretary/ Catholic priest
James Denholm — Felix's steward
Isabel Denholm — James's wife
George Denholm — James' son, gamekeeper
Tobias (Toby) Bentley — Felix's valet and factotum
Ann Bentley — Tobias's promiscuous wife
Ellen Bentley — Ann's daughter

Richard & Mary Banks	Servants to Tobias, Ann and later Ellen
John Corby	Constable and churchwarden
Hannah Corby	John's wife
Vincent Keddy	Corby's assistant, bailiff
Ursula Keddy	Vincent's wife
Thomas (Tom) Kitchin	Corby's assistant
Samuel Kitchin	Tom's father, island blacksmith
Martin Moore	Defrocked Anglican rector, uncle to Ann, Hannah and Isabel

Referred To

Henry (Harry) Bohm, esquire	Michael's twin brother, deceased.
Peregrine Neale	Previous Marquess of Nith
Jerome Tighe	A disappearing islander

Real Historical Characters

Charles II	King of England
Oliver Cromwell	deceased Lord Protector
George Monk, Duke of Albemarle	Commander-in-chief of the English army for both Republic and King
James, Duke of York	Brother of the King, his heir, and naval commander

1

An exceptionally cold winter penetrated the dales and moors, as Luke and Matilda awaited the birth of their first child—and England prepared to welcome the restored monarchy. George Monk assumed control of the English army in the last days of the republic, axed the parliament and called for new elections. These resulted in a Royalist majority, and the inevitable invitation for Charles Stuart to return as King Charles II.

Luke, a staunch supporter of the Parliament and Oliver Cromwell took no part in the last desperate attempts to save the Republic. His friend and ally, Sir Evan Williams, the Governor of York Castle, and commander of the republican government's forces in the north had already placed his men under the command of Monk, and thereby in the imminent service of the incoming King.

Monk, pending the arrival of the monarch ordered all magistrates, including dedicated republicans like Luke, to stay in their current positions until the King issued new lists after his arrival in England.

Luke faced a personal dilemma. After fifteen years of service to Oliver Cromwell, who was initially his company commander, then his commanding general, and finally for five years the Lord Protector of England, Scotland and Ireland, would he be able to adjust to the return of the monarchy?

He had met the young Charles Stuart on two of his missions for the English Republic, and was favorably impressed by the young man, especially when compared with his late father. Only six months earlier he had received a letter from the young King in exile, to arrange a meeting between a royal envoy, and the then leaders of the republican government.

Luke's future was dangerously uncertain. Would a vindictive Royalist Parliament order the arrest of leading republicans and Cromwellians? As the former head of military intelligence for the English Republic, he was an obvious target for monarchists seeking revenge. Many of his acts in the service of the Republic could justify his summary execution.

He need not have worried. Charles Stuart had not forgotten that Luke had saved his life in Scotland nine years earlier. The man about to be proclaimed King of England was very anxious to acquire the services of Cromwell's most effective agent for his own administration. As the late January chill deepened, and the snow impeded travel in the dales and moors, Luke was surprised by the arrival of three horsemen at his home at Abbey Grange. As they removed their heavy outer garments in the reception hall, Luke was delighted to recognize his friend, the Governor of York Castle, Sir Evan Williams.

"Welcome Evan! What is so urgent that you have made this trip in such outrageous weather?"

"When my current commander-in-chief, General Monk, and the man soon to be proclaimed King, issue an order, who am I to ignore it? I received orders from Monk, and this sealed letter addressed to Sir Luke Tremayne of Abbey Grange, Yorkshire. The letter was to be delivered by me personally, and its nature and source not made known to anybody. The seal is that of Charles Stuart."

"Come into the library while I read the letter. Your companions can stay here in front of this raging fire. I will have food and drink brought to them." Evan followed Luke into his library, and while the former warmed himself in front of a much smaller fire, Luke read the letter.

It indicated that when he was proclaimed King, Charles would offer Luke a similar position to that which he occupied under the Commonwealth and Protectorate—head of a special intelligence unit which would be directly responsible to the head of state.

In the interim there was an urgent mission that he would like Luke to complete. It was to save the life of a man revered by both his own late father Charles I, and by Luke's late commander, The Lord Protector.

Luke did not miss the not too subtle attempt to portray this first mission for the King, as something he could have been asked to do by the late Lord Protector. The incoming King was no fool.

Luke relayed the gist of the letter to Evan who asked the identity of the man he was to save.

"Felix, Marquess of Nith. I have never heard of him. Do you have another letter? The King indicates that I will receive all the details at the same time as I receive this letter."

"It now becomes clear. I have no other letter, but one of my companions who is warming himself in your reception room, and undoubtedly wolfing into the food you have provided, is a Royalist officer, who until very recently was on the continent at the King's court-in- exile. He is a local Yorkshireman, Sir Mark Cowper. He must be carrying the second letter."

"Call him in."

Evan left the room and almost immediately returned with a youngish man with long black hair and short beard that imitated that of the late King. Luke welcomed him, and slightly embellished his comments. "Sir Mark, I understand from this letter of His Majesty that should I accept the assignment offered, you will provide me with further details—and act as my deputy."

"His Majesty did not mention my role as your deputy. I was told to ensure that his letter reached you as soon as possible, and if the time was still available, to meet two men in Whitby who would give us all the details we needed, and provide the transport necessary to reach this mysterious isle of Nith somewhere in the North Sea—hopefully not far off the Yorkshire coast!"

"Who are these men?"

Mark withdrew a sheet of folded paper from his doublet on which he had scribbled a few notes and replied, "Tobias Bentley, a valet of the Marquess, and John Corby the constable of the island parish. They will be in the snug of the recently renamed Three Crowns until the end of the first week in February between four and six in the afternoon."

Four days later Luke, Mark, John and Tobias were seated in the snug of the Three Crowns enjoying the black licorice flavored Whitby ale. Luke asked Tobias, "What do you do for the Marquess?" Tobias replied very slowly, as if by rote, "I have been his personal valet for decades. I serve the person of the Marquess but have no role in the running of the estate, or any of his scientific, religious or business activities."

"I have spent most of my life in Yorkshire and was only aware that Nith existed when I was sent on this assignment. Why would the King send Sir Luke and I to a forgotten island to assist a nonentity?" asked Mark undiplomatically.

Luke smiled to himself. Perhaps this Royalist courtier was not the milksop Luke's prejudices had expected. He might make an admirable deputy.

"You may remember our master by the name he went by before he inherited the marquisate from a distant cousin. He was Doctor Felix Bohm, clergyman, physician, alchemist, astrologer and magician. Some would add showman and charlatan. He was apprenticed to the aging Dr. John Dee as a child, and in the thirties was very popular at the court of Charles I, at the University of Cambridge, and on the London stage," John explained.

"What side did he take in our recent civil wars?" asked Luke, anxious to assess the man's political loyalties.

"The outbreak of hostilities coincided with his acquisition of the marquisate, and he withdrew to the island. He has not left it since his arrival in 1642. Neither he nor any of the islanders that remained on Nith took any part in the conflict. But he continued correspondence with King Charles I and in recent times with the new King. He was also occasionally consulted by Oliver Cromwell, when he was Lord Protector," answered John.

"On what matters? Ill health, future predictions or turning base metals into gold," asked Mark somewhat flippantly.

"In his early days he was renowned as a physician, but since he has been on Nith he has dabbled more in the supernatural and on giving people advice regarding their future. All of this for people outside the island has been done by letter as Felix and most of the islanders never leave Nith. His sons, myself and the steward, James Denholm are the exceptions. Visitors are not encouraged, although over the years several newcomers have accidently reached Nith and have been allowed to stay by a very tolerant Marquess. This includes a number of Quakers whose pernicious ideas have poisoned the minds of some of the islanders. The most recent uninvited guests were two representatives of the King who appeared unannounced at the end of last year. Your assignment is a consequence of whatever went on then between the Marquess, and the King's men," said John.

"Who were they and why did they come?" asked Luke.

"Apparently the new King, remembering Bohm's friendship with his father asked Nicholas, Lord Ashcroft, who had been on a mission into then republican England, to visit us on his way back to the continent. The stated reason was to obtain a horoscope on the chances of young Charles returning to the throne, and on the success of his subsequent reign. While discussing this the Marquess remarked that Ashcroft's timing was fortunate because his own days were numbered. The tarot cards had revealed that he would die on the very day the new King was crowned, and the stars had confirmed it would be at the hands of a woman from his past."

"Well that should be easy to prevent. I have never known a murderer to alert his victim to the exact day of his demise," announced the skeptical Mark.

"Who said he would be murdered?" replied Toby who had remained silent while John answered the questions that had been put to them.

"What are you suggesting? Some supernatural occurrence?" Luke probed.

"The master is an astrologer and magician. Death is an elusive phenomenon. It will be contrived magically!" was Toby's surprising comment.

"Your island sounds a mysterious and intriguing place. Few mainlanders know of its existence," commented Mark, attempting to bring the discussion down to earth.

"For two decades his lordship has deliberately created such an impression of the island. It is perfectly located to remain concealed. The fishing fleet of Whitby sails much further to the north, and that of Scarborough to the south. The island is too far off the coast to be seen regularly by the coastal traders. Much of the time it is clouded in fog, and its waters are reputedly bereft of fish. This is a falsehood put abroad to discourage fishermen from the mainland for the benefit of the islanders. Those who venture towards the island are also discouraged by a volley of musket fire," admitted John.

"I still doubt that to save a mysterious magician from an imagined fate is sufficient justification for this mission as there are dozens of more vital issues confronting the King that we should be investigating," declared an increasingly unconvinced Mark.

"Lord Ashcroft spent a lot of time in the chamber where the master conducts his scientific experiments. Maybe the Marquess convinced his visitor that he could turn base metals into gold, and the new King would be loath to lose such a valuable resource—but you would know more of the King's motives than I," added John with a hint of sarcasm.

"I was never briefed by the King on that issue, but I gained the impression that our assignment was designed to make things easier for him on his return to England. Our success was to lead to a more harmonious reconciliation of the opposing forces of the last two decades. How trivial events on this forgotten island could possibly help in this regard is currently beyond me," concluded Mark.

"Yes, how an aging academic, living in glorious isolation could have any significant effect on the county or nation at large also baffles me," added Luke.

"There must be a hidden agenda of which we are both ignorant," he whispered to Mark.

"Perhaps, but the young King is very sentimental. There may have been something regarding Felix Bohm that the lad's father expected his son to continue to implement," added Mark modifying his skeptical approach.

Luke turned to John and asked, "Is the Marquess wealthy? Nith Island cannot be the source of any great wealth?"

"Nith Island cannot sustain itself, and the Marquess sends a boat under the steward's supervision weekly to Whitby or Scarborough for supplies, but in my time with him he has never been short of money. He is a very wealthy man. His lordship explains this by claiming he transforms base metals into gold, but the income is actually derived from the many properties on the mainland owned or rented by the Marquess, which his sons have added to over the years. He owns a large part of expanding London, the exploitation of which provides the major source of the family's income."

Toby was annoyed by John's comment and replied with some passion, "But he does turn other metals into gold. I have seen him do it."

Luke was about to denigrate Tobias's last comment but picked up on the now more diplomatic approach of his comrade, Mark who enthusiastically exclaimed, "That I cannot wait to see."

“When do we leave for Nith Island?” Luke asked.

“Tomorrow, on a fishing vessel that I have hired. Toby will accompany you. Normally the Marquess's skiff, under my control, would take you there, but I have to continue on to Scarborough this evening, before returning to the island late tomorrow,” replied Corby.

“Won't such a fishing vessel be driven away by the islanders?” asked an apprehensive Mark.

“Normally yes, but they have been alerted that Toby will return on the *Maid of Malton* with two special agents of the King. He is to fire two shots in rapid succession and stand on the deck waving his arms so that the lookouts will recognize him and allow you to land. You may need to remind him of this as you approach the island. Meet Toby at daybreak where the local fishing trawlers are moored!” said John abruptly ending the discussion.

John and Toby hastily withdrew, and Mark and Luke after a few more pints of Whitby ale retired to their bedchamber. A worried Luke commented, “Are we about to join a community of ignorant superstitious peasants who actually believe that their Marquess can turn base metals into gold?”

“Of more concern to me is the thought that the King might also believe such a claim, and we are being sent to protect a potential asset for His Majesty's later exploitation?” Mark uttered quietly.

Luke was surprised and pleased by Mark's cynicism.

The *Maid of Malton* left Whitby just after dawn, and in relatively light seas and a favorable wind, eventually came in sight of Nith Island. Its captain, who given the color of his hair, was simply referred to as Red, had maintained a constant banter with Toby throughout the voyage. Its subject matter involved the mythical creatures that various fishermen had reported seeing from a discreet distance as they sailed past the island. Did the fishermen really believe the island was populated by dragons, giant wolves and unicorns, and its surrounding seas dominated by enormous fish and trawler-devouring monsters? thought the mildly amused Luke.

He was not surprised that Toby, whom Luke had assessed as simple, did nothing to dissuade the captain from such beliefs. Luke was tempted to join the banter and denounce such alleged sightings as at best an illusion, when Mark probed Red further on the local lore regarding the island.

He replied in surprising detail. "Sir, over the centuries people have seen dinosaurs, dragons, unicorns and giant birds roaming along the cliff tops—and strange sea creatures have been caught in our nets. Nith is ruled by a magician who can conjure up demons, and creatures from the past. There may be a monster hiding under the sea at this very moment ready to swallow us up. The current marquess turns lead into gold and directs his magic against anybody who crosses him. You gentlemen must be very important to be invited to this malevolent isle. Let's hope we are not shot to pieces as we approach the shoreline?"

"If you have such a view of the island and the potential danger to your boat, why did you agreed to carry us here?" asked the inherently cynical Mark.

"The Marquess pays well, and in gold—and it is not wise to offend him or his servants. Too many people who have pried too closely into events on the island have disappeared, or become inexplicably ill, and subsequently died. Nevertheless, I will not to sail too close to the island. As soon as the islanders become aware of our arrival, they will row out to collect you."

As the *Maid of Malton* approached the island everything went as planned. Toby without prompting moved to the prow of the trawler and waved his arms towards the shore and fired two shots. Almost immediately a small rowing boat was launched from the island and headed towards the slowing trawler. Then the unexpected happened.

Another shot was heard.

Tobias fell backwards, hitting his head with a sickening thud on the deck.

Red was aghast. "I knew it. I knew it. We will be next," he muttered as he ordered his helmsman to steer the boat rapidly further offshore out of range of the marksman—and further away from the straining oarsmen.

Luke bent over the unconscious Toby. He eventually commented to Mark, "There is not much blood. The wound to his face seems superficial, but the heavy fall backwards has rendered him unconscious. The knock may have done no harm, or at the other extreme rendered him into a cabbage. We will have to await until he regains consciousness."

"If he ever does. I saw many head injuries during the hostilities and the victims often remained in a permanent coma," remarked a pessimistic Mark.

Luke turned to Red, "Those rowers will not be too happy with you moving further out to sea. It's getting quite choppy for those in the small boat."

"They have themselves to blame. Frankly if I were you, I would stay aboard *The Maid*. That shot may have been meant for one of you or me. Nith is an evil island. I have a mind to throw Toby overboard for them to pick up. My crew is on edge. If I don't leave soon, I will face a mutiny."

Eventually the rowers reached the trawler, and assailed Red regarding his relocation further out to sea. The complainant who introduced himself as Vincent Keddy, assistant constable of the parish and bailiff to the Marquess, was shocked to hear that Toby had been shot.

He explained, "We heard a shot as we rowed out, but assumed that it was someone shooting rabbits on the island. Is Toby badly wounded?"

"He has a flesh wound to the face, but he fell backwards and hit his head severely on the deck. He is still unconscious. We will lower his body down to you first, and then the two officers will follow," announced Red, anxious to be well away from the island as quickly as possible.

As the small boat approached the shore, Luke could not conceal his curiosity. "Mr Keddy do you have to row to the other side of the island to land. There appears to be nothing but towering cliffs in front of us?"

"There is nothing but precipitous cliffs around the whole island. That is why in past centuries it proved difficult to capture. When the Danes were expelled from England six hundred years ago, they remained on this island undisturbed for another century. Even William the Conqueror recognized the futility of trying to conquer Nith Island."

"Then how do you land us, and your regular supplies?" asked Mark.

"It is done at low tide, when the entrance to a large cave becomes visible. You can see the opening now."

The boat entered the cave where several men were waiting. Keddy organized them to carry Toby's inert body. They all then moved deeper into the cave, climbing as they went. After fifteen minutes of ascending through a number of interconnected caves, they emerged into the sunlight.

They were in the high street of a village and passed a number of houses—a blacksmith's forge, a tavern and a small church. Looming above them at eastern end of the high street was a very large manor house, Nith Hall—in appearance a combination of monastery and castle. As Luke and Mark entered its extensive grounds, they became aware of the building's unique layout. It was in the shape of a cross with four two storied wings emanating from a central tower block built in Elizabethan brick.

Keddy noticed Luke's interest and commented, "Nith Hall accommodates most of the inhabitants of the island. That is why there are few houses in the village. The inhabitants of the manor are carefully segregated according to status and position. The north wing contains the family, the south wing servants of the household while the east and west wings house the other inhabitants of the island, who may or may not have small holdings elsewhere on the island."

Keddy led Luke and Mark into the north wing, and to a room that would be their accommodation while on the island. They were to meet Michael, Baron Bohm, at twelve noon in the reception hall.

"Why are we to meet the Baron, and not his father the Marquess?" asked Luke, suddenly a stickler for protocol.

"It is not the task of a simple bailiff to question the decisions of his masters. Few people have seen the Marquess in recent weeks. The island is effectively run by his son and heir, Baron Michael. Only the comatose Toby, and his wife and daughter have access to the private quarters of the Marquess. You may have to await Toby's recovery, before you gain access to that inner sanctum."

An irritated Mark reacted, "This is not a social visit dependent on the whims of the inhabitants. We act under the direct orders of the King. We need to complete our task here, and report to him as soon as he arrives in London. There is little time to waste."

Keddy appeared startled by Mark's comment and moved quickly towards the door. He hesitated, turned around and addressed Luke directly. "Sir, I am glad you are both here. I did not know whether Lord Ashcroft was suitably worried by the information that John Corby had given him that he would convince the King to send someone to prevent a catastrophe involving the death of the Marquess. The attack on Toby suggests our fears were not misplaced."

"What exactly worried Corby?" asked Mark.

"This island has not had recourse to English law and its mainland agents for nearly twenty years. As constable, John Corby is forbidden by the Marquess to refer any criminal matters to the magistrates. The Marquess in person exercises ultimate legal authority. He is the law. Until recently this was not a problem. There was little crime of a serious nature, despite or perhaps because of the Marquess's tolerance of diverse views and unconventional behavior."

"What happened recently to change that situation?" probed Luke.

"While the Marquess sees himself as a tolerant humanist, his family, except for Mr Ralph, are all Papists. This Papist wing of the family led by the Baron and aided by the steward have exercised increased authority and influence. The Baron's secretary has openly revealed himself as a Catholic priest. More than half of the islanders are Papists, even though the Marquess himself has long discarded his family's Catholic traditions. He did so as a young man to enter university, and his youngest son Ralph did the same to become a lawyer. Neither attend the services conducted by the priest in the family chapel, but the rest of the ruling family and their co-religionists do. The Baron, and the priest in their different ways have undermined the authority of the Marquess—and not acted in the common interest," proclaimed an embittered Keddy.

"I wish you had not told me about the Papist priest. As a magistrate I am obliged to have him arrested and sent for trial," commented an alarmed Luke.

"That will complicate your dealings with the Baron," added Keddy with the hint of a smile as he finally left the room.

As a large clock halfway along the long corridor struck noon the two officers entered the reception hall to be greeted by a well-built, exceedingly tall man who introduced himself as Michael, Baron Bohm, and his much smaller wiry companion as James Denholm, steward of the manor.

"Gentlemen, I hope your visit will not be a waste of time. I tried to persuade Lord Ashcroft when he was here not to take the word of my father and a few troublemakers seriously. My problem is that I was not party to what went on between them other than a cock and bull story that my father was to die at the hands of a woman on the day the King is to be crowned."

3

"Why a cock and bull story?" asked Luke.

"It is the kind of story that father has been spreading across this island since we arrived eighteen years ago. It is designed to terrify the ignorant peasants, and exalt his own magical powers," replied Michael coldly.

"Do you deny your father's magical powers?" asked a surprised Mark.

"Not completely, but father is above all a showman, and most of his magic is an illusion—a trick."

"Why should Ashcroft have ignored what appeared to be your father's genuine fears?" probed Luke.

"In recent years father has withdrawn into his laboratory. He spends all his time on experiments. He has come to believe that he can actually achieve, what in his youth, he knew were illusions. Put simply, his mind has begun to decline. He can no longer separate fact from fantasy," replied the Baron, warming to the verbal assassination of his father.

"It was no fantasy that someone on this island tried to murder the one man who has constant access to him, and who would have an up-to-date view of his actual condition. From our perspective, the attempt on Toby Bentley suggests that someone does not want us to communicate meaningfully with the Marquess, or at the least it indicates that there is something amiss on Nith, which we, as officers of the law and agents of the King, must now investigate," declared Luke forcibly.

"Who would want that simple soul Toby dead?" asked Mark.

James Denholm answered. "Gentlemen, the common folk live in awe of the magical powers of the Marquess. They are frightened by his perceived ability to direct the forces of nature for good or evil. The ignorant do not understand the nature of his magical powers and confuse it with diabolic witchcraft. It is possible that one of them saw Toby as a familiar, a demonic servant of a diabolic master."

"Why would such a feeling rise to the surface now, and not in the previous eighteen years?" asked Mark.

James looked at Michael who nodded his head in approval of what was anticipated. The steward explained, "Gentlemen, this island has a large proportion of Roman Catholics, including most of the Bohm family and myself. We Papists have been served openly in recent years by a Catholic priest trained on the continent and imbued with the Church's mission against diabolic witchcraft. The Baron's secretary, William Perry is a Catholic priest. Father Perry has tried to re-educate the islanders with the reformed ideas of the Church, which now declares that all magic, other than that performed by the church, comes from the Devil."

"So rather than attack a humanistic Marquess directly, the priest undermines his authority by associating his powers with the Devil? How can you condone this insidious attack on your own father? It is creating an environment in which some misguided islander could even see killing him as obeying God's decree to be rid of all witches," Mark angrily asked of the Baron.

"Perry answers to God and the Church, not to me," was the limp response.

"Perry's threat to your father will soon be ended. Perhaps that was your intention. By informing me that Perry is a Papist priest, as a magistrate I have no option, but to arrest him, and incarcerate him in York Castle until his trial."

"You could turn a blind eye. Since the Reformation, English governments of all faiths, have permitted the great Catholic magnates of the land to maintain their religion, and shelter their priests. Perry is no threat to the established religion of the nation. Since he arrived here, he has had no contact with the Catholic enemies of England. As the new King's brother and heir is a supposed Catholic, as is his mother, the new government may not look kindly on any precipitous action against the Catholics of this island," was the Baron's careful but forceful response.

"The Duke of York is not a Catholic. There are rumors that he has secretly married an English Protestant gentlewoman," responded Mark angrily.

Luke subdued his rising anger and asked, "Is there no substance in the predictions regarding the death of your father? Who are the women on the island that might be involved? Which of them have the run of the north and south wings of Nith Hall?"

"Too many questions, Sir Luke! There are four aristocratic women— my wife Alice, Baroness Bohm; the widow of my deceased identical twin Harry, Lady Margaret Bohm; Lady Felicity Bohm, the wife of my younger brother Ralph, and Jane, Marchioness of Nith. She is not my mother, but father's second wife who is half his age," explained Michael.

"And there are four yeomen or gentry women including my wife, Isabel. Toby's wife Ann, Corby's wife Hannah and Vince Keddy's spouse, Ursula," added James.

"Have any of these women displayed antagonism towards the Marquess in recent years?" asked Mark.

There was a deathly silence.

After a while Michael commented, "As my father is still alive, it does not seem reasonable to impugn the reputation of any of these women for the sake of something that might never happen. Over time most of them have had their disagreements with father."

"Unfortunately, my lord, such disagreements, even over petty matters may be critical to our overt mission. To prevent the murder of the Marquess by a woman, we must examine every aspect of these women's lives," countered Luke.

Michael was livid at this projected intrusion into the private life of the eight women. "You will meet this bevy of potential murderesses when you dine with us tonight," he said, deliberately ridiculing Luke's comment.

An incandescent Luke followed by an equally irate Mark strode out of the meeting.

Luke had for over two decades sat at many a gentry and aristocratic table across several countries. The seating arrangement usually reflected the strict social hierarchy that was imbedded in upper class dining. The table to which a servant led Mark and Luke had seating for sixteen, three at each end and five on each side. Luke was intrigued as to how Michael, Baron Nith would reflect the family hierarchy to give his socially superior stepmother, Jane, Marchioness of Nith, her appropriate place, without diminishing his assumed role.

At one end of the table sat the Baron with his senior servant, the steward James Denholm on his left, and his wife Baroness Alice on his right. Along the left-hand side of the table were seated the household servants—Isabel Denholm next to her husband, then John and Hannah Corby and Vincent and Ursula Keddy. At the far end sat the Marchioness. Mark took his place at her right hand and Luke at her left. The right-hand side of the table catered for the rest of the family, and the priest. Next to the Baroness was her brother-in-law Ralph, his wife Felicity, the priest William Perry and the widowed Lady Margaret. This placed her next to Luke.

Michael welcomed his guests explaining that there were three absentees, his father the Marquess, Toby and Ann Bentley. He was interrupted by his brother Ralph who added, "And don't forget mad Martin!"

"That defrocked cleric is only welcomed here when father presides," replied the Baron tersely.

As Luke surveyed the group, he assumed that the potential murderer of the Marquess, and Toby Bentley's assailant was at the table. If a woman was to cause Felix's death there were eight possible suspects, the aristocrats Jane, Margaret, Felicity and Alice, and the gentle and yeomen women, Isabel, Hannah, Ursula and the absent Ann. All he could achieve over supper was to obtain as much information as he could from his two neighbors, the Marchioness Jane, and the widowed Margaret. He hoped that Mark might intensively question Ursula Keddy.

Jane Bohm, the Marquess's second wife was twenty or more years younger than her husband, and probably close to Luke in age, being in her late thirties or early forties. He opened the conversation with a pragmatic, but possibly controversial request. "My lady, our visit here is to meet with your husband. Your stepson has not moved to arrange such a meeting. Could you obtain from the Marquess a time for us to meet?"

Luke was taken aback at Jane's reply.

"I never thought that the late arch-demon's head of military intelligence would be asking me for a favor."

"And I never thought that the young king would select me for this particular mission, given the past you describe," replied Luke warmly.

"I am well aware of that past—cavalry commander, special agent, head of military intelligence, and more recently English ambassador to the Islamic states of North Africa."

"My lady, how does a former lady-in-waiting to the Queen Mother, who moved to this isolated island nearly twenty years ago, and from what I hear has never left it since, know such details about the largely secret activities of one of the King's leading opponents?"

"Not only do I know a lot more about you, than you know about me, I can explain to you why the King selected you for this mission."

"You certainly surprise and intrigue me—reveal all, my lady!"

"Well, it's simple really. We have a mutual acquaintance."

"I find that hard to believe. Our paths have never crossed, nor can I think of anybody we might know in common," commented a puzzled Luke.

"That is because you know nothing about me, except my service with Queen Henrietta Maria, and my subsequent marriage to Felix Bohm."

"Enlighten me!"

"I was the fourth daughter of the impoverished Viscount Dart with little prospect of a good marriage among the limited range of suitable Catholic aristocracy."

"You must have been clairvoyant to marry an alchemist gentleman such as Felix, well below you on the social scale—and not a Catholic himself. It's a wonder your father approved."

"He didn't, until he was persuaded by my godfather that Felix would one day inherit a marquisate, and considerable wealth—and whose family was Catholic. My godfather was no clairvoyant, but a senior Catholic peer with a network of connections. He is your one-time enemy, one-time friend and ally. A man, who while a courtier to the exiled King, was accepted by the late Oliver Cromwell as the voice of the Catholics who remained in England."

Luke smiled and muttered, "I should have guessed. My old friend Simon—in England, Lord Stokey; in Wales, Lord Kimball. It was only two years ago that we worked together in North Africa. So, he is the source of your information about me, but how do you remain in contact with him, isolated here on Nith?"

"We write frequently, and late last year he came here unheralded with Nicholas, Lord Ashcroft to talk to Felix. Ashcroft was immediately convinced that there was a problem that needed to be investigated, and Simon persuaded him that you, despite your loyalties to the late Protector, was the ideal man to help us."

"What exactly am I expected to uncover?" pleaded Luke with mock humility.

"This is not the place to discuss such issues. Our fellow diners have big ears—and vested interests. Visit me tomorrow at ten!"

She squeezed his hand as she turned away to talk to Mark. Jane, Marchioness of Nith was certainly not what Luke had expected. Her appearance was equally surprising. She remained a red-haired beauty with penetrating green eyes. She had a high aristocratic forehead and long neck, currently adorned with a silver and deep green peridot pendant, which her low-cut bodice amply revealed. During their long conversation she exhibited a cheerful and smiling face—and even to a happily married man, a smoldering sexuality.

Turning to his neighbor on the other side, Lady Margaret, widow of Harry Bohm, Luke was struck by the contrast. Her bodice was dominated by a large silk collar which covered her neck, around which was hung a large golden crucifix. Luke had noticed that while he was talking to Jane, Margaret had spent most of her time in earnest conversation with her other neighbor, the priest, William Perry. This was a very religious woman, perhaps the typical Catholic female devotee that he had met in Spain and Portugal.

Her round face with small lips and snub nose were completely overshadowed literally by the darkest brown eyes set deeply into a head which was topped by curly raven hair that came down to her shoulders. Most moon-faced persons that Luke had previously known had a perpetual smile and a sunny personality. Margaret's personality and physiognomy were the complete opposite.

When Luke spoke to her, she struggled to raise her head and failed to look him in the eye. This was a timid, probably scared woman who was much younger that Jane, in her mid-thirties at the oldest. She clearly lacked confidence. Why did Michael place her beside the guest of honor? Was it a deliberate attempt to curtail the amount of information he might elicit during the meal? Was the priest placed next to her to ensure her silence?

The anti-Catholic Luke was already sensing a Popish conspiracy.

Luke adopted the gentlest approach that he could muster. "My lady, you have received poor treatment from the Baron, being placed next to a visitor of whom you know nothing, and then be expected to indulge in meaningless chit chat throughout the meal."

"Sir, I am not totally ignorant of your background. You are a magistrate sent here to arrest my friend, mentor and priest, Father Perry."

"Only partly right. I am a magistrate, but I am not here to arrest Father Perry, although to be frank, as a magistrate required to uphold the law that the presence of a Catholic priest in England is illegal, I will eventually have to arrest him. However, if he cannot be found when the time comes for my departure, I would have to leave without him. But arresting a priest has nothing to do with why I am here. I am surprised that the Baron has not informed the whole household of the purpose of our visit. We have been sent here by the King to prevent a murder."

Lady Margaret showed signs of interest, "And who sir is about to be murdered?" she asked.

"The Marquess."

"Ridiculous. Nobody can get near him. He has created a series of obstacles with magical doors and mirrors to hinder anybody entering or finding their way around his apartment and laboratory. His magical powers have most islanders frightened of him. And he is well protected by the devoted Toby Bentley and his slut of a wife, the predatory Ann."

Luke was surprised at this vehement comment.

"When apprised of this mission I had a similar reaction, but the attack on Toby Bentley may be the first stage of an attempt on the Marquess.

Remove his man servant and bodyguard, and the task for the murderer, becomes easier. What still concerns me is a motive. If someone on this island is out to kill the Marquess, who would you suspect? And why would they be driven to such an attempt now, rather than anytime in the last eighteen years?"

Margaret ignored Luke and turned to William, "Father, did you hear what Sir Luke said? Someone plans to kill the Marquess. Is that likely?"

William spoke directly to Luke. "Have you thought of any possible motives?"

"Our investigation has hardly begun, but your presence may be a possible catalyst to such an attempt."

William expressed genuine surprise. "I am absolutely loyal to the Marquess who with his predecessors have entertained and protected a succession of priests. I have always preached a gospel of peace and harmony to my flock."

"Nevertheless, I suspect that like many of the more recently trained priests from the continent, you preach that all magic either comes from God or the Devil. If the magic that the Marquess espouses does not come from God through the church, then it must come from the Devil. You may have turned the Marquess, in the eyes of some into a diabolic male witch, and those close to him as demonic servants. This might explain the attack on Toby Bentley."

"I see that you are well aware of the Church's current teaching on magic and witchcraft, but I cannot recall ever preaching on the topic, nor even mentioning it in passing. My flock here are in desperate need of pastoral care, not ideological indoctrination. I inform and protect my flock mainly through the confessional, and not by cajoling and frightening them with the hell fire and brimstone sermons so common among the Protestant heretics."

Margaret spoke quietly to the priest who nodded his head in approval of whatever she had said. She turned to Luke, "You might find that any attempt on the life of the Marquess and the recent attack on Toby Bentley have their origins in a real murder that no one acknowledges."

She looked furtively across at the Marchioness and whispered to Luke, "This is not the place to discuss it. Meet me tomorrow at noon!"

Back in their room a concerned Luke confided in Mark. "We have talked to very few islanders, but I am already convinced that we confront major problems here. There are only the two of us to restore English law to this wild island, which in one simple example of defying the law, overtly protects a Catholic priest. This is in defiance of both the old republican, and the restored monarchical governments."

"I agree. I already feel uneasy, and we are yet to probe beneath the surface."

"Did you discover anything of relevance from your discussion with the Marchioness or Ursula Keddy, whom I noticed was flirting with you?"

"You are mistaken in that last comment. Ursula was very friendly, but extremely moralistic. She was not at all interested that I had spent time at King Charles's court in exile, which she considers a den of iniquity. She openly expressed the view that the death of the late Protector was a calamity for England—and a blow to the establishment of God's kingdom. Nor does she have much time for the island clergy whether Anglican or Papist, both of whom she views with disdain, if not a simmering hatred. She confessed to be a Quaker, who received instructions directly from God without need of King, Marquess or cleric. Her hatred of established authority is evident. God could easily tell her to remove the Marquess in preparation for His direct rule."

"Great, she could prove to be a good informant. She will probable reveal much more to me, who she might see as a fellow believer," said Luke, confident in his ability to empathize with Protestant extremists.

"Also, she was inclined to gossip, but confined her information to unimportant issues given her location at the table. She may be a good source of lower-class rumors, as she is responsible next to the relevant mistress of the particular establishment, for the appointment and control of many of the servants. She appears to be the overall housekeeper of Nith Hall, freeing up the aristocratic women from such a tedious chore. How do we progress our enquiry from here?" asked Mark.

"I meet both the Marchioness and Lady Margaret tomorrow, while you sail back to the mainland."

"What do you mean? You are removing me from the investigation?"

"Relax Mark! You will be back as soon as possible. Throughout my career, I have had troops ready to enforce my decisions. We will need such a force here should our investigations upset the locals—as they are most likely to do. Perhaps we were the targets of that lone marksman, and not Toby."

"So, what am I to do?"

"Leave the island early tomorrow. Make your way to York, and request half a company of musketeers from Sir Evan Williams, whom you know. As Governor of York Castle, he commands all government troops in the north. Have him also commandeer a frigate or armed merchantman to bring you back here under cover of darkness. Try to land, hopefully unseen, and get your men to surround Nith Hall before dawn. Have the frigate then patrol the island indefinitely to prevent anybody coming to or leaving the island—and if in an emergency, is in a position to bombard the island."

"What will you tell the Baron about my sudden departure?"

"A pack of lies—the investigation does not require the two of us, and that you have other urgent tasks to perform. I will play down the urgency of our mission here and suggest that our initial verdict is that there is little going on here that requires the King's intervention. I'll even concede that the question of the priest can wait until the new government clarifies its position on the issue. While you are away, I will speak to Ursula Keddy, as well as Jane and Margaret Bohm."

Next morning Luke implemented his plan, and within hours Mark was aboard the island's skiff heading for the mainland.

Sometime after the early afternoon meal Luke was confronted by an irate constable. John Corby expressed surprise and alarm that Luke had in such a short time decided that any problems on the island were of such minor significance that Sir Mark could depart the island.

Luke decided to trust the constable. "Quite the opposite John. For the moment I want you to keep this information to yourself. I am so worried about the potential problems here that I have sent Mark to York to obtain a detachment of troops to help us enforce any decisions we need to make in order to restore this island to English law and protect the Protestant faith. For the moment I will present my work to the islanders as simply preventing any harm befalling the Marquess."

A general discussion that followed was interrupted in late afternoon by Corby's deputy. A breathless Vincent Keddy burst into the room in quite a state.

"What is it Vince that leads you to so abruptly interrupt my discussion with the magistrate?"

Vince ignored the rebuke and turned towards Luke, "Sir, there has been a two-fold tragedy."

"What do you mean?" asked Luke.

"John asked that Tom Kitchin and I visit the Bentleys to check on Toby. No one answered when we knocked on the door of their apartment. It was not locked, so we entered. We went straight to the bedroom where Toby had been placed. He was still unconscious. I was about to leave when Tom leaned over the body. He told me that Toby was not unconscious—he was dead."

"Does his wife know? queried Luke.

"That is the second part of the tragedy. In the next room we found Ann lying face down on the floor. She was also dead."

"What did you do then?" asked an incredulous John.

"I ran here to inform you. Tom is with the bodies."

"We must examine the corpses!" announced John.

"I have examined a lot of dead bodies in my time. What is the protocol on this island?" asked Luke.

"The Marquess is a physician and alchemist, and when there was any doubt he was consulted, but in more recent years, the Catholic priest who has also had some training in medicine took his place."

Luke and John made their way to the Bentley's apartment while Vince went to fetch Father Perry. Luke carefully examined Toby's body, and commented, "The bleeding from the mouth, nose and ears probably a result of the massive blow he suffered to the back of his skull when he fell backwards on board the fishing boat, suggests that death was probably a delayed result of that blow. It must have caused massive internal bleeding. There are no other signs on his body indicating any further injury. Despite the long delay, we can consider this at least a manslaughter caused by the person who shot at him."

Luke moved into the next room and examined Ann Bentley's body. He turned to John who had followed him. "This is a clear case of murder. Look at her neck and throat. She has clearly been strangled or rather garroted. There must have been a major piece of information that the

Bentley's shared that somebody could not allow to be passed on to me—maybe, the identity of the Marquess's potential killer."

Father Perry arrived, and after a thorough examination agreed with Luke's diagnosis. He then asked, "Has anybody informed the Marquess, Marchioness and young Ellen?"

"No," replied John.

"Who is Ellen?" asked Luke.

"Toby and Ann's daughter! She was lady's maid to the Marchioness but has recently been seconded to the Marquess to help her parents," replied Perry.

"I will accompany you as you inform these three people," said Luke to him.

The priest objected, "For a stranger and outsider to impose himself on the Marquess who has just lost a lifelong friend and devoted servant, and a young woman who has lost both parents is insensitive and inappropriate."

"That may be true as far as Sir Luke is concerned, but it also applies to you, Father. It would not be appropriate for you to inform the Marquess or young Ellen, nor to minister any spiritual comfort they might need. They are not of your faith. You may inform the Marchioness who is, and I will break the sad news to the Marquess and young Ellen," insisted John.

Luke was impressed with John Corby—a solid Protestant ally.

Corby and the priest left. Luke remained with Tom Kitchen and the two corpses as company. Tom was a young man in his early twenties, over six feet tall and with a solid and muscular build. He explained that he was an apprenticed blacksmith, and a member of the constable's watch mainly because of his physical strength, and imposing presence.

He was anxious to talk. "Rumor has it, sir, that you were a close friend of both the late Protector, and the new King—and that you were one of the leading generals in the Protector's army. Some say you were an admiral and others an ambassador to the Great Turk."

"Rumor, as usual, Tom, it is only partly right. I was a friend of the late Protector and spent most of my service under him as a colonel of cavalry. I have met the new King twice but am hardly a friend. I only became a general recently as part of my new role as a diplomat in southern Europe and the Mediterranean. I understand that the Marquess shielded the islanders from the divisions of the civil war. Did you know what was happening during that period?"

"I was only a baby when it began, but during my childhood every fourth Sunday the Marquess, as part of his sermon, gave a summary of events to the congregation."

"The Marquess delivered the sermon? What happened to the parish priest who was defrocked? Was he not replaced?"

"He is still here although he was defrocked before I was born. The Marquess until a couple of years ago delivered a monthly sermon but permitted the defrocked rector to conduct other services in line with the

Anglican Book of Common Prayer. As a parish we continued to elect our churchwardens and constable. In recent years Mr. Corby as churchwarden and lay reader as well as constable, has taken over a minor preaching role."

"What is the pattern of Christian worship on the island at the moment?" asked Luke, anxious to confirm what he had been told.

"The Catholics to a person resort to the Bohm family chapel within Nith Hall, where Father Perry conducts mass. Most of the Protestants attend the parish church where Mr Corby reads from the Book of Common Prayer. Some of the islanders such as the Keddys who are Quakers ignore both communities. They worship with a few followers on a hilltop at the eastern end of the island, which the original Danes considered a sacred spot with its monoliths of stone. On one occasion some years ago, Vince Keddy took over the parish church physically preventing Martin Moore, the defrocked rector, from reading from the Book of Common Prayer. This led to a temporary falling out between the Keddys and John Corby. They now appear to be reconciled as Vince is John's deputy."

After a period of awkward silence Tom blurted out, "I am glad you are here. Many things have gone downhill these last few years. Put them right!"

"What do you mean?"

"We never see the Marquess. He could be dead for all I know. The Baron and steward rule the island and ignore the rest of us. And they never really explained the death years ago of the Baron's identical twin, Henry. In fact, our problems stem from the time of Lord Harry's death."

Luke asked, "Before his death, where did Harry fit into the family hierarchy?"

"Up until Harry's death, the Marquess ran the island, and everybody, his closest family included, jumped to his orders. The Marquess was a magician and most of us, even now, worry about his ability to harm his enemies with his supernatural powers."

"Your Marquess was essentially a showman whose real powers were limited," commented Luke.

"Not according to Father Perry who constantly refers to the Marquess's use of diabolical power. According to the priest all magical power comes from God or the Devil and not as the Marquess always claimed from man using nature."

Luke was interested in this statement—a direct contradiction to that of the priest himself. "The priest openly opposes the Marquess?"

"That is one other aspect of the changes over the last two years."

"You are a Protestant. How do you know what Perry preaches?"

"My best friend is George Denholm. He is a Catholic, although his mother was a Protestant, before she married."

"When the Marquess actively controlled the island and was constantly visible, what roles did Michael and Harry Bohm play?" probed Luke.

"The Baron then was a gentle soul who simply acted as an assistant to his father on the island. Harry managed the mainland affairs of the Bohm family which brought in an incredible income without which the island would be destitute. He was a hard man who showed little sympathy for the personal problems of the islanders. These were handled by Michael and his less likeable wife, Lady Alice."

Luke took on board the reference to Alice which he would pursue at a later date. For the moment he concentrated on the death of Harry.

"How exactly did Harry die?" he asked.

"He was murdered, but the Marquess has forbidden any discussion of the matter," was the surprising response.

"Was his death not investigated by the authorities?"

"Mr Corby as constable tried to get involved, but very quickly the matter was deemed a family affair with the Marquess and Baron excluding everybody else except Father Perry, and James Denholm, from their private enquiry."

"Was there no dissent from this procedure?"

"Mr Corby was not happy, and Lady Margaret, Harry's wife was livid. She was so upset that it was common knowledge that she had some sort of mental breakdown as a result. Ever since she has been prescribed heavy medication by our resident alchemist, the Marquess. It was doubt over this affair that persuaded Mr. Corby and Mr. Bentley to talk to the King's men, last year, that led to your visit."

"I thought I was here to stop some woman killing the Marquess on the day the King is crowned," responded Luke.

"They could hardly tell the King's men that they suspected the Bohm family of concealing a murder, when they were aware that the Marquess was a favorite of the King's late father. Didn't you think the stated reasons for your visit were a little farfetched? Mr Corby wanted to get someone here under any pretense and hoped that the visitor would uncover the truth behind Harry's death!"

Luke was surprisingly relieved. The young apprentice blacksmith had revealed the real reason behind his mission—a reason that made more sense than the predicted death of an aging magician. He would have to question John Corby. He turned to Tom and repeated, "What did happen to Harry Bohm?"

"According to the Marquess on the following Sunday, Harry and his brother, the Baron, with their wives and a few islanders went rabbit shooting in the forested warren on the eastern end of island. Harry's gun misfired. He was accidently shot and died at the scene, but rumor had it that his body was found at the bottom of the cliffs at the north eastern extremity of the island. The rabbit warren does not extend to the cliff face. The reaction of disbelief from many of the islanders must have pressured the Marquess into changing the official story. On the next Sunday he announced that on further enquiry it now became clear that Harry had simply suffered an unfortunate fall. After the rabbit shooting in the warren, Harry challenged Michael as to whom could bag the most seabirds that nested in the cliff face. In trying to retrieve one of the birds he had shot, Harry slipped and fell to his death on the rocks below."

"In addition to the ladies, Alice and Margaret which other islanders were present?" asked Luke

"Nobody except Michael was near the cliff face, and it was never revealed who remained in the general area while the brothers went shooting the seabirds despite Mr Corby's attempts to find out. I heard that apart from the wives, William Perry, and James Denholm were invited to the warren shoot, but did not move to the cliff edge."

They were interrupted by a woman who burst through the door.

"Is it true that Ann is dead?"

Tom restrained the woman from entering the room where the bodies lay, informing Luke, "This is Mistress Corby, the constable's wife."

Luke took her hand and led her to a chair. She asked, "Does Toby know, or is he still in a coma?"

"I am afraid that Tobias also is dead."

"Has Ellen been told?"

"Your husband is doing that while we speak."

"What happened to Ann?"

"I am afraid she was murdered," replied Luke.

"Murdered! I am not surprised," was the surprisingly response.

"Why are you not surprised?" asked Luke.

Hannah ignored Luke's question, "I will return with friends and prepare Toby and Ann for burial." She hurried away.

Luke turned to Tom, "Why was Ann Bentley murdered? Was it simply as Toby's wife she knew things that he knew, which their mutual killer did not want revealed to me?"

"If that is the case then there will be more killings. Toby confided in both John and Hannah Corby, and certainly with his daughter Ellen. In fact, Toby talked to everybody. He had no concept of keeping things secret. He was a simple soul, but I cannot think of any secret information he might have that could provoke such a murderous reaction—other than the truth about Lord Harry's death."

"There are no other major secrets on the island that one or more persons might want to conceal?"

"There are many. I am a simple apprentice blacksmith who only knows the doubts concerning Lord Harry because I have been one of the constable's assistants in recent years and have heard Mr Corby often discussing it with Toby."

Luke's fruitful discussion came to an end when Hannah Corby returned with several other women. Luke and Tom lifted the corpses onto a bed and left the women to prepare the bodies.

Next morning Luke visited the warren, and the cliff at the bottom of which Harry's body had been found. He asked Tom to accompany him. The young apprentice declined, saying that his father the blacksmith needed him urgently.

Luke found his trek to the fatal cliff took longer and was more difficult than he expected. After leaving the grazed fields around the manor house and then finding his way through the quite dense wood, he reached an undulating terrain dissected by several short streams that emptied themselves over the cliff and cascaded toward the surging sea below.

As he peered over the edge, he was astonished to see a petite female figure standing on a rocky edge at the base of the cliff—it was the widowed Lady Margaret.

She was about to jump into the raging surf.

He shouted, but his words were completely lost in the noise of the relentless waves crashing onto the shore. He looked for a path down the cliff, but he knew he could never reach her in time.

Running along the cliff top Luke finally found a path down which to descend. Then the urgency disappeared.

As he looked at the ledge, Margaret was still there, but now well back from its edge—and kneeling. She was praying. Luke was so intent on watching Margaret that near the bottom of the cliff, he lost his footing and tumbled down the last few yards, landing luckily in a rare sandy patch of the beach. As he brushed the sand from his clothes and his face, he was confronted by a concerned Margaret. "Have you hurt yourself?"

"No, my lady."

"What happened?"

"I was watching you and missed my footing."

"Why were you watching me?" she asked with a hint of a twinkle in her eye.

"I thought you were too near the edge, and likely to fall into the sea."

"Or rather, you thought that I might jump. Rest assured sir, that my faith sees suicide as a mortal sin. Yes, immediately after the death of my husband I did consider such action, but Father Perry helped me through that period, and I also took advantage of the visit of a Catholic peer who happens to be Jane's godfather to help me cope with the situation."

"I had heard that Simon, Lord Stokey visited the island with Nicholas Lord Ashcroft, a visit that led to myself and Sir Mark being sent here. Although it may surprise you, I, a Cromwellian general and Lord Stokey a Royalist courtier are almost friends. Less than two years ago we were on the same assignment in North Africa, and before that Simon prevented a Spanish landing in Wales, and seven years ago he saved a fortune in privately owned Catholic treasure falling into the hands of either the King or the republican government."

"That explains why he nominated a ruthless Cromwellian official to solve my problem," said a more animated Margaret.

"And what problem is it exactly that you asked Simon to help solve?"

"The murder of my husband, Harry."

6

"It has already been suggested that the real purpose of our mission is not to save the Marquess from a predicted murder, but to solve this past crime," admitted Luke.

"The Marquess in his dotage may have convinced himself that he was to die on the day the King is crowned, but I am sure Lord Stokey would have raised the question of Harry's death to convince His Highness to send you here. Your expertise, apart from killing Royalists, I understand is in solving murders—not preventing them."

"If your husband was murdered, do you have a suspect?"

"Of course! The Baron and or his wife, that depraved Alice," answered a clearly embittered Margaret.

Luke began to suspect Margaret's assessment of other women—Ann Bentley was *a slut*, Lady Alice *depraved*. Were these the views of a deeply religious woman, or that of a mentally disturbed person who if pushed too hard might become unpredictable and dangerous?

"Why would Michael and his wife want Harry dead?"

"Harry was having an affair with Alice. She probably tired of it, or her jealous husband to maintain his honor, was driven to kill his adulterous twin."

"If that is true, I am not surprised that it was not investigated. Preserving the family name, and the life of the heir apparent is paramount in any aristocratic family. Were there any other issues, apart from Alice, between the brothers,"

"Yes, although Harry was the younger twin by a few minutes, he was the most capable, and for years has run the family business in banking and land speculation. His older brother lacks ability in almost every aspect. He was content to simply assist his father in the daily ceremonial routine of island life. There were growing rumors that Felix would disinherit Michael and make Harry his heir. The Marquess was awaiting the return of monarchy to engage in this rather difficult legal exercise, which according to Father Perry was doomed to failure because of the peculiarities of English law with its obsession with the rights of the eldest son."

"Nevertheless, you certainly provide a powerful motive for Michael to kill his brother—a jealous husband determined to protect his honor. What actually happened on the day of the alleged murder?"

"I don't exactly know. So many different stories have circulated since the event. Initially I was told that the brothers were fooling around, and that Michael's musket accidently discharged, and Harry was killed. But the women who prepared the body for burial, a day after his death, told me that Harry had sustained a great fall. James Denholm later told me his men had recovered Harry's body from this very spot—at the rocky base of this cliff."

"Did you confront Michael over these discrepancies?"

"Yes. He had a perfectly logical explanation. At first, he said Harry was fooling around and fell. I asked why he had initially lied to me. He changed his story again. Harry had jumped to his own death, and as a Catholic such an act was a mortal sin. The family had tried to shield me from the thought of Harry's eternal damnation given this suicidal act."

"That seems a perfectly logical and plausible explanation. Why do you not believe it?"

"Harry had no reason to commit suicide. His father was anxious to make him heir, and I suspect his relationship with Alice was on-going."

"On the day of Harry's death were the two brothers alone on the cliff edge? Were there any witnesses?"

"A number of us went on the shoot in the warren but only the two brothers went to the cliff's edge to snare the roosting sea birds. I suspect they had a wager on who would catch the most They were out of sight of the rest of us, except the then gamekeeper."

"Don't tell me! This gamekeeper has also died in strange circumstances?"

"No, quite the opposite. With no legal training, he was appointed by Michael, acting for the Marquess, as the new steward. James Denholm is the only possible witness to what really happened, and he was some distance away, and his line of vision would have been obstructed from time to time."

Luke whistled aloud, "The plot thickens. Did you question James?"

"Yes. He claims he saw nothing. Just before the fall Harry had shot a brace of birds and disappeared over the cliff to collect them while Michael turned in the opposite direction to collect his along the top of the cliff. He could not have seen Harry fall—and they were yards apart when it happened. So goes the official explanation. It's a fairy tale. I do not believe a word of it. Lies from start to finish."

"But still plausible although Denholm's promotion is suspicious. Was it ever explained?"

"Michael claimed that with lawyer Ralph's impending relocation on the island, the steward did not need legal training, and James knew the island and its families better than anybody else. That is true. The Denholms have played a major role on this island for centuries. Like me, they are related to an earlier family of marquesses—a claim James strengthened by his marriage to Isabel Moore"

"You are related to a previous marquess?"

"Yes, I am a closer relative to the last marquess than Felix Bohm or Martin Moore, but as a woman without male heirs, I could not inherit the marquisate. If I had had a son before Peregrine died, that son would have been the new marquess, not Felix, nor the usurper-in- waiting, that corruptor of children, Martin Moore."

"You have lived on this island all your life?"

"Yes, I was born here, but when both my parents died, I became a ward of the previous Marquess. Father was a younger son of an earlier Marquess, and I was born Lady Margaret Neale. On the death of the last Marquess, I was of marriageable age, and when Felix Bohm arrived on the island, I appeared an obvious partner for his unmarried son, Harry. Michael had already married Alice in London."

"Thank you, my lady. You have certainly given me a number of issues to consider."

"One more thing. Please do not take William Perry away. He is my only friend on this island of intrigue, illusion and diabolic malevolence."

"I cannot ignore the law, my lady, but the arrest of Father Perry is not one of my priorities."

"A second request! Let me make my way back to the manor alone. In the current circumstances, no one should know that we have spoken."

Luke agreed.

As he watched Lady Margaret ascend the cliff face, he was convinced that his real mission, orchestrated by Simon, Lord Stokey, was to solve the murder of Harry Bohm. He would now hear what the Marchioness could add to this redirected enquiry.

Unfortunately given the death of the Bentleys, Jane could not keep her ten o'clock appointment. The meeting was rescheduled for an hour before supper. When Luke arrived, the Marchioness had already dressed for dinner, and looked resplendent in an emerald green bodice and skirt complimented by a myriad of golden and green jewelry. Luke was immediately attracted to her incredibly low-cut revealing bodice.

Jane did not miss Luke's focus and quipped, "Surely we do not have a return to the womanizing soldier that Simon warned me about. He told me that you were now a happily married man."

"Very true your ladyship—and my wife is expecting our first child."

"When is it due?"

"In about three or four weeks."

"Will you be finished here by then?"

"It depends on what my work here really entails. Why did you and others lobby Ashcroft and Stokey to persuade the King that the situation here needed investigating? I doubt that a prediction that the Marquess would die on a certain date would have convinced Ashcroft to lobby the King."

"What do you believe then?" teased Jane.

"Knowing Lord Stokey, he could have been convinced by Lady Margaret and the priest that her husband Harry had been murdered, and the family had covered up the crime. Did they?"

"Margaret has never adjusted to the loss of her husband. She is not right in the head. The people are now calling her Mad Meg. Fact and fantasy have become confused in her mind, and that devious priest Perry, does not help, working on her religious obsessions for his own ends. I am one Catholic who will not regret it if you incarcerate him in York Castle. He is a disruptive force in this community, which Felix has spent his life trying to bring together."

"That may all be true, but her husband could still have been murdered." "Given that that there were no witnesses, Harry could have accidently fallen to his death, jumped—committing suicide, or been pushed," commented Jane.

"But by whom?" asked Luke.

Jane ignored the comment and concluded, "The family, that is the Marquess and the Baron believed it was suicide, but to protect the family name, and Harry's eternal resting place, they declared his death accidental."

"So, you then accept that his death was either suicide or accidental?"

"I have known my step-sons, Michael and Harry for over a decade and have lived very closely with them on this island. I cannot conceive of the gentle Michael murdering his brother. Now if the situation had been reversed—if Michael had died in the same circumstances—I could readily accept that Harry had done it."

"Why?"

"Power and succession! It irked Harry, and most second sons that we English hand everything over to the eldest—and in this case the eldest by a few minutes. The French have a fairer system. There, all the children get something from their father's legacy."

"If we put Margaret's concerns to one side, why do you think I am here? What issues did you put to Ashcroft and Stokey?"

"To prevent a coup against the Marquess."

"By whom?"

"His daughter-in-law, the ambitious Alice."

"To what end?"

"To replace me as Marchioness."

"But what's the hurry? Michael in time will be the Marquess, and Lady Alice the Marchioness. And from what I hear about your husband's health, that may not be far off."

"You raise the very issues I put to Ashcroft and Stokey. What is it that Michael and Alice want to do that requires the imminent demise of Felix? And is Felix's declining health natural, or is it being orchestrated by that devious pair? And I believe my interpretation of events explains the death of poor Toby."

"In what way?"

"Toby waited on and served Felix every day for decades. He would be very sensitive to any change in Felix's health, and in the circumstances surrounding any such decline."

"What are you suggesting? That Michael and Alice are slowly poisoning the Marquess?"

"It's a possibility."

"I have had some experience in detecting the effect of particular poisons on the human body—arsenic, strychnine, mercury or lead. I will examine Felix as soon as possible. If Toby or you suspected such action against Felix, why did you not take counter measures?"

"We did. I told Felix that given his failing health I would have my lady's maid, Ellen Bentley, seconded to his service to prepare and serve all of his meals. As he refused to come to supper, and ate in his laboratory, this was easy to arrange without raising the suspicion of Michael or Alice."

"Maybe Ellen reported some recent event to her parents, which led to their death?"

"In that case Ellen's own life is in danger," said Jane suddenly aware of the implications should her view of the situation be correct.

"Take me to Felix now! I have been on the island for several days and still have not been received by the Marquess. Such a delay in receiving the King's envoy is certainly contrary to protocol. Why the delay?"

"Felix has not been himself the last week or so, and I reluctantly agreed with Michael that his immediate meeting with you would probably serve no purpose."

"What is exactly wrong with Felix?"

"His memory, if not his mind is going. At times he does not know who I am, yet at other times his intellect is as sharp as it ever was."

"Take me to him now!"

"I will, but when I saw him earlier today, he was still not himself."

Jane led Luke along the main corridor which took him into the central tower block. Several servants appeared as if to block his way until they recognized that he was accompanied by the Marchioness. The couple climbed a winding staircase which led to a large door on the first landing. The Marchioness knocked three times and announced her name and that of her companion.

7

Eventually the door was opened by an attractive young woman who Luke assumed to be Ellen. "Would you tell Felix that the King's man, Tremayne, is here to speak with him. Is he up to it my dear?" asked Jane.

"Yes, my lady. He is his old self at the moment."

Ellen disappeared and returned almost immediately announcing that, "The Marquess would see the Roundhead general, but the Marchioness need not waste her time here."

"Getting rid of me is probably a good sign. He probably wishes to pass on to you information that he believes I need not know," uttered a surprisingly relaxed Jane.

She left. Luke followed Ellen into what was a converted reception room with a large number of tables on which were various collections of bottles. Coming forward to greet Luke was a small sprightly man who directed him to a cushioned bench against one of the large windows, from which a magnificent view of the island could be had.

"Glad to meet you, Sir Luke! Life as the late Protector's head of military intelligence, and later as a diplomat in North Africa sounds fascinating. How are you adapting to the return of the King?"

"My presence here suggests an answer, my lord," Luke replied cautiously.

"Yes, I was surprised at your acceptance of the Royal directive, but I am glad you have come. When I explained to Lord Stokey my problem, he suggested that the best man to assist was unfortunately on the other side of the hedge, a fervent Cromwellian. He did not know at the time how you would respond to any request from the returning King, or whether the King would even agree to your appointment."

"What is your problem that needs a solution, and which Stokey and Ashcroft, and ultimately the King thought important enough to send Sir Mark and myself here?"

"My murder!"

"Who is going to murder you?"

"Given your reputation, you will already had deduced that my elimination is a possibility, and you will already have some persons in mind."

"I have been alerted to two possible narratives. Some blame you for the death of your son Harry and may seek revenge: others suggest that your son and heir, Michael, is anxious to succeed you sooner rather than later, and might speed up your demise."

"I know to whom you have been talking. Harry's widow Margaret is devastated by his death—and is certain that he was murdered. Whether she blames me or Michael, I am not sure. She is encouraged in her fantasies by that priest, Perry, who in recent years has been undermining my influence by pushing an ultra Papist line. He would certainly like to see the end of my humanistic, secular emphasis. England has had enough of religious intolerance under your Protector. Let's hope the King does not resort to a similar religious fanaticism in retaliation. Puritans and extreme Papists are an equally dangerous threat to social harmony—and an united kingdom."

"You are the Marquess. Why tolerate a Papist priest who undermines your authority?"

"I have tried to bring the islanders of conflicting faiths into developing a tolerant and harmonious community, but this island retains a majority of Papists, including all of my own family, except Ralph and myself. My successor Michael is too close to Perry. The attitude of the new King's government to this issue is uncertain, given that the King's mother and possible future bride are both of this ilk. It is not wise at this time when I seek favors from the King to be expel a Catholic priest. Nor can I anticipate what my Catholic islanders would do if I act too strongly against Perry. You know he was born here. He left the island just before I arrived. Margaret told me that only a week or so ago. Jane believes Michael would use any act of mine against Perry to declare me demented and seize the marquisate."

"So, you would not be unhappy if when I left the island, I took an arrested Perry with me."

"You might be confronted by a violent Catholic flock who would prevent you from doing your duty."

"I am not so sure of that. You underestimate the effects of your tolerant humanism on many of your Catholic families. I have picked up considerable resentment among some of them to Father Perry. As for any violent reaction from the islanders, I wish to advise you that within a few days a large force of troops will land on the island to assist Sir Mark and myself to effect any reforms that we think necessary—and in particular to protect you from any murder attempts."

"Stokey said you were an efficient and cunning operator. Michael told me that you did not think there were any problems on the island and had sent your comrade Sir Mark off on a new assignment. Does he or Denholm know of this coming troop arrival?"

"No."

The Marquess smiled, "I like you Tremayne. No wonder the republican government seemed to know every move we Royalists made with people like you in their intelligence. You have certainly lulled Michael into a false sense of security."

"Mark is at this moment obtaining troops from York Castle and hopefully a frigate to lie off the island with its guns trained on this manor house. It is too difficult to unload cannon onto the island."

"If it helps, I shall tell Michael that I have asked for military assistance, and that you have obliged. It will stop him becoming too big for his boots. Before Harry died Michael was a passive loveable soul. Harry's death has turned him into an aggressive, hardheaded businessman. He is now greedier than his rapacious brother ever was."

"My lord, what makes you think you are going to be murdered?"

"A year or more ago I received an anonymous letter indicating that because of evil I committed decades ago, an avenging angel would bring my life to an end."

"Why wait so long before you did anything about it?"

"I did not take it seriously."

"Why did you change your mind?"

"I discovered by accident, just before Ashcroft and Stokey arrived on the island, who had sent the letter. You can question the writer and establish her then motivation."

"How did you discover the author?"

"I came across a letter sent by one of my daughters-in-law. It was in the same hand as that of the writer of the murder threat."

"Lady Alice?"

"An interesting guess Sir Luke, but incorrect. It was Felicity."

"I nodded in her direction at supper, but I have not yet spoken to her."

"Be discreet! Probe into her background. Her husband Ralph, my third son, is in many ways the most gullible. Why he married this widowed French countess, I do not know. He stayed in London when I insisted the rest of the family move here. It was only with the death of Harry that I ordered Ralph to join us here—and surprisingly he complied."

"I did not realize that Felicity was French."

"She isn't. As a London teenager she ran off with a French diplomat. Why did you think Alice may have been the culprit?" probed the Marquess.

"In my brief time here, I have gained the impression that your son and heir is already running the place, and that his wife is a very ambitious woman. In fact, until I met you, I thought you might have already been locked in your room and treated as a person who was losing his wits. You should make more public appearances to dispel the view that you have sunk into a mental decline, and that Michael is Marquess in all but name."

"An interesting observation. Jane keeps saying the same thing."

Luke smiled. "Is there any major disagreement between the Baron and yourself concerning the running of the estate?"

"There are always disagreements, but Michael has never strongly advanced his views. After all I am the Marquess, and as far as I know he follows my direction."

"Is there a situation which if you died, Michael could change any of your policies to benefit himself?"

The Marquess stroked his chin and thought for some time without replying. Eventually he commented, "I have been remiss in recent years. Frankly I have allowed Michael, and the relatively new steward, Denholm, to run affairs unimpeded."

"What is the major area of your activities which Michael and Denholm would alter?"

"Tremayne, I could speculate—but you are the inquisitor. Interrogate Denholm! Pretend you are back in military intelligence and force the truth out of him. Ask him to explain in detail from where I derive my wealth, and what is the current state of my accounts? Your questioning has reminded me of a comment made by Ashcroft, which I did not quite understand. He said the King was anxious that the Nith estates be in order as it would make His Majesty's return to the throne much easier. At the time I thought it just a general comment that thriving Royalist estates would give strength to his cause."

"And now you think it may have been something more specific?"

"Possibly—question Denholm, and it might all fall into place."

"I can see why the King has sent me here. Your life could be threatened by a number of people for at least five reasons—Margaret seeking revenge for what she perceives as the murder of her husband and your alleged role in covering it up, Felicity for reasons we are yet to uncover but obviously related to some episode in your past, your son Michael and his wife Alice who are anxious to take over power—either for its own sake or because they wish to change your policy on matters that may affect the King's return, and I cannot rule out Father Perry who wants to replace your humanistic culture on the island with a new and more strident Catholicism."

"I took none of this seriously, despite the views put to Ashcroft and Stokey until the attack on Toby. Who do you think killed him—and why?"

"At the moment without any detailed investigation I believe he was removed to stop him telling me something someone else wanted to remain hidden."

"And you think that something had to do with my planned murder?"

"A reasonable assumption."

"Not if you knew Toby."

"Why? What was his problem?"

"Decades ago, in London, Tobias was a young tumbler intrigued with my magic. He often assisted me to present my act. Unfortunately, during one of his tumbling acts he landed on his head. He was never the same again. He became very slow and seemed to lack the ability to connect ideas. I took pity on him and when I inherited the marquisate, I brought him here as my valet. He devoted his life to assisting me in the basics, but he could not comprehend any of the broader issues swirling across the island. Therefore, why would anybody kill a man whose childlike personality and general ignorance could not harm anybody? He knew nothing, so he had nothing to tell you. Yet he was murdered!"

"You think he was murdered?" asked Luke.

"Initially I thought it was an accident. The shooter was aiming at you and hit Toby by mistake. After all you were, and to many Royalists here still are, a symbol of the hated military power of late Republic. The ordinary Royalist is not as forgiving as the King. But then Toby's wife was also killed."

"You could be right. I may have been the target, and then someone else took advantage of Toby's incapacity to murder Ann Bentley for entirely different reasons."

"Talk to young Ellen! She is aware of tensions within the Protestant families. She will return here any minute with my supper."

"Have you ceased permanently to dine with the household?"

"Yes, I can't be bothered with their trivia and point scoring. Jane keeps me informed of everything I need to know."

"My lord, in the current circumstances it might help if you reversed your policy of isolation and seclusion. Let the people see you still rule the island! They need your visible and effective leadership. Many do not trust the Baron and particularly his wife."

A few minutes later two servants arrived carrying food. Ellen then arrived and arranged this mini feast on a large table in the corner of the room. She then gave the Marquess a hug and asked was he ready to eat. He assented and introduced Luke as the King's man sent to prevent his murder.

Ellen became agitated at that remark and told him there was no substance to such a silly idea.

"If it is such a silly idea, why were two of my closest servants, your parents, murdered? Sir Luke would like to talk to you regarding all of this. You can go into the antechamber, while I start on the lamb stew."

8

In the quiet of the adjacent room, Luke was diplomatically sympathetic, "I am sorry for the way his lordship referred so casually to the death of your parents."

"There is no need to be so. The Marquess knows how I felt about my late parents, and why. We were not close."

"Why not?"

"Five years ago, I became pregnant, and my immediate worry was that the child might be slow like my father, Toby. I asked mother who was also an experienced midwife about his condition. She could have said that Toby was slow because of an accident, which I later learnt from the Marquess. Instead she chose that moment to tell me I had no concerns in that regard as Toby was not my birth father. I was devastated."

"I can understand such a revelation separating you from your adoptive father, but why did it lead to a break with your mother?"

"When I asked who my real father was, she refused to tell me—unless I revealed the name of father of my child."

"I have seen no such child. What happened to it?" Was an abortion forced on you?

"No, I had a natural miscarriage."

"Do you have any idea of your real father's identity?"

"Is my paternity relevant to your enquiry?"

"It might be to the death of your mother."

"I always assumed he was a member of one of the Protestant families. We are closely knit group; however, we did interact with the Catholic majority. Mother was descended from one of oldest Protestant families on the island. She was a Moore. Her sister Hannah married John Corby, and her uncle who was much the same age as her, is our disgraced Anglican rector who was defrocked before the current Marquess arrived."

"Your mother could have been raped by a member of either community, or conversely she may have fallen in love with someone whom she couldn't marry. It was obviously in everybody's interest to conceal the truth. Did anybody show a special interest in you over the years—someone who may have been your birth father?"

"No, only the Marquess took an interest in me—and mother was pregnant long before he arrived on the island."

"Have you asked your Aunt Hannah?"

"Yes, but she claims she knows nothing."

"Given her sister's murder, she may now be in a mind to tell me. I have heard whispers of the defrocked rector. I am told he is still on the island."

"Yes, but since the Baron took over the running of the island, he keeps a much lower profile. The Marquess allowed him to live in the rectory and paid him a small stipend as sexton of the church. The Marquess himself exercised the role of parish priest until very recently. The Baron wants to expel Martin from the island for his continuing philandering and drunkenness, but the Marquess continues to protect him. As a compromise Martin has been exiled to a tiny shepherd's cottage in the hollow near the cliffs on the northeast tip of the island, just below the old Danish sacred site which we call Big Head and the Three Trolls."

"That seems an irreverent name for a sacred site?"

"It's simply a hilltop with a number of stone monoliths with many rocks precariously balanced on top of each other. Although completely the work of nature they resemble one giant figure and three smaller ones. The top stone on the giant figure is almost as large as the stone beneath that provides the upper torso, therefore 'Big Head.' The Danes had originally named it after their pagan gods but for centuries it has been known by its current name. It has no religious significance to most of the islanders, but recently the Quakers on the island worship there."

"Since exiled to his hollow, does Martin have any contacts, and friends?"

"Myself, and possibly my aunts. The Marquess sends me with essential supplies, but Martin has developed into a very good hunter, keeping himself well stocked with rabbit meat, birds and pelts."

"Thanks Ellen. I must talk to your Aunt Hannah and Great Uncle Martin as soon as possible. Is there anything else you might want to tell me about the murder of your parents—and the projected murder of the Marquess?"

"A servant should not tell tales about her superiors, but there is immense tension between three of the aristocratic ladies in Nith Hall—Alice, Margaret and Felicity. Each is hiding a great secret that might be related to the future of the Marquess. On the other hand, the fourth peeress, the Marchioness appears surprisingly calm—almost carefree."

"What is the Marquess's attitude to the three?"

"He dislikes and distrusts Alice, he thinks Margaret has lost her mind, but his attitude towards Felicity has undergone a major change. Mother told me years ago that he did not trust Felicity yet in recent months she has become his devoted assistant."

Luke noted a possible contradiction between what Ellen had just told him and Marquess's earlier account. Had the Marquess's declining mind blotted out the more recent positive relationship with Felicity, or was he playing games?

Luke would keep a low profile and avoid provoking anybody until his troops arrived. In the interim he sought out the defrocked Anglican priest, Martin Moore. Luke headed for the north eastern end of the island and eventually found a semi-derelict cottage in a deep hollow just in from the precipitous coastline. It was well protected from the bitter North Sea winds and nestled below the towering monoliths of Big Head and the Three Trolls.

As Luke approached the cottage a white haired, bearded man emerged with a musket, which he recklessly fired in the general direction of the approaching visitor. Luke turned the delicate situation to his advantage, "A mere local magistrate does not require such a formal welcome. I am Luke Tremayne sent here by the King to protect the Marquess."

"You are that former Cromwellian general. The island, being overwhelmingly Royalist, is aghast that the King should send you on such a mission. But if you and your ilk had come twenty years ago, I might still be rector here. Watch your back, sir! Some of the fanatics here would not hesitate to kill a former agent of the hated Protector."

Luke was soon inside what proved to be a cozy snug and sharing a home-made strong liquor with the host. It tasted like the best French brandy, rather than the product of an ex-rector's makeshift still.

"And what really brings you here? I have been an outsider for twenty years, and for the last few forced to live here. The Baron will exile me the moment Felix dies. If Felix had not afforded me his personal protection, and ensured that I did not starve, I would be long dead, or at least driven from the island. Consequently, I cannot help you very much."

"But you can. Although I was sent here ostensibly to protect the Marquess from an anticipated murder, I am now more concerned with three other issues, —the death of Harry Bohm some time ago, the recent manslaughter of Toby Bentley, and the murder of your niece Ann Bentley."

"Poor Toby, I am sure that the shot he received was meant for you, but most of the islanders are hopeless marksmen. All of them avoided the wars, and there are so little game or even vermin that they get little practice. The Bohm family reserve the rabbit warren, and the killing of nesting sea birds to themselves. How can I help regarding Ann?"

"I originally assumed that the shooting of Toby and the murder of his wife were part of an orchestrated campaign to prevent them informing me of some secret that somebody did not want revealed. Now, if I accept that Toby was an accidental victim, then the death of his wife probably has nothing to do with my arrival on the island, and may stem from events in the distant past, perhaps when you were still rector."

"It may help your investigation if I start by explaining the position of the Moore family on Nith. They have been here for centuries, and next to the family of the then marquess, the Neales, were probably the most influential. So much so that the grandfather of the last Neale marquess married one of his daughters to a Bohm and another to a Moore. These daughters were twins and the eldest by a few minutes married the Bohm. When the last Neale died without children the marquisate evolved to the nearest male descendant through that earlier female line. Felix Bohm whose ancestors had long left the island for London and the south, inherited the title. Margaret Neale, Harry's Bohm widow, had she had a son before Peregrine died, that son would have been the marquess."

"So, the Bohm's were just lucky that circumstances fell the way they did? What did you do before Bohm took over the marquisate?"

"I studied theology at Oxford and was eventually appointed rector of St Nith by the old marquess, Peregrine Neale. My brother farmed the family property, and had a daughter Ann."

"Was she pregnant before the current Marquess and his valet Toby arrived on the island?"

"Yes."

"Who was Ellen's father?"

"I don't know."

"Surely your brother investigated who got his daughter pregnant?"

"No, unfortunately at the same time as Ann became pregnant my brother, his wife and their only son died of an influenza type epidemic that hit the island in 1642. Ann, her two sisters and I were the only Moores that survived."

"So, at the critical moment the new Marquess arrived with his valet who was hastily married off to the pregnant and orphaned Ann. Surely you objected to the marriage of your niece to such a disabled Toby?"

"At the time, no! We were not aware that Toby was as simple as he was, and Felix's gesture in the short term saved Ann and the Moore family from disgrace. Felix conducted the marriage ceremony as I had already lost my license. Felix continued to help our family. He let me stay in the rectory and assist in services, which he conducted for almost twenty years. I remained his unofficial curate until the Baron put an end to that. But as time went on, I deeply regretted my approval of Ann's marriage. Toby declined rapidly in recent years and I felt deeply for my niece."

"Over the years have you never wondered who her real father might be?"

"Not really. Once Felix arrived and found a secure place for Ann, and her child in his household, it ceased to be an issue."

"Except that now, Ellen wants to know the identity of her father."

"A dangerous idea. Such knowledge can benefit nobody. Ann should never have told Ellen that Toby was not her father. I do not know why she did that."

"So, Ann's pregnancy twenty years ago did not provide in your eyes a motive for her murder?"

"Less so than more recent events."

"What more recent events?"

"The death of Harry Bohm, and the gradual takeover of the island by the Catholic extremists led by the Baron."

"Do you have any comments concerning the religious and political sentiments of the islanders?"

"Twenty years ago, the former marquess was a Catholic and the Catholic majority on the island worshipped in his lordship's chapel. The Protestant minority with myself as rector occupied as required by law all positions within the parish including churchwarden and constable. There was no conflict between the two groups as the Catholics enjoyed a freedom of worship unknown on the mainland, except at the court of the then Queen. The Protestants exercised parochial authority and represented the island before the courts of Yorkshire. When I was sacked, Felix himself took over services in the parish church which were less Protestant and more humanistic. He tolerated the Catholics to an even greater extent, as all of his family other than himself and his youngest son Ralph were Papists. Both father and son had renounced the old church so as they could pursue their careers within the church and the law. He weakened the Protestant position by banning any appeals to the mainland authorities."

"Any significant changes in recent years?"

"Following the death of Harry, Felix withdrew from most perceivable activity on the island. Its day to day running fell into the hands of the Baron, Michael, and the steward Denholm. Both pushed an aggressive Catholic agenda. The steward developed his own team of henchmen that sought to rival and usurp the role of the Protestant constable and his men although Corby has more than held his own. In addition, Felix has retained enough of his wits to deprive them of any legal authority although they still exist as a private Catholic militia."

"Have the Protestants coped with this aggressive Catholicism?"

"With difficulty. When Felix withdrew from active participation the parish church temporarily fell into disuse. It was eventually saved by the Protestant laymen, particularly John Corby who on a Sunday afternoon read from the Book of Common Prayer. Corby alienated the Baron when he refused to allow the Catholics to conduct services there—a use that is completely illegal as you would know. The last straw for Corby and his co-religionists was the revelation that the Baron's secretary was indeed a covert Catholic priest. When you leave the island, take Perry with you—in chains."

9

"Why did the Papists suddenly flex their muscles?" asked Luke.

"With the death of the Lord Protector, and the collapse of the extreme Protestant Republic, the Baron expects the new King to be very favorable towards Roman Catholics. He constantly repeats the false rumor that the King's brother and heir to the throne is a Catholic and emphasizes the obvious fact that the King's mother is devoted to that faith. He has convinced some of the islanders that the returning King is himself a covert Catholic. I am sure that this is why many of the Papist flock here cannot accept that a King, so favorable to them according to Perry, should send one of the radical Protestant Protector's former henchmen to their island. You were a fool to come here without armed support."

Luke thought it wise not to reveal to Martin that a body of troops was on its way. He continued questioning, "How did Ann adjust to this changing situation? Could her failure to do so have contributed to her murder?"

"In the last few years the Marquess has not taken supper with the family. He takes his meals deep inside his private apartment to which only Toby, Ann, Ellen and the Marchioness had access. Somebody, and I suspect Ann, stirred up by sister Hannah and her husband John Corby managed to get a convincing message across to the King's envoys at the end of last year that the situation on this island deserved to be investigated. The excuse put abroad that someone had threatened to kill the Marquess on the day of the King's coronation was done to conceal deeper and more serious problems, the most urgent in my eyes being the death of Harry."

"What exactly happened to Harry? I hear conflicting stories."

"Murdered at the instigation of his brother Michael, or more probably orchestrated by Michael's wife, Alice."

"At their instigation—not by them?"

"Michael may have done the deed himself, but he has since constructed a convincing alibi."

"What evidence have you of the couple's guilt?"

"None."

"Then on what is this wild assertion based?"

"Intuition and common sense. Michael had motive."

"Such as?"

"The usual—lust and power."

"Surely as the heir apparent, and with the title of Baron, Michael already had the power. It was Harry who missed out."

"Not in reality! Michael had the nominal power, but he was increasingly overshadowed by his younger twin."

"Harry from what I hear may have been the more able, but this does not necessarily create a problem for Michael, whose future is totally protected by English law."

"Harry was carving out for himself a position more powerful than his elder brother and was exerting a dominant influence on the family."

"In what way?"

"This island and the hereditary possessions of the Marquess of Nith lack resources. The Bohm family before they acceded to the marquisate had begun to dabble in property. Harry made a fortune in land deals around London, and on the Yorkshire mainland. With the outbreak of the civil war Harry Bohm, nominally in the name of his father, purchased dozens of relinquished Royalist estates. Harry was efficient and ruthless, and openly referred to his older brother as a dithering incompetent."

"Michael panicked and removed his brother before the more ruthless sibling removed him? Is that your theory?" summarized Luke.

"Exactly! Michael engaged in a preemptive strike. He had his brother killed probably by the secret Catholic militia, before Harry had him murdered."

"No, not reasonable Martin! I cannot accept that either brother was under such pressure that fratricide was their rational solution," concluded Luke to Martin's obvious disappointment.

"You cannot ignore that this brotherly antagonism was further inflamed by the lust Harry had for his sister-in-law, Alice—Michael's wife. Their adulterous relationship has been common knowledge for years—a constant humiliation for the Baron."

"If that was the case, why would Alice join her husband in removing Harry?"

"That I do not know. Maybe Alice tired of Harry's affections. Maybe he refused to desist. Interrogate Alice at length. Most of the problems on this island stem from that woman's ruthless ambition!"

"This cottage is not far from where Harry's body was found. Where were you on the day of the murder?" asked Luke, suddenly changing tack.

"Watching Harry die."

"How can that be?" asked an astonished Luke.

"I had a direct view of his death. I was fifty yards offshore fishing from my dinghy. I looked up and saw a man's body tumbling down the cliff and crashing onto the rocks below. I rowed as fast as I could to the site. By the time I reached it James Denholm was already removing the body. He coldly informed me that Harry had climbed over the edge of the precipice to collect a bird he had shot, lost his footing and crashed to his death but someone could easily have pushed him."

For the next week Luke kept a low profile. He anxiously awaited the arrival of his troops, and hopefully a well-armed frigate whose cannons could coerce the island if necessary. He was delighted that the Marquess took his advice and resumed having the evening meal with the family and was seen out and about on the island—even conducting the Sunday service in the parish church.

This was well received by all, except the Baroness. Alice could not conceal her annoyance that the center of attention at the evening meal reverted to the Marquess and Marchioness, and little conversation was directed at her or her husband. Luke noticed the obvious alarm in both the Baron and the steward Denholm when Felix announced that he had asked Luke to provide troops to effect any changes that he may wish to introduce.

Luke delighted in Michael and Alice's scarcely concealed panic. He turned the screw further on these potential opponents when he explained that in addition to at least half a company of musketeers, a heavily armed frigate would anchor off the island to enforce the King's will, and tightly control access to and from the island.

James Denholm looked particularly depressed.

The following week the anticipated troops arrived under Mark's command. He explained that in authorizing the allocation of much needed troops, Evan was unable to free up any serving officer and had issued him with an updated commission as an active lieutenant colonel. Mark handed Luke a letter from Evan explaining this action and noting that he was busy securing centers of opposition to the returning King and could be of no immediate assistance to Luke should serious trouble arise on the island.

Luke and Mark were on their own.

Evan's postscript was revealing, "If your mission had not been specifically ordered by the King, General Monk would not have found the necessary troops, and cannot spare any senior officer. Mark has had no active military experience but under your overall command this should not be a problem."

Luke briefed Mark on developments during his absence and then organized with James Denholm accommodation within Nith House for his men. Very quickly, and deliberately Luke made their presence felt by instituting regular patrols and setting up small tented garrisons at each end of the island.

It was now time to confront the notorious Lady Alice.

She was in her early forties, neither tall or small, beautiful or plain. Her brown hair with tints of red was worn excessively long, covering part of her breasts that her low-cut bodice would otherwise have revealed.

Alice was not to be brow beaten. She began her confrontation with Luke by remarking that his invasion of the island now seemed complete and wondered what unwanted changes he intended to impose of them.

"My lady, you know that I am not here to reform the island. The purported reason for my presence is to prevent the murder of the Marquess, although most of those I have spoken to are more concerned that I solve the apparent murder of your brother-in-law, Harry. Another common attitude these people share is their apparent intense dislike of your ladyship."

Alice ignored this deliberately delivered barb.

"As you no doubt have discovered I am not a local. I arrived in 1642 with the Marquess and my husband."

"Does being an outsider account for your unpopularity?" asked a provocative Luke.

"In part, but most of the enmity stems from simple jealousy. I am the next Marchioness and have made it clear that under Michael and myself many people will lose their undeserved favors and special positions, especially those gentry and yeoman families that despise our aristocratic blood."

"I was not aware of your aristocratic lineage," commented a skeptical Luke.

"My grandfather was the notorious gambling Duke of Oare. He married my mother off to a very wealthy London goldsmith. As patriarch of the family, when I reached an age to be married, he discovered that a popular cleric, alchemist and magician was soon to become a Marquess, and offered Felix Bohm a dowry he could not refuse to marry me to his eldest son Michael."

"Why was the duke so anxious to marry you to the son of a man, many viewed simply as a charlatan?"

"I don't know. Grandfather died a short time after my wedding. I suspect that Felix convinced him, as he apparently convinced the then King that he could turn base metals into gold, and there would be a financial return for him through our marriage. Grandfather could not resist a gamble."

"And was there any return?"

"Yes, but not through the magical means my grandfather had hoped for. It was through the property purchases that Michael and Harry with the aid initially of my family accumulated. After we moved here, Harry, assisted by me greatly increased the family's property assets."

"So, you worked closely with your brother-in-law over the years?"

"Harry and I went to London on many occasions as I was often needed to negotiate with members of my family on many joint family acquisitions."

"What did these acquisitions comprise of?"

"Two quite separate areas of property. In the first place the Bohms bought up as much of the outskirts of an expanding London that they could manage. Secondly with the onset and continuance of the civil war they bought Royalist property from those anxious to prevent their assets falling into the hands of the Parliamentarian victors. These properties were handed over for almost nothing on the promise that when the war was over, they would be returned to their owners at the same price."

"That process is about to begin in earnest now with the return of the King, and thousands of his exiled supporters."

"And that, despite your denials is really why the King sent you here, and probably ordered you to invade Nith with his troops."

"What do you mean?"

"When the King's men were here last year Michael explained to them that those Royalist properties could not be returned at anything like the price, we had paid for them. In most cases a decade or more of outlays and the increased costs of living would force us to charge at least fifty per cent more than we paid. Ashcroft and Stokey were furious. They made it clear that in their eyes such exorbitant demands, especially on property transferred on trust, would not be permitted by the King. In addition, they believed it would make the return of the King, and his acceptance amongst the people much more difficult. No, you are not here to prevent some woman murdering Felix, nor discovering what happened to Harry. You are to make sure that we return the property of hundreds of devoted Royalists at minimal cost to them—and maximum plaudits for the King," Alice sneered.

"If you did accede to the King's demands would the Bohm family income drop considerably?" asked a dogged Luke.

"Not greatly. The immense wealth that the family has built up through its property investments will not suffer that much. It is an expanding London that continues to fill the family coffers."

"So, you could accept the King's demands, and comply with what you consider my purpose here, without too much angst"

Alice shrugged her shoulders.

Luke changed the subject. "The death of Harry nevertheless remains a mystery. If he was murdered, whom would you suspect?"

"If we were on the mainland, the possibilities would be limitless. Harry was not always honorable in his land dealings and made many enemies. None of these potential killers could ever make it to the island. As you have discovered, movement on or off the island is well controlled and publicly visible. If Harry was murdered, it was by someone on the island, and that could only be on the orders of one man."

"Who is?" asked Luke.

10

"Nothing happens on Nith without the knowledge of the all-powerful magician, Felix—undoubtedly manipulated by that two-faced Jane."

"The Marquess had his own son murdered?"

"Yes."

"Why?"

"A matter of honor."

"His affair with you?"

"There was no such affair. And that would not have annoyed Felix. He tried to jump into my bed himself when we first came to Nith. Harry's crime was much more serious than an adulterous urge. It was seen as destructive to the family. Harry's indiscretions started in about 1644 but was not widely known until a few weeks before his death."

"What do you mean widely known?"

"To the inner family—Felix, Jane, Michael, myself, Ralph, Felicity and Margaret. That is why the family won't discuss Harry's death. Several of us believe it was suicide. Harry could not stand the disgrace. Margaret won't accept Harry's guilt. She believes other members of the family were involved, and he was murdered to stop him revealing all. We therefore cannot refer to what for me is the obvious motive for his removal."

"Then why tell me?"

"I am tired of Michael and myself being blamed for things for which we bear no responsibility—and to be honest I want to be Marchioness, sooner rather than later. And for the time being the most powerful man on this island is you, Colonel Tremayne. I want your support to obtain what should be mine. You help me—and I will return the favor."

Luke ignored the plea for support, "What was Harry's crime?"

"In mid 1644 he went to London on one of his many trips—one of the few on which I did not accompany him. He disappeared. Michael went to look for him without any success. A month later a ransom note was delivered, purporting to come from officers of the Parliamentary London militia. It claimed that Harry, believed to be a Royalist officer escaping a battle, had been captured by the Parliamentary soldiers. As was the custom before Parliament re-organized its army, officers could ransom off their captives—if of sufficient wealth to be worth the trouble. The amount asked was immense. Felix utilized most of his resources and in fact borrowed a large amount from my family. Michael and I went to London, and using one of my brothers, as a negotiator, we obtained Harry's release."

"Did the islanders know of Harry's capture?"

"Yes, that part of the story was highly publicized. Felix increased rents to help pay for the ransom. The islanders suffered for a few years as they struggled to recover their economic position."

"How did the islanders relate to the returning Harry?"

"As nearly all of them are Royalists, Harry became something of a hero."

"What went wrong?"

"A few years ago, the family lawyer, and the younger brother of Michael and Harry, Ralph, who rarely left London, made a surprise visit to Nith. He was locked in conversation with Felix for hours, and then left, talking to no one. The next day Harry was summoned by Felix. A week or so later Felix informed the family that Harry's capture and ransom fifteen years earlier had been a hoax."

Luke was dismayed and drawing in a deep breath asked, "What actually occurred?"

"Harry was never captured by the Parliamentarians. He went into hiding with a few friends and the ransom money went directly to him. Harry used it to start his own landed empire, independent of the family. He consequently became a very wealthy man in his own right."

"What happened to Harry's ill-gotten gains?"

"As part of the deal not to reveal Harry's imposture beyond the immediate family, Harry signed over his properties to Felix. This proved too much for Harry, and not long after his capitulation, he committed suicide."

"Certainly, your story provides a strong motive for such an outcome, although it does create a motive for both Felix, and your husband Michael. There could have been a feeling that the disgrace Harry brought to the family needed to be more adequately punished."

"You do not need to include Michael among your suspects. The massive increase in the family assets that the acquisition of Harry's private empire created, assets that Michael will soon inherit, has obliterated any desire for revenge from his mind."

"How did Ralph uncover Harry's dastardly act?"

"I don't know. He refuses to discuss it. I understand from a few comments that Felicity has made that she, not Ralph, discovered the fraud."

"Well, your comments have determined who I must interview next—Ralph and Lady Felicity."

That evening Luke briefed Mark on his conversation with Alice.

"Lies!" was Mark's intuitive response.

"What leads you to that ill-informed and unsubstantiated conclusion?" asked Luke, half- jokingly.

"Why would the woman whom most see as the most powerful female on the island, reveal such a disastrous family secret to a complete stranger, when there is no need for it? She is leading you on. We may have the power on Nith at the moment, but in a few weeks, we will be gone. Any help you could give to Alice would be short lived. And why would Harry, who by all accounts was a tough and aggressive businessman, meekly hand over his vast assets without a murmur?"

"I must admit that initially I had similar reservations, but she was honest regarding her motives. She confessed that she was tired of Michael and herself being the major suspects for anything that happened, and she was simply out to show that Harry's death was either a suicide, or a murder ordered by Felix."

"Agreed, her story is plausible, but it need not be true."

Ralph Bohm kept a low profile. Apart from his presence at two or three suppers, Luke had not seen him around the island. He dressed as a London lawyer in black or dark brown clothing, softened by an elaborate collar that was almost a ruff. He had not adapted to the more relaxed style of country living.

Before endeavoring to find this elusive younger Bohm, Luke needed to know more about him. Ralph's stepmother, the Marchioness Jane, had been the warmest of Luke's earlier consultants. He sought a further audience with her. She readily consented and immediately attacked her would-be successor, the Baroness Alice. "You must have hidden charm which you did not use on me," she teased. "I hear Alice has been spilling the family's most intimate secrets."

"Yes—and that is why I am here. Before I question Ralph about how he uncovered his brother's fraud against the family, I need to know more about him."

"I can't help you very much. Ralph is the dark horse of the family and from the moment Felix and the family moved here, until Ralph's sudden arrival a few years back with his disastrous news about Harry, he had little to do with the family."

"Was there any particular reason for his split from the family? Why did he not come north with the rest of you?"

"He had not completed his legal studies when the family moved. Felix expected him to follow as soon as these were complete, but it never happened. Ralph placed his London legal career ahead of everything else. He had previously alienated his brothers by his renunciation of Catholicism. Only a practicing Anglican, could pursue a legal career. The older brothers said little at the time, as Ralph was doing exactly as their father Felix had done to study theology."

"Was this ultimate antagonism of Michael and Harry towards Ralph due to their loyalty to the family's traditional faith, or did they think the youngest brother was trying to ingratiate himself with their father by adhering to his pragmatic Anglicanism?"

"Michael was genuinely concerned about his brother's eternal damnation as a heretic, but Harry was influenced more by its possible effect on the family hierarchy, and his position within it."

"There was little contact between Ralph and the family for over sixteen years?" posited Luke.

"Felix corresponded with him quite regularly, but there was little physical contact. Harry may have met him on occasions when he was in London, but it was never a matter of note. None of the family attended his wedding to Felicity. We were not told of it for months," explained Jane.

"His marriage to an ultra-catholic Royalist who had been a countess at the court of France, must have softened the attitude of his Catholic brothers to him."

"Yes, in some ways. Before he married Felicity, the family had picked up rumors that like many London lawyers, he was becoming quite Puritanical and revolutionary. Felicity certainly put an end to that drift toward Puritan republicanism."

"Tell me about Felicity!"

"Apart from having been married previously to a French count who was one of the royal courtiers; being of English gentry birth; and initially employing Ralph as her lawyer, I know nothing. She refuses to discuss her past. If Felix's story about being murdered by a woman on the day of the King's coronation came true, Felicity would be my suspect. She is a woman of mystery who in her time on this island has done nothing to clarify her past, or reveal her attitude to the island's, or for that matter the nation's problems."

Jane who had been looking out of her window as she talked to Luke suddenly announced, "Speak of the devil! Ralph is talking to one of the gardeners at the entrance to the maze. Catch him before this most elusive Bohm brother disappears again."

Luke explained to Ralph his role on the island. "I am currently investigating three murders, one past, one present and one future—your brother Harry some years ago, Ann Bentley last week, and the Marquess on the day of the King's coming coronation."

"The last is a ridiculous piece of fantasy explicable only in terms of father's declining mind," spluttered Ralph.

"But the death of your brother is another matter. I have been told that it was your actions that led Harry to commit suicide."

"Was its suicide?"

"I hoped that you could clarify the situation. How did you come to uncover your brother's fraud against the family?"

"No great mystery! It was only in the last few years that I became involved in London real estate. One of my clients wanted to buy a property which was listed at an exorbitant price. Imagine my surprise when I noticed that the signature of the would-be seller was Harry Bohm. I contacted my father to express alarm that he was selling property at such an excessive profit and this would damage the family name—and also to get a reduced price for my client. He replied that the property in question was not one that the family owned. It did not take me long to uncover a portfolio of estates owned by Harry, independent of the family—all totally unknown to us. I immediately met with father and my two brothers to discuss my discovery."

"What happened when you revealed the situation?"

"Absolutely nothing! Harry claimed as a second son, unlikely to receive anything from the family estate, he was simply building up assets for his own future. He also convinced father that while doing this, he had not neglected massively increasing the family assets at the same time, which was true."

"How did you come to discover the ransom scam?"

"It was Felicity who noted that in the list of properties that Harry bought was a large part of north east London. This very expensive area of the expanding city cost a fortune—and it was one of the first group of properties Harry bought in his own name. She asked herself where he could possibly have acquired such a large sum to start his property development career in such a wealthy area."

"But how did you get from concern regarding the source of Harry's finance, to discovering the ransom hoax?"

11

"Luck on my part, stupidity on Harry's. The amount of his initial investment was very similar to the sum of the ransom. I employed a few men who eventually tracked down Harry's accomplices."

"Why did you pursue this vendetta against your brother? And why did you inform your father and brother of Harry's deception? As a third son your future would be better served by doing a deal with Harry for part of his assets in return for keeping quiet."

Ralph was speechless.

"I am amazed that such a suggestion should be uttered by a magistrate. We are both officers of the law, and as such obliged to report and act on any crime that we might discover. In addition to my duty as lawyer, loyalty to my family was important. In addition, Felicity argued that we had a duty before God to reveal Harry's sinful betrayal."

Luke was not convinced by Ralph's high-minded explanation of his motives which he immediately demolished. "Yet despite your profession of doing your duty by the law, in the end you covered up Harry's crime."

"Yes, family loyalty dominated, but justice was nevertheless served. Harry gained nothing from his deception. Father in return for Harry transferring the bulk of his assets back into the family, decided that his fraud should remain a secret. Consequently, I am surprised that any member of family mentioned it to you, especially Alice, who was complicit in many of Harry's covert dealings."

"Some family members believe this is the key factor leading to Harry's death—either murder by a disgruntled family member, or suicide in the light of the disgrace he may have felt. Which option is the most likely?"

"Neither, it was an accident. Harry in retrieving a shot bird on the cliff's edge slipped and fell to his death. The steward James Denholm confirms that Harry was on the cliff just before he fell. Harry was not a person who would commit suicide. If he was experiencing a low point in his life, he would immediately bounce back determined to succeed. None of the family wanted Harry dead."

"I don't believe that. Your father, brother Michael or even yourself may have considered Harry had not received sufficient punishment for his crime against the family. Given the religious obsessions of some of your family members, they could probably justify murdering Harry as delivering God's justice."

"The mental problems afflicting some members of the family might lead them to indulge in such fantasies, but for that very reason you cannot believe everything you have been told."

"Clearly you accept that Harry's death as an accident, and your father's potential murder as sheer fantasy—can you help me with the murder of Ann Bentley?"

"Surprisingly I can, although I was not on the island during most of father's tenure as Marquess. In the short time I have been here, I have come to know the Bentleys and their friends quite well. With father's withdrawal into his magic world, I am the only member of the ruling family who is an active Protestant. Father asked me with the help of John Corby to reactivate the parish church and counter the extreme Papist views of Father Perry. The Protestant families of Bentley, Corby, and Kitchen not only represent a different religious tradition, but are essentially lesser gentry and yeoman, rather than aristocrats of long standing, such as my wife and sisters-in-law, and the more recent elevations such as my father and eldest brother."

"What is your impression of the island Protestant community and the position of Ann Bentley within it?"

"Over the last year or so the Bentleys became a very dysfunctional family. As you are aware, Toby was never the full shilling, but made up for his deficiencies in his absolute loyalty to father, and his own family. The latter was partially shattered when Ann revealed to Ellen that Toby was not her birth father, but inexplicably refused to say who was. In retaliation Ellen refused tell her mother who had impregnated her. The sensuality of these Bentley women has caused many problems over the years—and right up to the present. There was constant tension between Ann and her sister Hannah, the origins of which I have not discovered, but I could advance an educated guess."

"Which is?"

"Ann slept with dozens of males. I doubt if her brothers-in-law were off limits."

Luke changed the direction of his questioning, "Have you dealt with the former rector, Martin Moore?"

"Yes, quite a lot. He has asked me to take steps, with father's approval, of having him reinstated as a clergyman."

"Has that progressed far?"

"No, I am awaiting the return of the Archbishop of York to his diocese, and the re-establishment of the traditional national church. I have yet to be acquainted with the grounds on which Martin seeks his defrocking to be reversed."

"Those grounds might explain a lot about this island immediately prior to your family taking up its inheritance."

Having ascertained from Ralph that his wife was in the apple orchard sketching, Luke indicated that he would question her immediately. "Don't be surprised if she is uncooperative. She is a devoted Royalist and becomes almost apoplectic when she hears that the King is rewarding enemies like yourself while neglecting many who have suffered in his cause."

Forewarned Luke adopted a firm but understanding approach. "My lady, I understand your attitude to me, but in this situation, I am not a former general in the army of the Republic, but an agent of King Charles II sent here to prevent a murder. Do you have any comments to make on the claim that the Marquess will be murdered on the day the King is crowned?"

"The Marquess, both on this island and in his earlier life, undoubtedly alienated many families, a member from which may seek revenge."

"But why would anyone wait so long? The Marquess will die from natural causes sooner rather than later—and why predict it would happen in such dramatic circumstances?"

"Felix is a showman, selling his alleged magical powers to a gullible audience. The nature of the threat against his life has the trappings of that sort of environment. The Marquess created this prediction so that when it occurs under his own direction, belief in his magic will be validated."

"You are one of the few people who accepts the possibility of the threat being real, even if contrived by Felix himself. Tell me about yourself, my lady!"

"What do you know already?"

"That as a young English girl you were married to a French count whose status required him to attend the French court."

"Both my parents died when I was little more than a child. I was brought up reluctantly by my uncle and aunt. He was a London merchant and goldsmith who had many dealings with the French. I was taken by my guardians to receptions at the French embassy, where I met and fell in love with one of the ambassador's staff. Although I was still in my mid- teens, uncle was anxious to get rid of me, and I equally determined to escape his control. We were married in the French embassy, and soon after I moved to France with my husband—an almost penniless younger son of a count. A year later his father and two elder brothers were killed when the Spaniards surprised a French unit in the Netherlands and slaughtered the whole company. As a result, my husband became the count, and we moved to Paris to become courtiers to the boy King, Louis XIV."

"How then did a French countess at the royal court become the wife of an English lawyer in London?"

"Misfortune and chance! My husband took offence at a remark made about me and challenged the offender to a duel. Both men died. I was not popular at court and had few friends. I returned to London and discovered that I could not transfer any of the assets I had built up as a French countess to England without the help of a lawyer. My aunt recommended Ralph."

"My lady, as you are aware preventing the murder of the Marquess has been overshadowed by two other deaths—what really happened to your brother-in-law Harry, and the recent murder of Ann Bentley?"

"I cannot help with either. I was in London until well after Harry's death, and unlike my husband, since my arrival here, I have no dealings with the inferior classes."

"But you have been here for several years after Harry's death. You must have picked up the gossip and rumors surrounding it?"

"You need more than rumors and gossip!"

"Our church courts worked on that basis for centuries," retorted an irritated Luke.

"The family's official position was drummed into Ralph and myself the minute we arrived. Harry had slipped in trying to retrieve a bird he had shot and fell to his death. It was an accident. But this was the never the view of his widow. Margaret believed he had been pushed—murdered. And Alice in one of her many mean moments claimed Harry probably committed suicide to get away from his wife."

"That is a piece of useful tittle tattle I have not heard before."

"It's a wonder Alice has not come running to you with a treasure chest of calumnies against everybody on the island. Although she is my sister-in-law, she is a nasty piece of work. Do not believe a word she says. Relevant to your enquiries, she did tell me once that Ann Bentley was available to every male on the island."

"Ann's relationships do seem significant in my enquiry. I am surprised that Lady Alice would make such comments. Her own relationships seem equally as important. Didn't she have a liaison with Harry?"

"So, rumor has it. But let's be clear, Harry was a womanizer, and he did not limit his activities to his own class. If Harry was murdered, it could have been any father or husband on the island, and beyond."

"Your knowledge of Harry's sexual adventures must largely be hearsay?"

Felicity laughed, "Not entirely!"

There was significant silence as Felicity determined how much she should tell her questioner. The experienced inquisitor, Luke, did not break the silence.

Eventually she continued, "Harry was a vile man. One of the reasons Ralph and I did not come to the island until his death was that during his many visits to London, he occasionally stayed with us. On a number of occasions when Ralph was absent, he tried to seduce me—and most of the women we introduced him to. I understand he was equally as free with his services on this island. Ironically the sister-in- law who did succumb to his wiles, the Baroness Alice, has probably managed to restrain him in recent years."

"Did Margaret put up with this without complaint?"

"You would have to ask someone who was on the island. Since we have been here, she has become a Catholic recluse, who talks to no one except Father Perry—and her single theme is that Harry was murdered. If I were her, I would be celebrating the fact, not seeking revenge. His death freed her from a monster."

Luke, as if guided by an outside force suddenly asked, "Regarding Father Perry, does he exercise his authority to the detriment of the Bohm family?"

"Our Catholic community on this island is diverse, if not divided. Most are appreciative of the Marquess, who while having converted to Protestantism to pursue his career, did nothing to inhibit the traditional faith of his family and most of the islanders. Perry's arrival alarmed some of us who feared his aggressive Counter Reformation attitudes would unnecessarily alienate the Protestant minority. There is a considerable antagonism within our community towards Perry. The Marquess prevented Perry spreading his Catholic reformist message, but in recent years strongly supported by the Baron and his wife and the steward Denholm, Perry has had a lot more freedom."

12

Felicity continued, "Why has Michael and Alice adopted such a strong pro-Perry stance? What links them together? When I raised the issue, I was told that that they had always wanted to assist Perry in his missionary activity on the island, but the Marquess had prevented them. I would also ask, why Perry ever returned to Nith in the first place?"

"What do you mean—'returned to Nith'?" asked Luke to confirm what he already knew.

"William Perry is a local who was a wild one in his youth, and greatly upset the Catholic community as he cavorted with the most lecherous of the Protestant wenches. He left the island just before the Bohms arrived. The answers to three further questions might assist your enquiries. Why did Perry leave? Under what circumstances did this wild youth transform into a devout priest? Is Michael and Alice's support of him related to his sordid past, or his current missionary enthusiasm? The distrust of Perry by many of the Catholic community has more to do with what they remember of his youth, than any lack of sympathy with his extreme doctrines."

"I am a little surprised given your own ultra-Catholic past that you are so critical of Perry," commented a surprised Luke.

"That's because you know little of my past. I was brought up by my parents in the Church of England. When I was orphaned, my Catholic uncle showed no interest in my religious affiliation, until he saw the opportunity to get rid of me as the wife of a Catholic French diplomat. At the French court I saw the destructive influence of fanatical counter-reformation Catholic priests. Luckily the two successive chief ministers of France, Cardinal Richelieu and Cardinal Mazarin, have kept this extremism in check."

"Perry tells me he does not act in any aggressive way and accepts that most of his flock are traditional English Catholics, suspicious of the continental reforms."

"Believe him at your peril—and that of future harmony on the island."

"One last question—although you may not be able to help me. Before the Bohm's moved here in 1642, did any of the family visit Nith to prepare the way for their succession?"

"Yes. When Felix heard that the death of Peregrine Neale was imminent, he sent Harry and Ralph north. Ralph dealt with some legal matters and returned to London within the week. Harry stayed on for a month or so, covering the period through the death of the old marquess, to the arrival of his father."

"Significant information! So many things seem to have happened just before Felix arrived. Now there is a possibility that Harry at least may have been involved in whatever occurred during that critical period. Why did Felix send Harry and Ralph, and not his eldest son Michael?"

"Felix never had any confidence in the business and administrative abilities of Michael. Michael was always considered less effective than his brother. It has only been since the death of Harry that Michael has become a competent businessman and administrator. He finally emerged out of the shadow cast by his ruthless and charismatic sibling."

Luke and Felicity reached the end of the orchard when Ralph appeared and jokingly cajoled his wife, "I hope you have not filled the colonel's ear with your fanciful view of my family?"

He turned to Luke, "It looks like I have returned just in time to correct any false impressions Felicity may have created."

"No, your wife has given me a very prosaic and factual account of matters with which she was concerned. Regarding your family two issues were revealed upon which I would like you to comment. Why did your father prefer Harry over Michael in building up the family fortune?"

"Not a great mystery. Michael was the eldest and would inherit the marquisate. He needed no profession or job. He just had to learn to be the lord of the manor. It is clear that given his performance in recent years

Michael would have been just as effective as Harry, but he was never given a chance by father."

"The second question—what can you tell me about your visit here in early 1642, just before the death of Peregrine Neale?"

"I was only here a few days, clarifying the will and testament with the Neale family lawyer, and negotiating some minor points regarding some codicils to the will that would not have been appropriate in my view. The discussion ended harmoniously."

"Why did Harry stay on?"

"Father wanted a family member on the spot when Peregrine died to oversee the succession. He was here much longer than anyone anticipated, because the old marquess took longer to die than was expected."

"Did Harry strike any problems during his period here?"

"I gather he clashed with the then rector Martin Moore. The details of this encounter, I have yet to uncover as I only heard of the problem from Martin a day or so ago."

Luke was delighted with what Ralph and his wife had revealed and informed Mark that they would now concentrate on Ann Bentley's murder. The role of her uncle and sister almost twenty years ago may be relevant. In addition, it was possible that Harry Bohm was involved in the life of the islanders in the month or so before Felix became marquess.

Luke next questioned Hannah Corby regarding her sister. Ann Bentley had been buried two days earlier after a service conducted according to the Book of Common Prayer by the Marquess, assisted by Martin who had delivered a moving eulogy of his niece.

Luke found Hannah making cheese. She immediately exclaimed that her husband was not at home.

"I have not come to see John, but to question you about long forgotten times. It seems that in trying to solve your sister's murder, I need to understand what happened on the island just before and just after the Bohm family succeeded to the marquisate."

"That does not seem logical," retorted Hannah. "If the motives for the murder can be found in that period, why would a killer wait almost two decades? The cause is more likely related to her latter-day closeness to the Marquess, and the feared revelations of your investigation."

"I was initially inclined to that opinion, but too many people have raised the controversies involving your family at that time—the pregnancy of your sister and the defrocking of your uncle. It would help if you could tell me who seduced Ann that led to Ellen's conception."

"I told you before, I do not know. Ann refused to tell Ellen and everybody else the name of her seducer—probably because she did not know."

"I find that hard to believe," retorted a surprised Luke.

"Not if you were the island slut, sleeping with whoever was on offer. Why do you think Felix married her off to the unfortunate Tobias immediately he was made aware of the situation—not that it stopped Ann's serial dalliances."

"They continued right up to the time of her death?" probed Luke

"She never stopped, but her role in recent years looking after the Marquess, did reduce her opportunities."

"Given the circumstances that you describe in the period around Ellen's conception, you must have known a range of possible fathers?"

"Ann preferred older men, and most of the likely suspects at the time are now dead."

"Did Ann confine her relationships to the Protestant community, and her own class?"

"Religion and social status never deterred my passionate sister."

"Were there any rumors at the time that one of her partners may have been Harry Bohm when he was here around the time of the late marquess's death?"

"Yes! At the time Ann boasted of such a liaison, but I doubt it. When the Bohm's arrived here, there was no acknowledgement of any prior meeting between the womanizing Harry, and my equally debauched little sister."

"Your uncle's defrocking! It seems to have occurred as a result of one of the last acts of the late marquess."

"Ask Martin! He previously refused to discuss it with the family but since he asked Mr. Ralph to petition for his reinstatement, he maybe more forthcoming."

"There must have been rumors as to its cause. A local rector is not suddenly defrocked without his flock asking questions and seeking answers, especially if they have not petitioned for it."

"Nor does such action occur over trivia. Uncle Martin must have committed a major offence in the eyes of the church."

"And something more important or significant than the occasional sexual discretion or drunkenness, both habitual with so many clergy before the Civil War. Have you ever thought that whatever Martin did, he may have been covering for someone else? He may have been innocent all along, and now because of changed circumstances, he wants to put the record straight."

"The only person who has ever advanced that theory is Ellen. Martin was never a saint. Women and strong drink were his constant companions, but as you remarked, hardly sufficient reason to be suddenly defrocked."

"It is strange also that it was achieved so quickly. Normally such matters drag on for years—and only succeed if pushed by a powerful figure. Did Martin upset any powerful locals?"

"On this island we are isolated. The only powerful local is the Marquess."

"Did the previous Marquess have any influential connections within the church?"

"I don't know. Even if he did, why would a dying man destroy Martin's career? Peregrine had tolerated Martin's known indiscretions over many years."

"Surely there were rumors at the time as to why Martin had been defrocked, other than his wayward lifestyle?"

"Just after the Bohms arrived there was some gossip that Martin was a male witch, and the women that he cavorted with were part of a diabolical coven. The current Marquess put an end to such speculation by refusing to allow him to leave the island and co-opting him to assist in his alchemical and magic experiments. The Marquess from the beginning protected Uncle Martin from whoever may have been behind his defrocking."

"Was there any truth in this claim of a witches coven presided over by Martin?"

"Not a diabolical coven, but there were two or three wise women who were expert with herbs, on whom the islanders relied on in times of sickness."

"Who were they?"

"My late mother and my two sisters."

"Two sisters, I am aware of Ann, who is the other?"

"Isabel Denholm. Isabel got herself pregnant to the then Papist gamekeeper—and he did the right thing and married her. Martin, as brother and uncle of these women was often thought to exert similar powers."

"If your mother and two sisters exerted such powers, why haven't you?"

"My husband! I married John when I was in my teens, and he, as a Puritan protestant, had no time for such superstition as he called it. I was forbidden to exercise any of the arcane knowledge that mother had passed on to me."

"Does this mean that the only wise woman now left on the island is Isabel Denholm?"

"Perhaps, but Ann probably passed on to Ellen much of her arcane knowledge, and Isabel may be doing the same to her two daughters who are still children."

That evening Luke discussed his conversations of the day with Mark.

"Two major pieces of useful information! Magic, in its peasant form was alive and well on this island before the Marquess introduced his philosophical brand. Secondly, Harry Bohm was here a month or so before the old marquess died and could have played a part in two key events of that period, the seduction of Ann, and the defrocking of Martin."

"You are wasting your time relating Ann's murder to what may have happened twenty years ago. Something occurred in the last month to provoke her murder. It is therefore more likely that current events, and not past history explain the killings. A more thorough probing of what actually happened on the day of those two deaths might be more fruitful," suggested a skeptical Mark.

"You could be right, but they are not exclusive considerations. Something that happened nearly twenty years ago may have become suddenly relevant in the eyes of the murderer, due to some recent event."

"Such as our arrival on the island," added Mark.

"Perhaps, but maybe we are not as important as we both initially thought," commented Luke. "So, what other major changes have occurred recently?"

13

Next morning Luke and Mark visited Toby and Ann Bentley's former servants who had been re-employed by their daughter Ellen. She insisted on being present at their questioning. Luke tried to relax the middle-aged couple, Richard and Mary Banks, by commenting, "Life must be easier under Ellen than it was under her parents."

Richard's surprising reply contradicted Luke's assumption. "Quite the opposite sir! Mistress Ellen keeps us busy in helping with the Marquess, and in assisting her uncle, the old rector."

Mark kept to the task at hand and asked, "On the day she died, when did you last see Mistress Ann alive?"

"Just after noon. We brought the mistress her meal in the room where she was sitting beside the unconscious body of Mr Toby. She asked me to bring her a small cup of hot water into which she dissolved one of her herbal cures, which she administered spoon by spoon down the throat of her comatose husband," answered Mary.

"Any visitors during this period?" probed Mark.

"Yes, the mistress had asked her sister to bring her some herbs. Mistress Isabel dropped in with them but did not stay."

"Any other visitors, before the constable's men discovered the bodies?" probed Luke

"No," said Mary.

"That may not be true, my dear. I saw Mr. Denholm in the yard. He commented that his wife had mislaid her cape, but I did not see him actually enter the apartment," contradicted her husband.

"Where were you when the constable's men discovered the bodies?" continued Luke.

"I was collecting washing from the stone wall where it had been drying, and my husband was at the woodpile cutting wood to fit the smaller grates in Mistress Ellen's apartment."

Ellen suddenly intervened, "Did mother see a lot of Aunt Isabel in the days before her death?"

Mary thought for a moment and replied, "They were in contact daily, but it was only on the day of Ann's death, that Mistress Isabel actually came to the apartment."

"How did they maintain contact before that?" asked Ellen.

"I took letters to the Denholms, and often Mr Denholm came here with the goods Mistress Ann had asked for," answered Richard.

"So Mr Denholm visited his sister-in-law regularly in the days before her death?" probed Luke.

"Yes," was the reply.

Ellen looked surprised—and concerned.

Luke gave Mark a knowing glance and continued, "Did the Bentleys and the Denholm's socialize?"

"Not in recent years. Up to five years ago they saw a lot of each other socially, but since Mr Denholm became steward, there was no contact other than that which I have just outlined—and in the work that the sisters did in common. Mistress Ann and Mistress Isabel were the island's midwives and herbalists. As midwives they often assisted at the same birth There was never any contact at all between Mr Toby and Mr. James Denholm," replied Richard.

"In those last days, did your mistress visit or receive a visit from her uncle Martin Moore?" asked Mark changing the subject.

It was Ellen who answered. "No, there was a falling out between my mother and great uncle. Mother strongly resented me seeing Uncle Martin and was apoplectic when he took my side during my pregnancy."

"Do you know why they fell out?"

"Not really, but Martin implied my mother had a guilty conscience in making him the scapegoat for her past misdemeanors. His attempts to have himself re-instated as rector with the help of Mr Ralph, seems to have upset her considerably."

"Why?"

"I don't know," replied Ellen.

"But I do," was Mary's unexpected response.

The two soldiers and Ellen were astonished and waited expectantly for her to elaborate.

"I overheard the mistress tell Mr Toby that her uncle was being unfair. In making a case for his reinstatement, he would reveal facts that would harm her."

"What facts?"

"I do not know," was the disappointing conclusion.

But Mary Bates had not finished.

"It is not true Mistress Ellen that your mother and great uncle did not see each other in the week before her death. She spent a lot of time at his cottage, and he visited her in Nith Hall on several occasions. She told me she had made an important discovery that Martin had to know about— and act on. His and her life would depend on it. And so, it appears to be."

After leaving Ellen and her servants another visit to Martin Moore was now necessary. As they trekked across the island Mark asked, "What did Martin do that he now wishes to undo—to the apparent detriment of his late niece?"

"He confessed years ago to something he did not do. Such a confession would account for the apparent speed of the defrocking. Without a confession the procedure would have taken years. He probably lied to save others, and now the need for that concealment in his eyes has gone," said Luke.

"But not apparently in the eyes of Ann," commented Mark.

"An interesting difference. What could have happened that changed the opinion of the uncle, but left the niece unmoved?"

"Maybe one of them had a piece of information that the other lacked," commented Mark.

Luke suddenly changed the topic as he sniffed the air. "There is a strong smell of smoke, although I cannot see any," remarked Luke.

"Yes, there has been a fairly large fire that has only recently been extinguished," explained the pragmatic Mark.

As they approached the hollow in which Martin's cottage was located Luke's anxiety accelerated. The grass surrounding the area was burnt black, and a large number of his troops armed with leafy branches were putting out spot fires beyond on the edges of the burnt area.

Mark addressed the young officer, "What happened here, Ensign?"

"Early this morning the men on watch at our post on the north east extremity of the island noticed a fire in this hollow. When we arrived on the scene the building was aflame, and quickly burnt to the ground. The fire then spread in all directions in the dry grass, which while not dangerous has taken a long time to completely put out."

"And what of the inhabitant of the cottage?" asked Luke.

"My men are currently sifting through the ashes and rubble, but up until a few minutes ago they had not come across any human remains."

"Thank God for that," remarked Luke. "Order our men throughout the island that their immediate priority is to find Martin Moore. I will return to Nith Hall and alert everybody there."

Luke spent the rest of the day questioning islanders who might know where Martin would go, if not at home. He sent his men to each location suggested without any success.

That evening Mark and Luke rued a most unsuccessful day. No one had seen Martin. He was last observed the day before by Ralph Bohm when they met in the church to discuss Martin's case for re-instatement.

Next morning Luke spoke to Ralph. "When Martin left you the day before yesterday, what sort of mood was he in?"

"He was delighted when I told him I had just heard that the King's appointment as Archbishop of York was the peculiarly named Accepted Frewin, who is a distant relative of our family, although there was no indication when he would arrive in York, or whether he or lesser officers of the church would deal with our projected petition."

"Did he expand on the evidence he was about to produce as part of his case?"

"No. He was to see me today with that very information."

"Does it not strike you as suspicious that the day before Martin is about to provide you with what must be scandalous information that could affect a lot of islanders, his habitat is burnt to the ground, and he disappears, possibly murdered?" suggested Luke.

"I am a bit more positive than you. Martin is a wily old bird and very fit for his age. He may have heard the arsonists coming, and quietly slipped away. If he suspected that they were out to kill him, he has probably gone into hiding. He knows every nook and cranny on the island from what I have been told."

"I hope you are right," replied Luke.

"You have soldiers stationed all over the island. Surely they saw Martin over the last few days?" asked Ralph.

"On the evening before he disappeared, he was seen returning to his cottage from a fishing expedition. Their next contact was early the next morning, when they confronted the burning cottage, but there was no trace of Martin."

"It's a pity that the island is bereft of night walkers. There are no poachers, other than Martin himself. Maybe one of your men has developed a liaison with an island woman and may have been out and about during the night."

"That's a good thought. I will interview our small garrison located on the north east of the island. If any of them are courting women in the vicinity of Nith Hall they would have travelled over an area that any arsonist or would-be murderer probably traversed."

Luke continued, "If Martin is in trouble and seeking help, to whom would he go?"

"Ellen Bentley or my father."

"No one else?"

"I don't know how close he remained to the women he cavorted with in his younger days, which if you accept his bragging, seems to have included most of the females on the island."

"I'll see Ellen immediately."

Luke failed in this endeavor. Ellen was not at home, and Mary did not know of her whereabouts. He then checked with Mark as to whether their troops had discovered any trace of the missing man. Nobody had seen Martin since the fire.

An unexpected break occurred later that afternoon. Luke was interrupted by a young naval officer.

"General Tremayne, I served under you on *The Cromwell* in the Mediterranean three years ago, I am Lieutenant Philip Bates. I have just come ashore from the *Deadly Arrow* patrolling the waters of the island on your behalf. My commander, Captain Hutton wishes to report in response to your appeal about a missing islander that our lookout sighted a man and woman in a small boat moving along the southern coast of the island. He launched one of our long boats to intercept them. They disappeared around a small cove. The rocks and seas were too treacherous for our men to land and follow the suspicious couple. I have already alerted Lieutenant Colonel Cowper who has sent men to the area. He suggests that we join him there."

"Great work Lieutenant. It must be our missing man and one of his supporters trying to escape the island."

"We have made that impossible, sir. They were stopped heading for the mainland and forced to double back and have come ashore to escape our closer supervision."

Luke and the naval lieutenant found Mark on the edge of a south easterly precipice. Some of his men had descended the difficult cliff face and were making their way along the cliff's base, which was being pounded by heavy seas.

"What's the situation?" asked Luke.

"We saw the boat just below us, but it was putting back out to sea. It contained an older man who clearly was very fit given his rowing prowess in such seas, and a young girl. Probably Martin and Ellen," Mark suggested optimistically.

"Why has the frigate not moved to obtain a better vision of the couple as they move along the eastern edge of the island. Where they are, they have an excellent view of the southern shoreline, but cannot follow their quarry along the eastern periphery."

"There is a reef just offshore along the whole length of the eastern shoreline. Captain Hutton would not risk putting our ship into that dangerous area. Further out to sea, given the intermittent fog, they would see very little, especially as the whole coastline is made up of dozens of little cays, at various angles to the sea. This type of landscape obscures any sea-based vision into the inner parts of most of the inlets."

"That is why I have sent a party below, and hope they make their way around each promontory into the next small bay. We can move from one cliff top to the next, and hopefully keep the couple in sight," explained Mark—which they did.

14

The officers moved along the cliff tops. Luke finally reached a spot that he recognized. "This is where Harry fell to his death, and the path just below us is one used regularly by Martin returning from his fishing trips."

"And there is our man!" declaimed Mark.

"Yes, a boat has just entered the narrow inlet below us and is being rowed to the base of this cliff. With the low tide there is a considerable stretch of sandy beach. They seem to be unloading buckets of fish and lobsters," added the naval Lieutenant to Luke whose attention had been momentarily diverted.

"And the woman beginning to climb the cliff path is definitely Ellen Bentley, although I cannot see the man's face," announced Mark joyfully.

"Let us surprise them at the top of the path!" declared Luke.

The couple were halfway up the path when the man took the lead, carrying two heavy buckets of seafood.

Suddenly to everybody's amazement several shots were heard.

The man fell.

His buckets rolled out of control down the precipice, spraying fish and lobsters as they went.

The woman screamed as she slid down the precarious slope.

A fatal fall was averted by a narrow ledge.

Luke shouted, "What idiot fired those shots. Stop firing!"

"It's not our men. They are under strict orders not to fire, unless they receive a direct order from you or myself," said Mark. "The shots came from near the rabbit warren."

Luke ordered his men to seal off the area and detain anybody they found. He was already scrambling down the slope to the two prone bodies. He ignored the male, and reached Ellen balanced precariously on what was an unstable ledge. She was conscious. After a quick examination, Luke concluded her wounds were slight, but she was in a state of shock. He ordered her not to move an inch.

The soldiers hastily constructed a stretcher, and deftly removed her from her dangerous position, and carried her back to Nith Hall.

Luke cursed himself. Martin who could have helped him solve many of the problems that he confronted had been killed while he watched, powerless to intervene.

He, with Mark turned the body over to ascertain that Martin was indeed dead. They were astounded.

It was not Martin.

It was Ellen's man servant, Richard Banks—and he was dead.

Next day Ellen had fully recovered from her minor wounds having received expert attention from her herb and potion wielding Aunt Isabel, and the alchemist Marquess himself.

When Luke visited her, he was immediately aware of a deep sadness that had enveloped this normally bright personality, but it did not modify the bluntness of his first question.

"What were you doing being rowed for some time in the choppy waters of the North Sea, and heading for the mainland?"

"We were not heading for the mainland. Surely our activity was obvious. I was fishing, and in his absence inspecting Martin's lobster pots."

"To what end?"

"That's a stupid question—to provide the Marquess with the fish and lobsters that have become a favorite part of his diet. In recent years Uncle Martin provided this sea food. As I have been on many such fishing trips with him, I thought with the help of an able rower, I could fill the gap until his return."

"So, you were not deliberately trying to mislead us by creating the impression that Martin had left the island—a plot stymied by the *Deadly Arrow* when it forced you to turn back before you left the south westerly tip of the island?"

Ellen did not answer.

"Don't treat me as a fool young lady! It was only after you had been thwarted that you began fishing and lobster pot gathering."

Tears began to trickle down Ellen's face. "Whatever I was trying to do I did not expect that it would end in the death of old Richard."

"Or yourself. Those shots were probably meant for you as well as for the man whom the shooter misidentified as your Uncle Martin. Who wants you both dead?"

"Whoever killed mother. Someone is obviously trying to wipe out the Moores."

"With that I agree. I am stationing more of my men here for your protection. For the time being do not leave this apartment unless in their company."

"Did you find anybody in the area that may have fired the shots?" asked Ellen.

"Two persons were caught in the cordon. The steward's son, your cousin George, the acting game keeper fired a warning shot at a number of youths who were loitering on the edge of the rabbit warren. The other person in the area was Lady Felicity who was gathering mushrooms under the guidance of one of her servants."

Luke rose to leave and as he reached the door, he surprised Ellen by a last question, "Is Martin safely hidden here by you or the Marquess?"

"No, but I wish he were," she replied and burst into tears. "They have killed him."

"Who are they?"

"Whoever killed my mother," was the uninformative reply.

Later Luke explained his latest interpretation of events to Mark.

"Martin is still alive, and Ellen knows where he is. She would be much more distressed, if she thought Martin was dead. I was not convinced by her outburst of tears. And her answer to my question whether he was in her apartment was delivered with such confidence and lack of concern that I suspect she was relieved that I had asked that question, to which she could honestly render a negative answer. I will have her, and her servants watched and followed. I expect they will take food to the hidden Martin."

This plan bore fruit sooner than expected. Within the hour a soldier reported to Luke, "Sir, two women have just left Mistress Ellen's apartment, both carrying covered baskets. They are both heading this way."

"Good work soldier. Return to your position! We will follow the women," announced Luke.

Two women passed through the reception hall. One was Ellen who had completely ignored Luke's request that she travel abroad only in the company of a bodyguard. The other was her servant Mary.

Luke followed Ellen, and Mark set out after Mary.

As Luke kept a reasonable distance from his quarry, he thought that Ellen was making it too easy. She was heading towards the church. No doubt Martin was hiding in his parish church, and Ellen was taking him provisions.

Ellen entered the church by the main door. Luke found the vestry entrance and then quietly opened the door to the main body of the church. He expected to find Ellen and Martin together. The church was deserted except for Ellen who knelt before the communion table deep in prayer. The basket had been placed on a seat in the first pew. She would undoubtedly leave it there for Martin to retrieve later. This girl was cleverer than he had first imagined.

He left the church by the door he had entered and was making his way through the churchyard when he saw Ellen leave the church by its main door.

He was flummoxed by what he saw. She was still carrying her basket.

He was annoyed with himself. Martin had obviously taken the food and she was leaving with an empty basket.

At least he could check on that. He appeared suddenly from behind a large tombstone, which startled the young woman. "Ellen, what are you doing here? A mission of mercy to the needy with a basket full of food?"

Ellen pulled the covering off the basket and exclaimed, "Not quite a mission of mercy, but refreshments for the acting sexton, young Tom Kitchin. He is digging the grave for Richard's burial tomorrow. Mary thought it would be a nice gesture. Would you like to share the bread, cheese and cold chicken?"

Luke saw his opportunity, "Why didn't Mary bring the basket herself?"

Ellen blushed. "I thought it might be more meaningful coming from the mistress, rather than the servant."

"Even though that servant was the wife of the deceased, for whom Tom is digging the grave?"

Ellen's face was very red. "If you must know Tom and I have been on and off sweethearts over a few years. I took advantage of this occasion to catch him alone, but unfortunately he is not here."

Luke could not ask where Mary had gone with her similar basket in case Ellen realized her movements and those of her servant were being monitored by the intrusive military.

"Thomas can't be far. His hat and shovel are beside the unfinished grave under the young oak. Wait for him in shade of the tree!" advised Luke.

"And what are you doing in the churchyard, Sir Luke," asked a now suspicious Ellen.

Luke chose to be partly honest. "I came to the church driven by a naïve thought that Martin may be hiding there."

"I was just in the church but did not see you."

"I searched the main body of the church some time ago and spent the last fifteen minutes carefully probing the vestry."

Just then Tom re-entered the churchyard and Ellen moved immediately towards him. Luke waved her goodbye, cheerfully greeted Tom, and returned to Nith Hall.

"Let's hope Mark had a more successful pursuit," he muttered to himself.

Mark had kept his distance from Mary, who was trudging east across the island in the direction of Martin's burnt out cottage, and the path where her husband had been shot dead.

Both promised much for the investigation. Mark did not have a complete view of the cottage area, but he saw Mary place her basket on the ground, and begin to move burnt beams, and other items of debris. Several bushes obscured his view, but if he moved into a better position, he was likely to become visible to the apparently pillaging Mary.

He risked discovery. He crawled into a better viewing position from which he established that there was no one else at the site. Then it dawned on him. Martin had sent Mary to retrieve something that had been lost in the fire. Given the intensity of the conflagration it could only be a metal item of considerable value—perhaps a silver or golden heirloom although even these might have melted in the heat.

For a moment Mark wondered if Mary was not also assessing whether the burnt-out ruin could be rebuilt, as she moved bricks and stones into new positions. Eventually she picked up her basket, as yet untouched, and headed for the coast.

Mark made his way to the ruins, but nothing appeared to him to explain Mary's behavior. He could spend little time there as his quarry had almost disappeared from sight. She was heading for the path on which her husband had been killed.

By the time Mark had reached the top of the path, Mary had stopped at the spot where her spouse had been killed and was scattering flower petals from her basket into the breeze. She then withdrew a flask from her basket and poured liquid over the spot where Richard had died.

Mark removed himself from observing this private ritual and returned to Nith Hall.

Later that evening the two officers discussed another fruitless day of investigations. Ellen was feeding her on-and-off lover for his work in digging Richard's grave, and Mary was conducting some ceremony of her own on the spot where her husband had died. Neither act appeared related to Martin Moore.

A stubborn Luke was not totally convinced. "I am sure young Ellen has played us for fools. Maybe Tom Kitchen was to take the food to Martin when the opportunity arose, or he may have left the basket in the empty grave for Martin to collect in the middle of the night. Send a soldier to look there now! And why did Mary spend so much time at Martin's burnt out ruin?"

The soldier sent to inspect the freshly dug grave discovered no basket of food but did find a number of chicken bones. It suggested that someone, probably Thomas had eaten the refreshments provided by Ellen.

On the other hand, Luke did not dismiss the possibility that it was Martin who was there earlier in the night and had consumed the food

15

Next morning Luke acted decisively. He ordered the complete removal of all trace of Martin's shanty and had his men re-search the area thoroughly. For hours his men worked relentlessly. Several cartloads of rubble were removed. The only trace of the old cottage that remained by noon was part of the slate floor.

Mark suddenly said to Luke, "It has just come to me as something of possible significance. I saw Mary moving bricks and stones around Martin's burnt out shack for no obvious purpose. In the end most of these were as we have just seen placed on what remained of the slate floor. Maybe she was making sure that no casual passerby would lift any of the slates?"

"Then let's lift them!" replied Luke.

The soldiers raised the slates. There was nothing concealed beneath them. No hidden trapdoor to a world of underground caves and tunnels was found. The final raking and levelling of the site was halted when an unseasonal downpour moved in from the North Sea. The soldiers, including Luke and Mark found shelter against a brick retaining wall that had been erected when somebody dug out what was to be the floor of Martin's cottage.

The heavy shower passed, and men returned to the task of filling another cart with the remaining rubble. Luke was frustrated. He had convinced himself that Martin's ruined cottage concealed secrets that would have helped in their investigation.

Another downpour forced the men to shelter once more against the retaining wall. This time Mark and Luke found a more effective shelter under a bush.

Then, even over the noise of the rain, the two officers heard their men shouting. One of them ran through the rain and declaimed, "We have found a cave."

When Luke and Mark reached it, the men explained that a couple of them had pushed heavily against what remained of the retaining wall, trying to obtain a few more inches of dry space. Suddenly the wall collapsed inwards revealing a large opening.

Luke sent for tapers and large candles. It might only be a tiny grotto, or if similar to the situation on the other side of the island, it could be an entrance to a connected network of caves and tunnels—the perfect hiding place for Martin.

Mark raised another thought. "We may have been told a lot of lies. The stories that the Bohms made their money from the Marquess turning base metals into gold is clearly fanciful. The story that their wealth comes from their land deals, especially on behalf of exiled Royalists might also be false. You may have been right all along Luke to suspect that they may be making their money from smuggling. That would account for the family's very negative reaction to a government frigate patrolling its coastline."

"And a more plausible reason as to why the King sent us here. To prevent the Bohms defrauding him of his excise is a much more believable royal motive than preventing a murder, planned for his coronation day," added Luke.

While they waited for the tapers, Luke whispered to Mark, "Keep the men away from this entrance. I will take a preliminary look and declare it a small cave with nothing of interest. If this is part of a smuggler's network of tunnels, the fewer people who know that we know of it the better. In fact, it might be opportune to transfer all the men on this detail to have their rostered turn aboard the frigate. You and I will return later and explore it at our leisure."

Luke lit a taper and entered the cave. Within minutes he re-emerged declaring it a small cave that led nowhere. He immediately ordered his men to replace the entrance stones and conceal these with branches torn from surrounding bushes. To the casual observer no cave entrance was visible.

Mark could hardly restrain himself as they reached their apartment. "Was what you said true, or is there something we should follow up?"

"Initially it appeared to be a very small cave, but when I went to the far wall there was a narrow passage that you and I will explore this evening. As most of the island can be seen from the towers of Nith Hall, we will leave our adventure until it is dark. If last night is any guide, there won't be a moon."

The two soldiers stumbled across the pitch-black island and eventually found the entrance to the intriguing cave. Luke moved aside the branches and stones and slid through the narrow gap. Once inside Luke opened the ember box, he had brought with him, and lit one of the tapers. Mark carried two spares that would be lit when necessary and commented, "You expect a long journey—three tapers worth?"

"There is nothing worse than being lost in a pitch-black cave. It is the one thing I really fear," admitted Luke.

They had to walk sideways along the narrow tunnel. Eventually it opened out into a natural cavern. By the cobwebs along the walls of the narrow passage, and the undisturbed dust on the floor Luke surmised that it had not been used for sometime. The cavern also accommodated an underground stream that hardly flowed. The way through the cavern was a yard or so above the current water level, but Luke mused as to the situation should the river be in flood. Perhaps the danger of flooding accounted for its lack of use.

A more pressing reason for the neglect of this underground network appeared after they left the cavern and descended rapidly along a narrow tunnel. Several yards into this passage the roof had collapsed, and the sides did not appear stable. Luke scrambled over the rubble and waving his taper into the darkness beyond announced optimistically, "Further on it looks more stable."

Mark reluctantly followed, but in the process fell heavily against one side of the wall, which began a series of rockfalls. He was hit many times by several medium sized rocks and eventually reached Luke, bleeding from cuts to the head, and bereft of the two spare tapers.

Luke appeared unsympathetic to Mark's personal plight commenting simply that the rockfall prevented them returning along the way they had come. They had no option but to press on in the hope of finding another exit.

Nevertheless, a highly anxious Luke returned to the pile of rubble blocking the path in search of the missing tapers—but to no avail. The one lighted taper had burnt down to half of its expected life. If the journey took too long, it would have to be completed in the total darkness that Luke feared.

Luke's increased desire to speed up their progress was thwarted by other injuries that Mark had sustained to his legs and back that made movement quite painful. Luke had to half carry his companion through a series of tunnels and caverns. The final tunnel ended in a sheer drop into a very large cave accessible down a metal ladder. Mark could not manage its rungs. Luke reaching the bottom first, persuaded Mark simply to slide down using the rungs as brakes on his progress, and Luke's own body as the final safety net.

The nature of the complex now changed dramatically. The rocks of the upper reaches of the network now gave way to a limestone vista that mirrored a variety of colors seen in the dying flickers of the taper. It also revealed that they had reached a dead end. There was no way out of this last cavern which was mainly under water. Luke assumed hopefully that one might be able to leave the cavern at low tide.

The one good piece of news was when Luke tested the water it was salty. It was tidal and would probably subside.

As the taper flickered out Luke comforted Mark, but both men realized their predicament. It was pitch black and the only way to progress was via the water, if it receded. If it didn't, they would have to swim under water into the unknown. Luke's experience in the Netherlands as a young soldier breaching the dykes to flood Spanish held territory gave him confidence in water, but how would an injured courtier fare?

"Can you swim, Mark?" he asked gently.

"The current King and his brother swam most summer days they were in exile. His habit to do so naked more than gained the attention of many a young lady. As a companion to the King at court you had to swim. Under normal conditions, I could face what lies ahead with confidence, but at the moment every muscle in my back and legs ache. I don't think I can swim."

"We are close to the sea. We can only sleep. Let's hope some sign of daylight, and the lowest of tides saves us."

They slept.

And the water level dropped.

When the two men awoke, the water had receded leaving an archway through which rays of sunlight lit up the cave and provided an avenue through which the men could progress.

The floor of the cavern was not as deep as expected and both men waded through the water into the ultimate cavern in which small waves were lapping around a number of elevated pathways and a couple of small boats. One looked very much like the one that Ellen and Richard had used, and which belonged to Martin.

The exit from this last cavern opened directly onto a rock-strewn cove.

Luke left Mark beside the boat within the cavern and climbed the cliff to seek help from the troops stationed nearby. He lied to his men, pretending that Mark had been injured when he slipped from the path and landed on the rocks below.

Later that day Luke visited Mark who was being nursed by Ellen and her Aunt Isabel. Mark reported to Luke that Isabel was quite aggressive in her questioning of how he obtained his injuries. Luke noted this and whispered to Mark that he would return to the network of caves and tunnels as he had noted that there were several passages leading off the last cavern in addition to the one that they had come down. Where the other passages led was a question Luke was determined to answer.

"When will you go back into the caves?"

"Tomorrow. As I imagine these other passages lead upwards to other places on the island, I should not be faced with any danger of being cut off by water."

"Nevertheless, it will not be wise to venture back into that system alone, even if you are entering it at sea level and climbing upwards. You must take someone with you?" suggested Mark. "Wait a week and I will be able to accompany you!"

"No, you rest up and fully recover. There will be plenty to do when you are back on your feet. I have the perfect man to come with me—the young naval officer, whom I now remember from my days commanding one of the country's most powerful ships. He is currently ashore facilitating the transfer of our soldiers from ship to shore."

"Be careful and take plenty of tapers," cautioned Ellen.

Luke and Mark smiled.

"And I will not be there to lose them," Mark commented.

Philip was delighted to be re-associated with his former commander. Luke asked, "What happened to *The Cromwell,* and why are you not still aboard her?"

"It has been renamed after the new naval chief, *The Duke of York* and is now under his command. It is escorting the King from the Netherlands as we speak. With so many Royalists wanting to serve under the King's brother, and with my strong republican views well known, I was transferred to an insignificant frigate, which was to patrol the waters between Newcastle and Hull, until you seconded it to blockade and monitor this island. What do you hope to find in the caves?"

"It would answer a major question if we discover that it is a warehouse for smuggled goods, and that the Bohm money comes from such illegal activity."

"Will we wait until dark?"

"No, for us to discover the coastal cave in which locals moored their boats would have been considered only a matter of time by our clandestine opponents. I am surprised that our patrols had not discovered it before Sir Mark and myself stumbled into it from the depths of the island."

16

Philip and Luke with two soldiers, carrying spare candles and tapers, entered the eastern cave at low tide. They examined every inch of it.

To Luke's frustration the only evidence found indicated that it was used by fishermen who had recently scaled and gutted their catch on a large stone bench.

Martin's rowboat and a small skiff were the only sea craft moored therein. Philip with his nautical experience suggested the skiff was the ideal vessel for quick clandestine visits to the mainland or out to sea to meet larger ships. It was faster than Martin's rowboat but probably unable to carry as much merchandise.

Luke was worried. Perhaps his lockdown of Nith was not as secure as he thought. Why were these vessels moored at this end of the island and not with the rest of the local vessels at the opposite end of the island?

At the far end of the cave, easily missed amongst columns of limestone, was a narrow slit through which the four men eventually left the entrance cavern. They were soon on a well-structured staircase that led into another massive cavern, from which several exits were visible.

In the center was another large stone that Luke thought may have been an altar. Around the edges of this cavern were several cubicles which contained many shelves carved out of the soft limestone. Each was full, not of the smugglers' goods that Luke had hoped for, but of bones. Some contained headless skeletons, and others rows and rows of skulls.

"There must have been a massive massacre to fill this cavern with so many bodies," exclaimed an intrigued Philip.

"Not so, sir," said one of the soldiers. "I come from Hampshire and have seen something similar. It is a burial barrow of people who died even before the Romans came to Britain. Anything of value buried with them was stolen centuries ago."

"Yes, soldier, I agree. I have seen similar burial mounds in the south west," said Luke.

"In that case this little adventure amounts to naught—no trace of smugglers, little evidence of current or regular occupation, and no Martin Moore," concluded Philip, somewhat arrogantly.

"There is much more to this complex than we have traversed. We need to find out where all of these other exits lead," explained a disappointed Luke. "For now, let us climb this short staircase."

Philip readily agreed being disinclined to attempt the other exits which seemed initially to involve narrow descending tunnels.

At the top of the stairs that they did climb was a loose stone that was moved aside sufficiently for the men to squeeze through. On the surface they found themselves in a corner of a field at the intersection of two rather tall stone walls. Emerging from among the stones, the men realized that the exit had been partly concealed by the surrounding rocks.

As Luke made his way back to his apartment, he developed a new mantra which he repeated to himself countless times, as if willing its content to become true. "There is more to that complex of caves than we have uncovered. There must be."

Luke visited Mark, who was nursed by Ellen in a room within the private apartment of the Marquess. After Luke informed him of the disappointing mission into the network of caves, Mark whispered that he had some good news that might lead to a break regarding the murder of Ann Bentley.

"The disappearance of Martin Moore has spooked Ellen and she is now willing to tell us more about the circumstances leading to her mother's death. Initially she was only willing to tell me. She remains suspicious of your Cromwellian past, and ruthless career in army intelligence. I persuaded her to talk to us both. Ring the hand bell, and she will come!"

Luke put on his most relaxed and friendly demeanor, but wisely decided to leave the questioning to Mark. Such caution was unnecessary.

Ellen was clearly disconcerted and seemed obsessively anxious to unburden herself of built- up tensions.

"Mother was murdered for something that happened a long time ago, but which only recently became an issue. When I sought to know the name of my real father, mother said that up to a few months ago she would have told me, but something she had discovered very recently would put my life in danger, if some people knew I was aware of his name. This I thought was a lie because she refused to tell me the name of my father when I was pregnant Then just before her death, I raised the issue with Uncle Martin who confirmed her fears. He thought that not only mother, but the whole Moore family was in danger. With his disappearance, and mother's murder, I am scared. Two nights ago, when I went for my usual walk before retiring, I was followed."

An agitated Mark interrupted, "From now on you are not to leave the apartment at night until this matter is solved. How did you evade the guards we posted to protect you?"

"There are more secret tunnels than you think," she replied.

"Have you told anybody else about being followed?" asked Luke.

"No, but Uncle Martin has discussed the general family situation with one or more people. This probably led to his disappearance, if not murder. To whom can I reveal all I know?"

Luke was surprised at his own response, "You can trust us, who act in the name of the King."

Ellen began to sob. Mark comforted her in a manner that suggested to Luke that they were becoming quite close—perhaps too close.

This became obvious two days later as an almost recovered Mark discussed additional protection that he believed should be provided for Ellen.

Luke disagreed and suggested that they delay intensive protection. They could use Ellen to trap her stalker. She would take her usual walks apparently alone but followed by the army who when the stalker appeared, could arrest, or at least identify the culprit.

Mark strongly objected. "You cannot put the girl into any more danger. There is a serial killer abroad."

"And identifying the stalker is the first step towards catching him," responded Luke. "Let the girl decide!"

And that was not an easy matter. Mark made known to her his feelings on the matter. She agreed. Initially she was strongly opposed to the idea. Her nightly walk had turned in her mind into a nightmare of outlandish possible ghoulish outcomes. She broke down and wept uncontrollably.

Luke was disappointed. He had not assessed Ellen as a tearful emotional woman. Or was it all an act?

Luke, the professional interrogator and negotiator was quietly determined to win her over to his plan. He gently explained that if she followed the same route every night until the stalker was caught, there would be soldiers hidden at intervals along her whole journey. They would only reveal themselves, if she needed protecting. She must surely want the man who was stalking her, and possibly the killer of her mother and great uncle, brought to justice.

She finally agreed. Mark gave her a prolonged hug, which she returned with a passionate and long-lasting kiss.

That evening Luke briefed his men. Their task was not initially to apprehend the stalker, but to identify him. They must not reveal themselves. They could only break cover if Ellen was attacked.

Mark was still troubled. "Ellen tells me that the whole island knows of her routine. People who wanted to talk to her outside the apartments of the Marquess, where she spent her working day, often intercepted her on these regular walks. Her aunts and great uncle in particular took advantage of this opportunity to catch her away from the Marquess. She was regularly accosted by any number of innocent islanders, who might frighten off the stalker."

"I have a more serious concern," announced Luke. "There may not be a stalker. Ellen is a very troubled young woman, naturally quite fearful in the current situation. It is very easy in such an environment to imagine things."

Mark, not anxious to hear criticism of Ellen changed the subject. "Have you got any further on the murder of her mother?"

"Not really! The person with the opportunity, apart from her servants is her sister Isabel which, despite her husband, is most unlikely. That is why identifying and arresting this stalker is so important—if he exists."

"Or she?" added Mark.

"Do you know something that I don't?" asked a surprised Luke.

"No, but a number of women would have a motive for murdering Ann and silencing her daughter."

Luke deployed his men and hid himself near the rehabilitated site of Martin Moore's cottage. He was accompanied by Philip who would be his runner ready to inform other groups of what was occurring. Mark insisted that he follow Ellen from a distance. It was symptomatic of Mark' state of mind and concern for Ellen, that though an officer, on this occasion he carried a musket—unbeknown to Luke.

Ellen began her walk. It took her passed the hidden entrance of the barrow, and the site of Martin's former cottage until she reached the cliff top below which both Harry Bohm and Richard Banks had died. She returned along the same track.

On this return part of her walk a group of women fell in with Ellen and stayed with her. Luke hoped that this would not deter any stalker.

It didn't.

A figure wearing a long coat, and with his head and neck covered in a scarf and large hat emerged from behind a stone wall near the barrow entrance. There was no way that Luke could recognize such a heavily disguised figure.

Would the troops hidden along the track have any better view?

They did—as far as the women were concerned. The two adult women who had joined Ellen were her aunts, Hannah Corby and Isabel Denholm. They stayed with her until they all reached Nith Hall. The stalker watched them enter the building, and then disappeared.

Luke was disappointed. He now feared that during her long discussion with her aunts she may have revealed the precautions being taken by the soldiers. He did not want these plans revealed beyond his men.

Mark was delegated to discover what had transpired between Ellen and her aunts. He was disappointed. What he thought was a burgeoning love affair, dissipated in his latest discussion with Ellen. She seemed distant and more suspiciously, cagey.

Her reply to his question was simple, "My aunts were worried about me. They advised me not to walk on my own, but I did not tell them that I had protection. They also wanted to know if I was hiding Martin, or if he had contacted me. To that I could honestly answer, no."

Any further progress in Luke's plan was delayed. For three evenings rain squalls blew in from the North Sea drenching the island and confining Ellen to Nith Hall. During this period Philip sought permission to stay onshore and explore the island before returning to the *Deadly Arrow*.

Luke agreed with Mark that he could conceal himself somewhere along Ellen's path, and Luke would follow her—and hopefully the stalker.

When Ellen set out the following evening to Luke's disappointment she was immediately joined by Vince Keddy. A terrible thought hit Luke. What if the potential killer no longer felt it necessary to stalk Ellen but instead joined her on her walk. What if Vince was the potential killer? No one was close enough to stop him killing the girl. He would be caught just after the fatal act, but that was no protection for Ellen.

Much to Luke's peace of mind Vince left Ellen after a short distance but the tall over-dressed semi-disguised figure of several evenings ago suddenly appeared from behind a stone wall. Luke nearly knocked into him as he rounded a corner on the path. Luckily, he was not seen by this figure who seemed very intent on getting closer to the now isolated Ellen.

Luke fell back, but for most of the time he could see both Ellen and the stalker, but bends in the path, and dips and rises on the landscape obstructed his view from time to time.

As he reached a slight rise and looked ahead Ellen was nowhere to be seen, but the stalker was rushing in the direction of where she should have been. Was he taking advantage of some mishap to finish her off?

Luke ran towards the stalker and found him towering over a prone Ellen. He feared the worst and tackled the man from behind. Within seconds the nearest concealed troops were on the spot. They held the man, while Luke tended to Ellen. She was conscious.

It was a frustrating anti-climax.

She had not been threatened by anybody. The alleged stalker had seen her fall and twist her ankle and had come to her aid. Mark arrived on the scene, helped Ellen to her feet, and accompanied her back to the manor.

Luke turned his attention to the man he had tackled.

17

It was George Denholm.

He was taken back to Luke's apartment to be interrogated. Luke allowed a couple of hours to pass while George sat in a small room, surrounded by six menacing and intimidating soldiers. Luke finally began his inquisition. "We are holding you as the suspected stalker of Ellen Bentley, how do you answer?"

"Sir Luke, I am no stalker. Quite the opposite. I was following Ellen in case she got into trouble. I was helping my friend Tom Kitchen who had to leave the island for a couple of days."

"Why did Tom Kitchen think Ellen needed protecting?"

"Her great Uncle Martin asked Tom to keep an eye on her, as he believes someone is out to destroy the whole Moore family, which includes my own mother. That is why I offered to help."

"Did Martin asked Tom to do this before his house burnt down and he went missing, or since?" asked Mark.

"It was a day or two after the fire," replied George.

"So, Martin was still alive a few days after the fire and his suspected murder?"

"Yes, but ask Tom. He should have returned to the island last night," replied a much-relieved George.

After George was released, an angry Luke smashed his fist on the table. "What a fiasco! We are no further advanced. The suspected stalker is in fact a protector put in place by her great uncle and sweetheart."

"Relax Luke! We at least now know Martin is probably alive. We just have to find him."

98

After a few drinks Luke and Mark were about to retire when a servant knocked frantically on their door and informed them that they must come with him to the Baron. There had been another death.

"Maybe the body of Martin Moore has been found," muttered Luke to Mark as they made their way along the main corridor of Nith Hall.

Luke and Mark entered the apartment of a clearly distraught Michael who indicated that they should follow him. They were led along the corridor and entered what they realized was the Catholic chapel. Crumpled in front of the altar, dressed in full ecclesiastical garb, lay the body of William Perry. It was obvious that the priest had had his throat cut and had bled to death. The pool of blood was extensive.

Luke immediately looked for any bloody footprints. There were none.

A cursory search of the chapel revealed a blood-stained knife that may have been wrestled from the killer in the priest's dying moments. Luke had seen it, or one quite similar before. It had belonged to Martin Moore.

He intended to keep his thoughts initially to himself, but Michael did not hold back. "He was killed by that degenerate, Martin Moore."

"Did you see Moore do it?

"No."

"Had Perry been threatened by him?" asked Luke.

"No, but he is the obvious killer—if you know their past relationship."

"Which was?" probed Mark.

"I only became aware of it just before my brother Harry's death. Harry confessed that when he visited the island helping to prepare for our father's accession, he teamed up with the local degenerate rector Martin Moore, and two local wild lads Jerome Tighe and William Perry. Tighe had apparently raped a local teenager Ann Moore and escaped from the island. That episode left the girl pregnant and with a reputation as the island whore. Why William left I do not know. Years later William contacted Harry seeking to return to the island in his new persona as a Catholic priest. Perry probably knew what really happened at the time of Ann Bentley's rape, or Moore simply believed that Perry not Tighe was the rapist of his niece."

"It is very plausible story, but it immediately raises another major issue that your previous silence on these matters may have helped create. To me it suggests the possibility that Perry was the rapist who murdered

Ann Bentley to ensure her silence. He then tried to kill Martin Moore by setting fire to his house while he was within suspecting that Ann had finally told her uncle the truth surrounding her rape. Moore then became an avenging angel," uttered Luke.

"Perry could not have murdered Ann. He was a man of God," said Michael.

"Nevertheless, what if he was Ellen's father? Indeed, was he really a priest?" asked Mark of Michael.

"I cannot answer all of those questions. What I can answer is what I heard from Harry. According to him, Ann, the teenager was no virgin and had slept with several men anyone of whom could be Ellen's father. He also claimed that Perry was a genuine priest who had taken holy orders to make amends for his wild youth. This degenerate past is why many of the local Catholics have not warmed to him. Under pressure from some secret and imminent revelation by Ann or her uncle, he could have reverted to the wild and violent person of his youth. We can only surmise—but let's not speak ill of the dead. I still think your prime suspect is Martin."

"Will you ask your father to examine the body?" asked Luke.

"Not if we can avoid it. Father is old and gets easily confused. As a soldier who has examined many a dead body, if you agree that Perry was murdered by having his throat cut, it need go no further. I shall arrange for his funeral and burial."

Luke acquiesced, but back in their own apartment he and Mark reconsidered what they had been told. Mark was jubilant. "It has solved the murder of Ann, and probably the attacks, genuine or imagined on Martin and Ellen."

"I wish I could agree, but it seems just too convenient. Perry's death attributed to Martin Moore—a perfect cover up to my mind," declaimed an obstinate Luke.

"By whom, and why?" was Mark's incisive question.

"As yet I do not know. Perry may be being blamed for the crimes of others, and despite the compelling evidence of his knife, Martin may be innocent."

"You have spent too much time in military intelligence. What we have is sufficient before the law to apprehend Martin for the murder of the priest."

Next morning Luke visited Ellen. "You have heard of the murder of William Perry?"

"Yes, and that Martin is the prime suspect."

"Is he capable of such an act?"

"In his younger days Martin was apparently quite wild for someone who was a clergyman. If provoked he would be capable. He was certainly a fit man for his age. But what would be his motive? Sectarian hatred was never part of his life."

"It has been suggested that Martin was avenging your mother."

"For what reason?"

Luke was thrown by this naïve response and momentarily wondered whether he should tell Ellen what he had been told. His hesitation was noted. "How could my mother and the priest be in anyway connected?" she asked.

"According to my source, William Perry along with Jerome Tighe who both disappeared from Nith just after your mother was raped, could have been her attacker. It is possible that recently your mother or great uncle tried to blackmail Perry. The priest murdered your mother before she could spread her information, and Martin, aware of what was happening, took his revenge."

"Absolute rubbish. How could you reach such a silly conclusion? Another lying source out to belittle the Moores!"

"How do you know it is rubbish?"

"Mother did discuss her salacious past from time to time but refused to mention names as she claimed I would only fret about which of the men may have been my father. She only ever mentioned one name from the past—Jerome Tighe. And she was very clear about his role in relation to her. She said they put all the blame on an innocent, who was forced to leave the island before the new marquess arrived."

"Who were 'they'? Could it have included your uncle and Perry?"

"I do not know. With Martin missing, maybe my aunts will be more forthcoming. They have never been with me in the past, particularly regarding my mother's unacceptable behavior."

"Did that behavior extend beyond her obviously wayward youth?"

"Toby could never satisfy mother's obvious needs, but she was very discreet—and always denied the rumors circulating about her, although most of them were true."

"I ask, because I wondered, given your mother was murdered only a few weeks ago, that a recent liaison, rather than something that happened in 1642, provided the motive for her death. What men were linked with her in these rumors?"

"I am sorry to say the name that occurred most often was her brother-in-law, John Corby, and now since his arrival Ralph Bohm. Consequently, anything that aunt Hannah says about mother will be biased."

"Did your aunt Hannah know of your mother's affair with her husband?"

"There is no guarantee that such an affair ever happened. Mother was forced to marry Toby. She was always jealous of Hannah's marriage to the handsome and able John Corby. Mother probably made it up, just to annoy Hannah."

"Is it any more likely that she had an affair with Ralph Bohm?"

"If Ralph took after his brother Harry there may have been a liaison and if his wife Lady Felicity was aware of it, she would have acted against my mother. That mysterious countess is a strong and ruthless woman."

"Strong enough in every way, to murder?"

"I had not thought so, but now as things develop; it is a possibility."

"It is a recent affair that more likely led to your mother's death than what happened before the Bohms arrived. Your information opens up new possibilities. I will pursue both avenues."

Later that day Luke visited Felicity.

"My lady, I have received new leads regarding the murder of Ann Bentley, which could involve your husband and yourself."

"Not that old rumor that Ralph was having an affair with Ann?"

"Yes, true or false, and how did you react to them?"

"Ralph denied them."

"Did you believe him?"

"Ralph has always had trouble relating to women. Initially I believed him, until Jane claimed that Ann had the ability to inflame the passions of even the most disinterested of males."

"If he had, how would you have reacted?"

"Not an issue, aristocratic men have always considered the women of inferior classes readily available. It has no bearing on relations within an aristocratic marriage. Now if Ralph had had an affair with one of my sisters-in-law, it would have been an entirely different matter. I would certainly have acted. After all, I did spend time at the French court where extra-marital affairs were commonplace. I counselled a lot of distraught wives—some of whom went on to poison their wayward husbands. I can still conjure up a useful potion for such a purpose. So, if anybody on the island dies from poisoning, I am your prime suspect," was Felicity's teasing response.

"When I ask Ralph about these rumors. How will he respond?"

"Denial, or refusal to answer on the grounds that these are personal matters and irrelevant to any legal enquiry. After all he is the family lawyer."

Felicity knew her husband well. He considered Luke's question regarding an affair with Ann Bentley as inappropriate, and not relevant to Luke's enquiry. The soldier had dealt with lawyer's quibbling about words and relevance in the past. A direct, and if necessary extra-legal approach was called for.

"Don't try that legal rubbish on me. You had an affair with Ann and now she is dead. I could arrest you for her murder and send you under cover of darkness to York Castle. No one here would know of your whereabouts, and I am sure I could create enough witnesses to lead to your conviction."

"But that is illegal."

"Yes, but do not forget I was in military intelligence, and often acted illegally in the interests of the state, much longer than I have been a magistrate upholding the laws of England. I might occasionally regress to my former life, —if I suspect I am being lied to."

Ralph was sufficiently intimidated to modify his stance.

"I did not want to discuss this matter, not because I killed Ann, but because my brief encounter with her was a disaster. I could not satisfy her demands, and in her disappointment, she suggested, I might be happier with a man. She was not a pleasant person. At that point I could have killed her."

"I tend to believe you, but for a court of law you have provided a very clear motive for murder—her negative assessment of your manhood, and the possibility she would spread such information throughout the island."

18

Hannah Corby was not happy to find Luke knocking on her door. He sensed the antagonism and decided to counter it in the same way he had dealt with Ralph Bohm. He exaggerated.

"Mistress Corby, this is not a social visit. In investigating the murder of your sister, evidence now points to a possible role in it of yourself and your husband. Put bluntly, I have been told that your sister slept with your husband—which gives you the strongest of motives."

"John never slept with Ann. For nearly twenty years she tried to tempt him. Because of his consistent refusal, in recent years she has tried to discredit him—the moralistic constable and churchwarden sleeping with his sister-in-law. In addition, she never ceased trying to provoke me. She had Toby, a tragically disabled person. I had John. She was insanely jealous of my very happy marriage."

John repeated the same story with an interesting addition. "What finally turned my wayward sister-in-law into a vindictive and evil enemy was my attempt to reform her. I accept the teachings of Jesus Christ and try to uphold the highest moral code. My attempts to persuade Ann to follow it for the sake of the family, and her eternal salvation, only resulted in her more outlandish attempts to corrupt me. She continued to mock me on every occasion. With the help of the Lord Jesus Christ, I never succumbed."

While outwardly convinced that the Corbys were telling the truth, Luke could not eradicate completely the thought that many religious and moral men, when confronted by evil, took it upon themselves to administer what they defined as God's justice.

Was the honorable John Corby such a man?

The next day just before noon, Luke received a sailor who had come ashore from the frigate earlier that morning. He carried a letter from its captain, Peter Hutton, informing Luke that he had been temporarily ordered off station to sail to Hull to collect a very important aristocrat who would expect an update of the Tremayne investigation immediately on his arrival on the island.

Luke speculated whether it would be Simon, Lord Stokey, Nicholas Lord Ashcroft or someone else. Mark was concerned. "Whoever it is, what can we tell him? We have an increasing number of problems, but few answers."

"Let's go through them and clarify in our own minds where we are at. We were sent here overtly to prevent the murder of the Marquess on the day of the King's coming coronation."

"The consensus is that this has been concocted by the Marquess himself—and if it does happen it will be his ultimate act to prove to the islanders the effectiveness of his magic, of his prophetic ability," commented Mark.

"I can see a showman such as Felix concocting this last dramatic act, but only if he were on his death bed. Is Felix ill? His mental decline does not seem serious enough for him to cut short a life that to him still has many experiments to conduct. Check on the Marquess's state of mind and on his physical health!"

"But with whom? He has been his own doctor for decades."

"The *Deadly Arrow* has a surgeon on board. When they drop off their important visitor, I shall ask Hutton to send the surgeon to us for a few days," replied Luke.

"Others suggested that it was a fantasy concocted by Corby and others to persuade the King to send us here, playing upon the fact that Charles II may have wanted to do a favor for a man well respected by his late father, Charles I. A clever ploy to get us here to investigate something else that really worried them," added Mark

"But there are two women who think it might happen, and both of them could be the instrument to bring it about. Felicity has already sent a threatening note to the Marquess foreshadowing revenge for some grievance he committed against one of her relatives. She could be a killer. She is the cleverest women on the island, and the one we know least about. We need to know more about her past. The other possibility is Margaret. She is convinced that the Bohm family headed by Felix murdered her husband, but she is so timid and religious that I cannot see her hurting anything," concluded Luke.

"I am not sure. Her religious fanaticism could give her strength emotionally, and perhaps physically to kill a person who not only could have ordered the killing of her husband, but who through the preaching of her beloved priest was being depicted as an agent of the Devil, dabbling in satanic magic. Although with the death of Perry, this explanation now seems less likely," countered Mark.

"But there are some who have deliberately and maybe falsely presented Margaret as completely mad, and who in this state of declining mental stability could act completely irrationally. The truth or otherwise of these claims also needs to be further probed."

Luke continued and raised another possibility. "Then there is the least likely—the claim by the current Marchioness that the Baron and his wife Alice want to succeed to the titles and estates of the marquisate sooner rather than later. Unless the Marquess has discovered the secret of eternal youth, he cannot have many years left. The Baron and his wife already exercise most of the powers of the Marquess. They run the island. Felix has become a recluse, although I have tried to persuade him to take a more active role."

"Despite all of this, both of us agree that Felix's fate is not why we are here."

"Yes, and there are five other issues that may be relevant to our real mission. Hopefully our important visitor will enlighten us on that simple matter—the real reason why the King sent us here."

"What are the five issues you think demand our attention?" asked Mark.

"The three murders- Harry Bohm, Ann Bentley and William Perry; the disappearance of Martin Moore, and the possibility of a smuggling network centered on the island."

"Corby and his friends certainly believe that most of the troubles on the island stem from the time of Harry's death. Three explanations have been advanced for that—accident, suicide or murder. If murder by whom and why?" added Mark.

"Murder appeals to me, and there are a host of possible suspects, stemming from his activities on the island and in London. He had disgraced the family so both Felix and Michael may have been involved, he was a womanizer who may have raped Ann and many others. She or her uncle may have killed him. Then there was Margaret who put up with his continuous affair with Alice. It could have been Alice herself who may have tired of his attention, or her put-upon husband, Michael. If Felicity had not been in London at the time, she could have sought revenge for his alleged attempted seductions of her," summarized Luke.

"We cannot rule out an accident. I have been up and down that cliff face. It is very treacherous, especially if you leave the path. But we can both rule out suicide. Everything we have learnt about Harry indicates that he would never take his own life. Why would he?" Mark concluded.

"Ann Bentley's murder is the most difficult to solve. As a woman who has slept with dozens of men any past lover or their wives could have a motive. Her sensuality and lies complicate the issue. The only positive is that as her murder occurred only a week or so ago whatever the background, long term or recent, something happened recently to provoke the murderer to act."

"Her claims to have slept with John Corby and Harry Bohm could have led to her death, but in both cases, why wait almost two decades from when she claimed an initial contact?"

Luke quietly announced. "There is a simple explanation to all of this."

"Which is?"

"Ann Bentley, in addition to being the island whore, was a blackmailer. I have no direct evidence at all, but it would explain the timing of her death. She only recently threatened someone, and they retaliated. Maybe it was Father Perry. Ann may have threatened to reveal something from his wild youth."

Mark shook his head in disagreement. "Ann may have threatened Perry, but he was a genuine priest, and I believe killing Ann or anybody else would have been anathema to him."

"Perhaps he confided Ann's threats to his closest confidante Lady Margaret who in her disturbed state could have carried out the deed.

At the moment I would not put it past her own sister Hannah. Ann had tormented her with claims of sleeping with her husband, and there is no doubt that Ann brought disrepute upon the family. In most murders, close family are the prime suspects. Is Martin's disappearance and possible murder also related to Ann and maybe Martin's blackmailing activities?"

"An obvious possible connection is that Ann told Martin and possibly other members of her family whatever it was that provoked her murder. Consequently, the murderer has to get rid of all those he thinks might share the damaging information."

"We cannot avoid a possible motive stemming from Martin's notorious past. He was a womanizer and possibly more. He too could reveal many secrets from the early life of many of the islanders. He may have been a life-long blackmailer. Michael and Harry Bohm detest him, as do the Quaker Keddys. Perry could have been one of Martin's victims, as a youth and now as the subject of blackmail concerning what went on in those dark days. On the other hand, as one of few people on the island who went abroad at night in recent years Martin may have seen or heard something detrimental to somebody. I hope we find Martin alive because tracking down his killer, if there is one, will be difficult," concluded Luke.

"Relevant to the Martin Moore case is to discover exactly why he was defrocked? Equally significant is why Felix intervened and has protected him on this island from the rest of the Bohm family ever since? And thirdly why Martin thinks the time is right for him to seek reinstatement? Why did you include smuggling on our list of problems? There is absolutely no evidence of it, is there?" queried Mark.

Luke smiled. "At the moment it is based on intuition, and the existence of all the facilities that would support a smuggling network—the collection of caves and hidden tunnels to store and conceal the goods; rowing boat and sailing skiff to transfer the goods from a larger vessel off shore and to take to the mainland. And I have just realized the significance of a drink I had during my first visit to Martin Moore. He claimed it was a home-made spirit from his own still. At the time I was amazed that its taste was similar to the best French brandy I have ever sipped. Now I know why. It was French brandy. Above all, to put an end to a smuggling network, and save the King a fortune in lost excise and duties seems the most plausible reason for our mission here."

"Tomorrow we may get a definitive answer to that question of why we are here."

"Don't count on it! Both Ashcroft and Stokey are politicians as well as courtiers. They will reveal as little as they can. The King himself would probably tell us more."

"It has been a long day. In the morning you might be more optimistic. We will review the murder of Perry in the morning before our guest arrives," concluded Mark.

19

Next morning Mark and Luke discussed their imminent response to the King's representative regarding the murder of Perry.

Luke summed up the unsatisfactory situation. "His murder is a surprise and we have not even begun any investigation. It will be as difficult as Ann's to solve, given the cause may lie in a variety of areas—his wayward youth, his aggressive counter reformation Catholicism, or a specific problem perhaps revealed in the confessional. Until we uncover the details of his youthful indiscretions, we cannot advance far on the first possible motive. Martin Moore would be a prime suspect from that earlier period."

"And on ideological grounds there are a string of possible murderers. Corby the staunch advocate of a puritan Protestantism and bearer of the traditional anti-Catholicism of the typical Englishman, the Marquess himself who must be devastated that the tolerant humanism that he has preached for two decades is being undermined by Perry's extremism, in particular his equation of all magic if not presented through the church, as diabolic. In addition, there is resentment from some Catholics to Perry's continental aggression. Someone even Denholm although loyal to traditional Catholicism may have found Perry's new emphasis untenable," added Mark.

"The Catholic Bohms themselves may have found his extremism in dividing the community was making the island more difficult to govern. They may also have worried that if Perry accepted Margaret's view of her husband's murder, he might force the re-opening of the whole issue. Perhaps they also feared that he, as a close confident of the family might reveal too many of their secrets to us. The man did have a conscious. Maybe he had to be silenced to protect the family's honor," suggested Luke.

Mid-morning the longboat from the frigate approached the island. Within the hour Nicholas, Lord Ashcroft was in deep conversation with Mark and Luke as they outlined at length the issues they had discussed earlier.

Nicholas was impressed. "You have lost nothing of your incisive mind dogged determination and intuitive flair, Luke. The situation justifies Simon's feeling that something was amiss on the island. The King will not be crowned for several months. When the time approaches, he wants Felix removed from the island and confined for his own safety in York Castle with visits of all females completely forbidden. That must be the easiest of your problems to solve."

"Mark and I doubt that the King sent us here to solve that problem. It is such a fanciful story—and so easily prevented in the way you have just outlined. Why are we really here?" asked Luke.

"Why do you think?" asked Nicholas with a broad grin.

"Luke thinks it is to crush a smuggling ring that is depriving the King of much needed revenue but given how miniscule such an operation would be in the bigger picture, I do not agree," replied Mark.

"Your explanation then?"

"To uncover the murderer of Harry Bohm."

There was a long silence.

Nicholas eventually commented, "Harry's death did interest Simon and myself, and ultimately the King, but it was not in itself the major reason, although it may be related to the King's basic problem with the Bohms of Nith."

"Which is?" uttered Luke and Mark in unison.

"Betraying fellow royalists in shoddy land dealings. Luke, you and Simon were involved together some years ago in saving the individual treasure of countless Royalist Catholics who had combined their assets to prevent them falling into the hands of the victorious Parliamentarians. Simon managed to stop both Cromwell and the King from getting their hands on this treasure. At the moment the returning Royalists are receiving these goods from the safekeeping organized by Simon. The same cannot be said for their real estate."

"How did the Bohms get involved in this?" asked Luke.

"Led by the late Harry, the Bohms misled countless Royalists into selling their property at a token price to save them from parliamentary sequestration. The Bohms promised their former owners that once the monarchy was restored that they would return the properties to them at the same low price the Bohms had paid."

"Surely they would be protected by the law?" asked Mark.

"No, in most cases any agreement was verbal, and it has been brazenly ignored. If returning Royalists want to regain their property, they face prices often double or triple what they received. The government has already intervened in individual cases to reduce the exorbitant prices being demanded by the Bohms."

"Why does this interest the King?"

"His Majesty has a major problem. In his wisdom, he has decided to win over many of his enemies, such as yourself Luke, by not ousting them from properties they received during the Republic, which seriously limits the amount of land he can return to their previous owners who were his fervent supporters. Therefore, the more Royalists who can regain their land on the market the less supporters the King has to appease."

"I see the difficulties. If there is little in writing, then even the King cannot seize the properties of the Bohms and return them to their pre-war owners. Even the most despotic ruler would be loath to risk such an action. A newly restored King in such a precarious situation as we are now in can only exercise moral pressure," said Luke.

"Precisely," answered Nicholas.

"Then why are we here?" asked a confused Mark.

Nicholas moved to the door of the room, suddenly opened it and peered along the corridor. He then signaled Luke and Mark to join him in the middle of the room and whispered, "You are here to gain sufficient evidence against the Bohms to enable the King to deprive them of the marquisate. All of the issues you have uncovered will provide some basis for the King to act. It's a pity that Harry is dead. At the moment it appears that Felix took no part in any of the hundreds of nefarious acts, nor can much be held against his ultimate successor Michael. You can see why Simon had little trouble in convincing the King that you Luke was the one person who might be able to deliver to him what he required."

"Unfortunately, you can report to His Majesty that while there are many possibilities that we can pursue that might lead to a result that the King desires, at the moment progress is very slow," admitted Luke.

Mark asked, "My lord, given what you have said it appears that the King is pursuing a vendetta against the Bohms. We were led to believe that the current King's late father was close to Felix and had probably asked his son to assist the Marquess when he returned to England—the opposite to what you have stated."

"What you have said was very true of the late King's opinion of Felix in 1642 before he moved here. Between 1642 and his death in 1649 Charles I received many complaints against the Bohms, not only regarding their land deals, but the tricking of many into losing much of their silver in investing in Felix's schemes to convert base metal into gold. They never received back the value in gold that they had paid Felix in silver to convert their lead and copper into the precious metal."

"So, the current King's father changed his view of the Bohms?" Luke asked.

"Decidedly, and the distrust went deeper. While pretending to be loyal to the King there is some evidence that the Bohms assisted individual Parliamentarians and Cromwellians. One or more of them were traitors to the Royalist cause, but so far, I have not found any convincing evidence. The fact that Cromwell himself kept in touch with Felix is some indication that at least the Marquess remained friendly with both sides."

"From what I have gathered while on the island, although the majority of islanders were Royalists, the Marquess kept them neutral during the whole proceedings. What his sons got up to on the mainland may be a different story, but I doubt that Felix betrayed the late King", countered Luke.

"My lord, given the majority of Papists on the island and the recent murder of a Catholic priest, to know the King's future policy in relation to Papists would be useful before we plan our next move," asked Mark.

"The King is not a covert Papist, nor has he any intention of converting to Rome. He will allow his mother to worship as such and will not alter the long-standing policy of allowing Catholic aristocrats to remain Catholic without penalty. He wants to be an inclusive King. As long as Roman Catholics and extreme Puritans do not seek to undermine his government, they will both be tolerated. As Queen Elizabeth did a century ago, he will not impose a rigid religious doctrine on his people. Loyalty to the Crown, not a common Christian dogma is his emphasis," Nicholas declaimed with surprising passion.

"That will not be easy. The majority of loyal Anglicans that I know want him to punish the Protestant dissenters—Presbyterians, Independents, Quakers, and Fifth Monarchy men; and the Roman Catholics. He will have trouble with his new loyal, but Anglican Parliament. It is bent on revenge. As I have told Luke, the English people are not as ready to forgive the people who rose up against his father, as he is himself," said Mark.

"Will you return to the King immediately?" asked Luke, changing the subject.

"No. The official reason that I am here is to negotiate with the Bohms a further reduction in the price of the properties they are selling back to the former exiled Royalists. I will have a minor success with some pitiful reduction."

"I cannot understand why the Bohms persist in their greedy behavior. The Baroness herself told me that the bulk of their wealth comes from the expanding London market. They could conform to the King's wishes without seriously affecting their income," Luke commented.

"I shall use that piece of information, perhaps suggesting that the favor of the new King is worth a lot more than the money they would lose by agreeing to His Majesty's request."

"You could also give the Bohms a foretaste of what could happen if they continue to defy the King. I could ask the frigate that brought you here to fire a few salvos at the island."

"You have lost none of your ruthlessness Tremayne," remarked Nicholas. "I was sent to this island to achieve three things— an update on your investigations, to negotiate with the Bohms over their property resales, and to give you this sealed letter from the King."

Nicholas removed a letter from inside his doublet and handed it to Luke. "You must open it in my presence so that I can take an answer back to the King," he added.

After carefully reading the letter Luke asked, "Nicholas, do you know what it contains?"

"Only in general terms. The king is offering you a position similar to the one you held under the Protector. You will not be subject to me as head of security, nor to George Monk who now as the Duke of Albemarle commands the Royal army, nor to whomever the King appoints as head of civilian intelligence. You will head a small unit responsible directly to the King. I imagine you will do for the King those deeds which he, given his position, is unable to do for himself."

"Yes, in addition he does not think my final Cromwellian rank as major-general fits this new position. He has recommissioned me as a full Colonel, re-appointed me as a magistrate for Yorkshire, and also for Middlesex, and confirmed my possession of Abbey Grange. He recognizes that I may wish to spend sometime in Yorkshire with my wife and imminent child and suggests that the future can be decided when we meet in London within the next three months. Tell His Majesty that I accept his offer on the condition that I can reconsider my position in twelve months. I will create the organization that the King has in mind, and both of us can reassess the situation after a year."

20

"I look forward to working with you in London. I am sure some matters regarding the security of the King's person will be referred to you. After I speak with the Baron, I shall return immediately to the frigate. If it fires a salvo at the island as a parting gesture you will know that the Bohms have not been cooperative. I shall tell Michael Bohm that it is just a farewell gesture so as not to make him suspicious. Indirectly it may impress on him what a Royal navy vessel could do in anger."

Nicholas left to negotiate with Michael.

Luke and Mark agreed to concentrate on Perry's murder and with a small detachment of soldiers commenced another search of the Catholic chapel. The initial search had only produced a knife very similar to one owned by Martin Moore.

The chapel was dirty. Despite some rudimentary efforts to clean it away remnants of the priest's blood still stained the floor in front of the altar. The upkeep of the chapel following the death of the priest appeared to be nobody's priority.

The soldiers swept it clean. All finds were placed in a calico bag.

A few minutes later Luke heard a salvo from the frigate.

The Bohms were to be treated as the King's enemy.

"So, what has the second search of the murder site revealed?" asked Mark eyeing the bag.

"Let's see!" replied Luke as he emptied the findings onto a table.

"Two pearls probably from a broken necklace, a silver button, a plug of tobacco, and two silver amulets. One is a V shape of a bird with extended wings and an oval of silver at right angles to the wings, and the other an oval ring of silver divided in half by another jagged link of silver."

"The pearls have an unusual bluish tint to them," noted Mark.

"I will visit the aristocrats and enquire about their pearl necklaces. Fortunately, the yeomen women don't wear such status symbols."

"You cannot be sure of that. During your Republic many of the traditional status regulations were ignored. I saw many an inferior class of woman wearing pearls," remarked the pompous former courtier, Mark.

Luke visited his favorite amongst the Bohm women, the Marchioness Jane. "My lady, may I see your collection of pearls?"

"Is that some sort of coded proposition?" she replied with a chuckle and a twinkle in her eye.

Luke for once was not diverted from his mission—but he did smile. "No, but the pearls may tell me who murdered the priest."

Jane produced two jewel boxes from which she removed a pearl necklace and two pearl brooches.

Luke saw immediately that none of them matched the pearl found in the chapel. Jane's had a pinkish tint and were all of a much larger size. He asked, "Did any of your step daughters-in-law have a grievance against William Perry?"

"I would not know what grievances and what issues Felicity had with anyone. Margaret was emotionally besotted by the priest. If he rejected her in any way, in her delicate mental state, she could have snapped and killed him. Alice would be capable of such an act if she believed he was obstructing her and her husband's grip on power. In recent months Perry was exhibiting a strong moral position which may have interfered with some of the more nefarious schemes of the Baron and his wife."

"That's a great help, your ladyship," Luke replied. He withdrew from a pocket the pearls found in the chapel and placed them on the table beside those of the marchioness."

"Have any of the ladies mentioned pearls similar to these?"

The Marchioness gasped, "They certainly do. These gems are part of the family's famous blue pearls which Felix gave to his two new daughters-in law in 1642. Both Alice and Margaret have a necklace, a pendant and a brooch incorporating this variety of pearl. Alice flaunts her all the time, but I have never seen Margaret with any jewelry since Harry's death. It is part of her eternal mourning," remarked the unsympathetic Jane.

Luke took his leave and received a very tight and sensuous hug as he left the room. He headed for the apartment of the Baroness and asked to see her collection of pearls.

"Why?" Alice aggressively asked.

"To solve the murder of William Perry. Do you wear any of your collection to mass?"

"Always, both my necklace and brooch."

The items were produced and while the pearls were identical in size and color to those that had been found, none appeared to be missing. "My lady have you lost any similar pearls in recent weeks?" he asked, desperate to confirm his hope that the pearls discovered in the chapel belonged to Alice.

"What is all this about?" she asked a little more civilly.

"Similar blue pearls were found in the chapel under the front of the altar, not far from where William Perry was murdered. In his death struggle he probably pulled a necklace from his attacker and scattered the pearls everywhere. The female murderer picked most of them up but missed those that had rolled under the front of the altar. Did you murder Perry?"

"Why would I? If Perry annoyed Michael or I we could dismiss him from our service, and he would return to the continent, or we could hand him over to you to incarcerate in York Castle to await trial and execution."

Luke was annoyed at the confidence and arrogance of Alice and responded angrily, "I will not dismiss the role of your husband and yourself in the murder of Perry. He may have been about to reveal some secret that would destroy you both. Despite his wild youth, he had developed into a very moral man, anxious to do the right thing in the eyes of his God."

"You are still a Roundhead turd who does not know how to behave himself as a gentleman. Leave the room at once!" demanded a suddenly irate Alice.

There was no hug from Alice.

He was lucky to escape without a slap in the face. It now appeared that the missing pearls belonged to Margaret who in recent weeks had made the chapel her second home. Luke would need to tread carefully in dealing with a woman who had not recovered from the alleged murder of her husband, and whom now with the loss of her only friend and mentor, might be in a very disturbed state.

She was. A servant advised Luke to come back another time because Lady Margaret was not feeling well.

As Luke was about to leave Margaret emerged telling her rosary, interspersed with pathetic wails. The sight of Luke surprisingly brought her to her senses. "Sir Luke, have you come to tell me who murdered my beloved Harry, and friend William?"

"Not quite, but very soon I will have answers for you. I have come now to seek your help to find William's murderer. Can I see your collection of pearls?"

Margaret did not ask why and retrieved her jewel box. Luke opened it and saw a brooch, a pendant and a broken string of pearls.

He commented, "You had an accident with your pearl necklace?"

"Not so much an accident. I deliberately broke it."

"How did that happen?"

"I was praying in the chapel and an angel came to me proclaiming that if I wanted to know the murderer of my husband, I would have to cast aside all worldly goods. Spontaneously I ripped the pearl necklace from around my neck. The individual pearls rolled all around the chapel floor. William saw what I had done and told me that it was not God who had spoken to me but some diabolic demon. He picked up the pearls and here they are. I have not yet had them restrung. They were given to me by the Marquess when I married Harry. Why are you here?"

Luke had a convenient reply. "To return two of the missing pearls to you. My men found them under the front cover of the altar."

She thanked Luke profusely and began to recite her rosary. Luke let himself out of the room.

He had just left Margaret's apartment when the servant who had tried to turn him away accosted him. She appeared very nervous. "What is it girl?" Luke asked gently.

"I do not wish to tell tales against my mistress, but in her current state of mind she is a danger to herself and perhaps to others."

"Any evidence to support what you say?"

"Yes, the day Father Perry died she returned from the chapel with blood on her clothing, and only yesterday she tried to poison herself. I saw her place poison in a cup, but I managed to swap cups so that she drank an un-poisoned drink. I have since removed all the poisons I can find lying around the apartment. I need at least two more helpers if I am to keep her safe. I reported the problems to Mistress Keddy but have so far received no response."

"Thank you. I will raise Lady Margaret's state of mind with the Marquess himself. You do not happen to have the blood-stained clothes that she wore on the day of the murder?"

"Normally they would be laundered immediately they were taken off. Given the heavy and constant showers we have had over the last few days they are yet to be washed."

"Can I see them?"

Luke examined the clothes in detail. There was indeed blood on the bodice and on both sleeves. Luke turned to the girl. "Hold this bodice in front of you. Walk up behind me and pretend to stab me." Luke turned his back on the girl who hit him in the back. Luke spun around to confront his pretend attacker.

"Thank you my dear, you have just saved your mistress from a murder charge. If Lady Margaret had stabbed Perry in the back the blood would have been in a different place. I think Lady Margaret found Perry, perhaps still alive, and then held him in her arms until he died. This accounts for the blood on her sleeves. I will not confront her over this at the moment, but I will send two soldiers here to protect her from herself and safeguard your own situation."

Luke reported his discoveries to Mark concluding that Margaret could have killed Perry, but more likely she found his dying body and comforted him. Unfortunately, he could not pin the crime on the nefarious Alice.

Later that day Luke visited the Marquess to seek assistance for Margaret. He acted immediately. Margaret was transferred to a secure room in his own apartment to be cared for by her own and the Marquess's array of servants.

21

“The plug of tobacco might tell us something. The pearls were a dead end,” Luke remarked as he re-examined the contents of the calico bag.

“Not much! The murderer might lose pearls, knife or amulets in a struggle with the victim but it is unlikely a would-be murderer would have a plug of tobacco with him in a position from which it could easily be dislodged. It probably belonged to William Perry,” commented Mark.

“It will be relatively easy to identify the owner of that wad. Felix must have banned tobacco from the island as I have not seen any trace of chewing, smoking or sniffing that poisonous substance since I have been here. I’ll ask Ralph Bohm concerning the habits of the aristocrats and you question John Corby regarding the rest of the islanders.”

Luke asked Ralph, “Did your father ban the use of tobacco?”

“Yes, he has always frowned upon it and prevented its import onto the island. Since his withdrawal from an active role however I have come across the occasional use of the substance. Just before his death my late brother Harry took up the French fashion of sniffing flavored ground tobacco leaves which I believe is called snuff. My wife who saw a lot of snuff used at the French court tried to persuade me to take it, using Harry’s left-over supply. I found it revolting. Michael has never indulged in any form of tobacco use.”

“What about Perry?”

“As a protestant, I am not the person to ask. But I have certainly known a lot of pipe smoking clergy of various faiths. Why all these questions about tobacco?”

"A plug of tobacco was found at the scene of Perry's murder. I hoped it might help us find his killer."

"There are two pipe smoking islanders. One has ignored father from the beginning, and the other a recent convert. Martin Moore has smoked since his teens. In my dealings with him over his attempt to have his defrocking reversed I have had to negotiate through columns of blue smoke as he puffed aggressively on his pipe. The new user is James Denholm."

"The wad that was discovered was probably destined for a pipe. It was not the chewing variety."

"Nor was it rolled into a small cylinder shape, lit at one end and inhaled from the other? These are common in London, but I have seen none in the north," added Ralph.

"Some of the troops at York Castle smoke tobacco in that way," revealed Luke.

Mark received the same information from John Corby. The only two persons using tobacco on the island were Martin Moore and James Denholm—and both smoked a pipe.

"I'll question Denholm, he will know if William Perry smoked," said Luke.

Denholm was quite forthcoming. He had felt much better and less stressful since his wife's Uncle Martin had introduced him to smoking. Martin provided him with his initial pipes and continued to supply the tobacco.

"Did Father Perry smoke?"

"Yes, he first took up smoking as a teenager, corrupted by Martin two decades ago. He took it up again only recently, probably again supplied by Martin, but he tried to keep this renewed habit a secret from his parishioners."

"We found a wad of tobacco at the murder scene. From what you tell me it could only belong to Martin, William or yourself."

"I doubt if Martin has ever been in our chapel, and I do not take my pipe and tobacco with me when I attend mass. But I have seen William sitting at the back of the chapel puffing away. Was the wad in the shape that it may have been ejected from his pipe during a struggle?" was James's surprising question.

"We never found a pipe and the wad had not been finally formed into a usable shape. William probably dropped the wad we found while filling his pipe."

Luke later reported to Mark. "While the plug could have belonged to Martin, the fact that William himself smoked suggests the more plausible explanation is that it belonged to the victim, not the murderer. It is probable that Martin supplied the tobacco to both known users. If we do find that Martin had actually entered the chapel it was probably to resupply Perry with tobacco, not to murder him. I gave the knife we found at the scene to young Tom Kitchen to see if his father recognized it. I should have a response regarding the weapon at any time."

Later that day Tom delivered his report. "Sir Luke, father says that this knife and dozens like it were made by my grandfather for most families on the island. It is an all-purpose knife worn by most men as they would a dagger to aid them in their work around the island. Whereas a dagger is a stabbing implement these knives, which father continues to make, are a cutting tool. Women also use them around the kitchen for cutting meats and vegetables. There is only one way of knowing who owns the knife you gave me. You must ask every family on the island to produce their cutting knives. If a family cannot, they may be the owner of this one."

"There could be so many other explanations as to why they could not present their version of such a knife that such a widespread survey would not be warranted. No, my only hope is with Martin's return, I can ask him to produce his knife. If he can't, then this could be his."

"He might reasonably argue that his knife was lost in the fire that destroyed most of his goods," added Tom.

"We found no knife, nor melted metal that may have been one," responded Luke.

A disappointed Luke and Mark bemoaned another fruitless day. Neither the knife nor the plug of tobacco had brought them any closer to a solution of Perry's murder. Tomorrow hopefully the amulets would trigger a better result.

Luke tried to see the Marquess but was told by Ellen that he was not having a good day, and it would be impossible to carry on a meaningful conversation with him.

Luke responded, "I may not need to see the Marquess. You may be able to help me. You have been close to him in recent times. Has he passed on to you any of his magic?"

"Yes, until his mind started to decline, he had begun a systematic program of teaching me many of his secrets. He was very disappointed that none of his family are interested in his extensive almost unique arcane knowledge."

"Did he teach you about magic symbols and amulets?"

"Yes, a lot."

Luke produced the two amulets and gave them to Ellen. "What do they mean?"

Ellen handled both amulets with care and commented. "I was present when Felix made these. As an alchemist he developed quite a skill in crafting fine metallic emblems and tokens. These are both created with the thinnest of silver thread."

"And what do they mean?" repeated Luke.

"The one that looks like a bird in flight linked by an oval of silver represents dominion, the other oval of silver joined through the center by a jagged piece of silver denotes silence."

"Why and where would a magician deploy these symbols?"

"He would deploy the dominion amulet in a place where he wanted his magic to dominate. It is designed to obstruct the spread of views that rival his own. The silent amulet would reinforce the dominion amulet—it would silence whatever false view were emanating from the location where you placed both amulets. Where were they found?"

"In the Catholic chapel. Did you place them there?"

"I have never been in the Catholic chapel, but your search of it could not have been thorough. You should have found at least a dozen of the Marquess's magical charms hidden in that Papist den."

"Did the Marquess insert these devices himself?"

"No, it was carried out by the Marchioness!"

"The Marchioness!"

"Don't be misled. The Marchioness and the Marquess work together effectively as a team. He does little without her knowledge. She is a much more powerful and influential figure than you or most of the island realize."

Luke thanked Ellen and went straight to Jane's apartment. A servant took him into an antechamber where he was warmly received with a tight hug, and kiss on the cheek. "This is becoming a habit, Luke. What is your excuse today?" she teased.

"During our investigation into the murder of William Perry, my men discovered several amulets in the Catholic chapel. I have it on good authority that you placed them there. Is that true, and why?"

"Very true and done simply to preserve my husband's legacy of a tolerant and harmonious community."

"Tell me more!"

"You have already upbraided Felix for his withdrawal from the affairs of the island and his acquiescence in the takeover of most aspects of island life by Michael and his wife. I discussed this issue with him many times, but his view has been that Michael is the heir and will take over immediately on his death. The Bohm dynasty will continue. What he was adamant about that must not occur was the destruction of the tolerant society he had spent his life on this island creating. He quickly realized the danger of Perry's appointment and preaching of Counter Reformation Catholicism. He believed sectarian conflict would be created. He decided to fight it at the level he believed was the most powerful. He would pit his magic against the teachings of the Catholic Church as promulgated by Perry. I placed a dozen magical charms in the chapel all designed to counter, obstruct and render useless the ideas that emanate from Rome. It would give Felix great satisfaction, if he could prove that his magic was more powerful than the teachings of the Catholic Church. The death of Perry has in some ways sidelined his major battle between magic and Catholicism."

"You did not hide any magical devices that might have led to the eventual murder of Perry?"

Jane looked shocked. "You are a believer after all? No, not even Felix contemplated using magic in the battle between life and death. To Felix life was a battle for the minds of people, not over their life or death."

"You did a good job in concealing the amulets. My men found two, there must be another ten still in the chapel!"

"I would hope so. The poisonous ideas that Perry sowed in the minds of many of my fellow Catholics still need to be contained. May I keep the two you found. I will reinsert them into our chapel."

Luke handed over the two amulets. Jane kissed him on the mouth. Luke did not resist. There was a knock on the door and without waiting for a reply, Ellen entered the room. She addressed them both. "I told the Marquess what Luke had asked me, and that I had referred him to you, your ladyship. He wants to know what has come from Luke's discussion with both of us.

Luke used this intervention to leave. "The Marchioness will bring you up to date," he said as he departed.

22

The silver button was the last piece of evidence retrieved from the chapel that might lead to the killer.

Luke removed it from the calico bag and examined it thoroughly. Suddenly he jumped to his feet and exclaimed, "God's truth!"

He hit the table several times with a clenched fist and shouted, "I am a fool. I missed the obvious!"

An alarmed Mark asked, "What is it? Are you alright?"

"The silver button—I should have recognized it immediately. When I commanded *The Cromwell* in the Mediterranean, all my naval officers wore blue jackets with silver buttons identical to this one. They are engraved with the letters OCLP—Oliver Cromwell, Lord Protector."

"How did a button from a serving officer of the now defunct English Republic finish up in a Catholic chapel on the isolated island of Nith?" asked an astonished Mark.

"It is so obvious that we missed it. It is staring us in the face. The only naval officer that has been on Nith for decades is our comrade, Philip Bates, a man who served under me in the Mediterranean."

"The location of such a button in a Catholic chapel certainly needs explaining, but I doubt if Bates had any role in Perry's death. What could be his motive, and when did he have the opportunity. Most of the time he was on this island he was with us," cautioned Mark.

"Not so. He spent a couple of days sightseeing on the island before he returned to his ship, and he could land on the island without our knowledge at any time. He fought in the Mediterranean where English ships sent ashore troops to massacre the local Catholic and Moslem population, which in the former case included a number of priests. Bates is probably a Protestant extremist, who sees the murder of Catholic priests as a God given duty. He has both motive and opportunity."

Luke continued, "Let's find out! Mark, visit the frigate and ask Peter to free Bates to assist me for a couple more days. Have him return to the island immediately. You remain on board and obtain as much information that you can concerning Bates from Peter and his crew."

Mark carried out Luke's instructions. As he watched Bates being rowed back to the island, Captain Peter Hutton opened the conversation. "Before you begin whatever it is you wish to discuss, let me formally invite Sir Luke and yourself to supper aboard ship sometime this week—on whatever night is most convenient. I shall send the longboat ashore to collect you."

"That is very kind of you, Peter. Tomorrow night would be ideal. The boat that puts me ashore in the morning can bring us all, including Bates, back here that night."

"Given your constant use of Lieutenant Bates I had anticipated an invitation from Luke to dine ashore before this. After all, we served together in the Mediterranean. I was then an officer on *The Wildfire,* part of Blake's fleet, but seconded to Tremayne, while he dealt with problems on Benbali."

"I am sure if Luke knew that you were a senior officer under his command in the Mediterranean, he would have invited you. I am a little surprised that you mentioned our constant use of Bates. As far as I know he has only been ashore twice although he did extend one visit into a few days."

Peter looked puzzled. "Perhaps Luke has not kept you up to date, but why are you here?"

"On this very matter—to ask some questions regarding Bates, and you have already touched on the most critical. How often has he been ashore?"

"He told me Luke had requested his services a couple of days a week. Since we have been on station here, he has been ashore at least five or six times, not the two that you refer to."

"Why would he come ashore so often. He could hardly have found a lover in the short time he has been assisting us," said Mark half in jest.

"He had a believable reason. He has been looking up friends from his childhood and youth. Bates is a local lad, Nith born and bred. He left the island at the outbreak of war to join the navy."

Mark was jubilant. Luke would be delighted with this piece of information. He continued his questioning. "Is Bates a good officer?"

"When we were part of Blake's fleet and in the service of the Republic he was dedicated if not obsessed. He has very extreme protestant views."

"He delighted in the killing of Catholics?" probed Mark.

"I would not put it as strongly as that, but he was the first officer to volunteer to lead a shore party to terrorize the locals. He is finding it hard to adjust to the new regime. Serving the King does not seem to create in him the zeal I saw when he served the Republic."

Mark slept aboard the frigate that night and was returned to island next morning. Luke was delighted with his report. "Great, let's find out from the islanders who were here in 1642, all we can about Philip Bates."

Luke returned to Mark after his initial enquiries crestfallen. "How bad is the news?" asked the observant Mark.

"According to Denholm there have never been any Bates on Nith. Philip Bates was never a boy from this island who ran way to sea in 1642. He lied to his captain."

Both men were silent for some time. What promised to be a major breakthrough in their enquiry had fizzled out.

Then Mark chuckled. "Luke, we are simpletons. The man who calls himself Philip Bates was born and bred on this island, and left to join the navy, but Philip Bates is an alias. He has changed his name. If he is still on the island have him confront a number of the locals who are about his age, and who might recognize him, despite the passage of the years."

"It's worth a try. But twenty years changes a person's appearance considerably, and his bearded naval face could further confuse people who might remember a clean faced teenager. We will not confront him with the islanders directly. Let's gather our evidence in secret"

"And just how do we do that?"

"I shall talk to Bates in the small antechamber next to our bedchamber. The door to our room has a discreet peephole through which you can see into the antechamber. We shall have a selection of islanders in our room who can watch Bates at their leisure without being seen."

"Who do you want?"

Let's start with James Denholm, John Corby, and their wives—the sisters Isabel and Hannah."

Philip spent the day, assisted by several soldiers, exploring more of the tunnel and cavern network. Luke pretended that catching a smuggling ring was now his first priority, and the navy's role in this enterprise was paramount. Philip reported to Luke in the antechamber that they had discovered nothing of importance, except that one of the tunnels which they followed ended up in the crypt of the parish church. Philip suggested that it could have been there since early Viking days for the Christian clergy to escape the marauding Danes.

"Or for current ex-clergy to hide and move about the island unseen. Any trace of Martin Moore in your exploration," asked Luke.

"He may have spent some time recently in the crypt. There were the crumbs of a recently eaten meal."

"Good work, Philip! Mark and I are returning to the ship with you. Your captain has invited us for supper. You did not tell me that he was an officer on *The Wildfire* during our days in the Mediterranean."

"The captain is a very quiet man. I knew he had served in the Mediterranean, but I did not know that he knew you, let alone served under you."

"Wait for us beside your longboat. We will join you in about half an hour. We can't miss the tide."

Philip left, and Luke in eager anticipation almost ran into the adjacent room. Giving the level of agitated conversation the islanders had something to report.

James Denholm spoke for them. "At first neither John nor I recognized him, but both our wives immediately said despite his ageing that the man who calls himself Philip Bates is definitely Jerome Tighe who fled the island in disgrace at the same time as William Perry."

"Jerome Tighe was the young lad that your sister Ann said had been wrongly accused and who was forced to flee," commented Luke.

"Yes, Ann always thought he was the scapegoat for what others may have done," replied Hannah.

"What sort of lad was he?" asked Mark.

"Anxious to please. He was one of the youngest youths to attend Uncle Martin's lecherous parties," continued Hannah.

It was Isabel who then made a surprising but most revealing comment. "At the time he was considered the favorite of those older men who preferred boys to girls." James was about to rebuke his wife but thought better of it.

"It would then be a reasonable proposition to suggest that young Tighe had sex with one or more males on the island who given the arrival of a new Marquess thought it best to get rid of the lad, and he was terrorized into leaving the island almost immediately," suggested Luke.

"A possibility," answered Hannah.

John turned towards James, "You were a member of Martin's group of delinquents in your youth. Do you know why Jerome left?"

James was initially taken aback but did not deny the inference. "Every young male on the island, except yourself attended Martin's parties as did most of the women who are now respectable matrons. I met Isabel at one of them. They were not all devoted to scandalous sexual deviance. Most of them were simply a way of getting the males and females on the island to mix. They were essentially match making events helped along by some excellent beers, wine and strong spirits."

As Luke and Mark made their way down through the caverns to the main entrance cave, they were jubilant. Philip, or rather Jerome certainly had motive and opportunity.

"Maybe the lad was raped by the wild William Perry, forced off the island by Martin, and is now exacting his revenge. If he murdered Perry, he may also have killed Martin." said Mark.

"Let's see how he explains the button found in the chapel. I shall raise it at dinner."

"By the way when I told Michael that we would not be in for supper and were dining aboard the frigate, he gave me two bottles of the finest brandy as a gift for Captain Hutton."

Luke examined the bottles. "They look the genuine article. How the inhabitants of this isolated island have such a stock of the best French brandy remains a mystery," concluded Luke. "They must be smugglers."

Dinner was a delight, except for Mark who could not join in the reminiscences of Peter, Philip and Luke regarding their time fighting for Cromwell in the Mediterranean. Luke eventually turned the conversation in the direction he wanted. He spoke to the two naval officers. "I see you are still wearing the blue jackets with the silver buttons that were issued to the fleet at the time we were in the Mediterranean."

Mark noted that while the captain's buttons were uniform those of the lieutenant appeared mixed. Only one appeared similar to the captain's, the others had a slightly different silver sheen. He deliberately made his observation explicit.

Peter replied, "Easily explained! The original buttons carried markings referring to Cromwell and the Protectorate. They have recently been replaced with those that simply show the Crown. I am wearing the new buttons. Bates here is finding it difficult to adjust to the new environment, and until recently continued to wear the old Cromwellian buttons. I had not noticed that he had succumbed to change, and now has at least one Royalist button."

"A concession to change Philip, or did you lose one of your original buttons?" asked Luke.

"I lost it clambering through that network of caves with you, and of course no replacement Cromwellian buttons now exist. They have all been melted down, and reminted with the crown," was the unflappable response.

23

Mark saw the opportunity to keep the discussion on a track that might lead to Philip incriminating himself. "Gentlemen, the three of you have or are still facing the same dilemma. How do such strong supporters of the Republic and the late Oliver Cromwell, adjust to this new Royalist regime?"

Luke noted the hesitation in Peter to discuss such a fraught political issue with a Royalist courtier, so he broke the ice. "My initial dilemma was how to cope with the death of Cromwell rather than any possible return of monarchy. I resigned from the military but found myself a new life due to the largesse of the late Protector. I concentrated on my new roles as a magistrate and landowner. Since then I have tried to keep out of national politics, other than that which those new responsibilities forced on me."

"What changed your mind?" asked Peter.

"Last year I received a request from the now King to arrange a meeting between his envoy, Nicholas Lord Ashcroft, whom you have just transported to and from the island, and representatives of the dying republic. Although in my role as a local magistrate I eventually led a military expedition to ensure that Nicholas left the area. It was after he left the mainland as a result of my pursuit that he made his first visit here. With the collapse of the republic, I intended to concentrate on my local responsibilities anticipating that with the arrival of the King many Royalists might wish to take their revenge on leading supporters of the Protectorate as I was."

"There seems to be an almost unbridgeable gap between driving Ashcroft out of Yorkshire and now working with him," commented Philip with a hint of sarcasm.

"Absolutely! Yes, I was pleasantly surprised that the King in an effort to create a harmonious society, is not punishing many of his opponents. He has added many of them to his inner circle. Cromwell's military governor of Scotland and more recently commander-in- chief of the republic's army, George Monk, is head of the King's army and Cromwell's naval chief Edward Montague, is the Duke of York's deputy in leading the Royal navy. Offering me this position is another but entirely unexpected example of the King's attempt at reconciliation. Nicholas only the other day delivered me another offer from the King to take up a position similar to one I had in military intelligence under Cromwell. Despite my unflinching loyalty to Oliver Cromwell, England now faces a new era. These are different times, and I am fully reconciled to serving the new administration—as long as it serves England."

Given Luke's open admission that he will serve the King, Captain Hutton followed suit. "My approach has been similar to yours. I was never political. I joined the navy before the war and spent the first few years supporting the King. Then in the mid- forties, a flotilla of Royal navy ships left the fleet of Prince Rupert and joined the Parliamentary navy. I was aboard one of those ships. The change of loyalty had nothing to do with me. Parliament and then Cromwell built an entirely new fleet and gave the navy resources to take on the world. I certainly enjoyed my role in assisting Cromwell to make England the great naval power that it became. I too will serve the new King, although with more limited resources the navy may be cut severely, and some of us might lose our positions. My future is not secured."

"What about you Philip?" probed Mark.

Perhaps with his tongue loosened by several large glasses of Bordeaux wine, Philip did not hold back. "Unlike you gentlemen, my first few years in the King's navy were humiliating and degrading. When I ran away from home, I became a sailor on a Newcastle based collier. Then during a drunken binge after we had returned there after delivering much needed coal to London, a press gang for the King kidnapped us, and placed on an undermanned Royal ship. I was treated like a slave. It was only when a gunnery officer took an interest in me and made me his unofficial assistant that the situation improved. About this time my ship deserted the King and joined Parliament's fleet. I rose through the ranks and joined your ship in the Mediterranean as a junior gunnery officer. My future is very precarious, With the number of sailors likely to be reduced and hundreds of exiled Royalists wanting to replace people like us, I will be demobilized at any time. I will not serve the King for much longer. My hope is to join the Dutch or Swedish navy as a mercenary and carry on the fight against the Papists."

"You hate Papists?" continued Mark, confident that he was about to trap Philip into a confession.

"That is a strange question. Of course, I do. I am English. The Papists have tried to destroy us since the days of good queen Bess. No Englishman can trust a Catholic."

"Especially their priests," added Luke pulling the noose tighter.

Philip ignored the question and changed the discussion entirely. "As gunnery officer on this ship, I have bad news for you, Sir Luke."

"That's been my luck over the past few weeks," bemoaned Luke. "What is it now?"

"Any thought you had of using our ship's guns to bombard the island effectively is not possible. This frigate's guns are old, not the modern long-range weapons you had available on *The Cromwell*. These have neither the range nor appropriate elevation. Given the precipitous cliffs and inability to get close to shore, it is impossible for our cannon fire to reach any targets on the island. The only effective weapon in these circumstances would be mortars, and there are no ships in the English navy in this area equipped with such weapons. In fact, only the Ottomans have used the mortar effectively at sea."

The four men moved from imbibing Bordeaux wine to attacking the bottles of fine French brandy that the Bohms had sent to the captain. Luke could hold his liquor better than most but, on this occasion, drank very little. He hoped to spring a trap on Bates and needed his wits about him.

"Philip, or rather should I call you Jerome? Why did you leave this island in disgrace in 1642, just before the arrival of the current Marquess?"

Philip looked surprised, but quickly regained his composure despite, or perhaps because of his semi-drunken state.

"No doubt, given your investigative skills you would have already questioned the relevant islanders as to the circumstances of my departure.

I was forced to leave the island because of the actions of the then rector Martin Moore, Bill Perry and others."

"How did you react on discovering both those men were still on the island," niggled Mark.

"You can imagine my amazement to find that Bill had returned as the Catholic priest, that someone was trying to kill Martin and that the other person involved in the assault on me was a son of the current Marquess who was probably murdered a few years ago. That trio raped me and then made out, I was the aggressor, and unless I left the island I would be handed over to the authorities. It was my word against an Anglican priest, and although I did not know it then, the son of a next Marquess. Only Ann Bentley knew the truth, but pressure from her family, I suspect Martin, forced her to remain silent."

"So, you blame Martin Moore, Harry Bohm and William Perry for the downturn in your fortunes and perhaps for the ensuing early life as a sailor?" questioned Mark.

"Your rape by these three men preyed on you for years and built up in you an overwhelming desire for revenge." added Luke.

"Not at all! I suffered much worse in my early days at sea. The events of 1642 had been almost erased from my memory until by sheer chance this frigate was designated to assist you bring order to Nith. In going ashore my memories of 1642 came back to me. I was incensed that Perry was now a revered catholic priest, and that Moore was still on the island exerting his evil influence. I was delighted to hear that Harry Bohm had fallen or been pushed to his death."

"Then you decided to take revenge by killing Perry, and presumably Moore as well," announced Luke.

"Not at all! I did not seek revenge, I simply hoped that with your presence on the island, justice would finally be achieved. Perry should be arrested and executed, and Moore charged with all the offences that he committed on the youth of Nith. The Greek, Socrates was officially poisoned for corrupting the youth of Athens, Moore deserves the same fate for all those young girls he deflowered."

"Sex with women is not necessarily a capital offence," said Mark.

"Sex with your own sister, and at least one of your nieces is, as is sodomy and buggery," was the specific reply.

Luke was shocked. No wonder none of the Moore women would elaborate on who impregnated Ann, and on Ellen's paternity. It was beginning to make sense. Was Ann's death related to Martin's predatory behavior. Could Martin have murdered his own niece? He turned to Jerome.

"Would Martin murder Ann?"

"Yes, if she was about to reveal his history of multiple incest, buggary and sodomy."

"Did his possible murder of the only person who befriended you two decades ago give you even more justification to kill Martin?" asked Mark.

"Have you found a body? I thought Martin has simply disappeared," Jerome replied with an insolent smile.

Luke was stymied. Without a body he could not effectively pursue this line of questioning. He decided to play his trump card even though it amounted to little more than bluff. Martin could still be alive, so he turned attention back to the murder of Perry.

"Jerome Tighe, also known as Philip Bates, I arrest you for the murder of William Perry. You will be incarcerated in the brig of this ship, and then transferred to York Castle to await trial."

"You will never convict me without evidence—and you have none," replied an unfazed Jerome.

"But we do," whispered Luke.

Luke threw a silver button on the table. "This is a small part of our evidence. You lost this button in the Catholic chapel as you struggled with William Perry. It was found under his body. In addition, we found a knife that probably belonged to Martin Moore. You murdered Moore, stole his knife and then used it to cut the throat of the priest. You had opportunity—and motive."

Captain Hutton who appeared in state of shock sent the steward who had been serving them their drinks and meals, to have two soldiers come to the cabin to escort the lieutenant to the brig.

Luke, Mark and Peter were taken completely unawares by what happened next.

Jerome stood up and overturned the table momentarily pinning down the other three men. He ran to door of the cabin. By the time Luke reached the deck, he saw Tighe running headlong towards the stern of the ship. In full pursuit Luke was gaining on his quarry, when suddenly Jerome did a right-angled turn, and jumped headlong overboard.

There was no moon. Nor could Luke hear anyone splashing about. According to the captain, the lieutenant could not swim.

Back in the captain's cabin Mark was upbeat. "We have solved two murders, Perry and Moore and possibly a third, Ann Bentley."

"You are the optimist. We have solved one murder. By his suicide Tighe probably confirms he killed Perry, but Martin may still be alive, and a lot of other factors could be involved in Ann's demise," maintained a pessimistic Luke.

The steward poured another round of drinks as two of the three officers congratulated themselves. He suddenly spoke, "Captain, I have to correct you. Philip Bates can swim. He quite often jumped overboard from the long boat and swam the rest of the way to the island. He is a very powerful swimmer. Do not assume that he is dead!"

Luke gave a gasp of frustration.

Throughout the next day the long boats of the frigate and a motley collection of local vessels plied the waters around the island looking for Tighe, while Luke's troops searched the foreshore. Ironically the only evidence that emerged during that day was the naval jacket with the incriminating replacement button.

It did not help.

Tighe could have removed it at any time to help him swim to the island, or even the mainland. They quickly accepted the rumor that William Perry's murderer was Jerome Tighe, who was motivated by events which had happened almost two decades earlier.

Luke decided to risk a local panic by suggesting that Tighe might not have drowned and was possibly planning his revenge against other enemies from that time. All potential victims would be given protection by the allocation of more troops to guard their persons and households.

Mark was troubled. He confronted Luke. "The neat explanation that Tighe, because of the rape, murdered Perry and Moore may not hold water in regard to the latter's presumed death. Someone else is after Moore. When old Richard Banks was shot the assailant obviously thought he was Moore but at that time Tighe was with us on the top of the cliffs. He certainly did not fire that fatal shot."

"True. In addition to Tighe's desire to execute justice on Martin Moore, someone else is anxious to remove as many of the Moore relatives as he or she can. The murder of Ann and the attempt on Ellen are probably just the beginning."

Luke brought Ellen up to date with his current thinking. He emphasized that she must not go anywhere without her guards. If she did it could be fatal.

Ellen looked a little sheepish and confessed. "Luke, I have been keeping something from you which appears increasingly important in these attacks on Martin and myself, and probably in the murder of my mother. I only became aware of it just before Martin disappeared."

"You mean to tell me that the Moores have upset somebody for reasons I have, so far, no idea about?"

"Yes, mother and Martin ran a smuggling ring that apparently is very profitable for its members."

"Who are?"

"I was never told but I assume the Denholms, the Kitchens, and perhaps the Keddys were members. Martin specifically excluded the man he called an interfering busybody, John Corby."

"Were any of the Bohm family involved?"

"I do not know, but I cannot believe that the ring which has been in operation from before the arrival of the Bohms could have functioned without their acquiescence, if not their active participation."

"How does it operate?"

"For years, more recently from the security of the Marquess's apartment, my mother organized the activities, kept the books and distributed the profits. Martin would row out into the North Sea and meet a French trawler which would unload its cargo of fine fabrics, Bordeaux wines, French brandy, and exquisite jewelry."

"Surely he would have to make many trips. His rowboat is very small."

"When he was on a smuggling run, he attached two dinghies to the back of his boat. He could always claim they were there so he could bring his lobster pots back to shore. He seems to have managed large loads without much trouble. Some of the smuggled goods remained on the island for the benefit of members of the ring—and possibly the Bohms."

"Yes, your great uncle served me the finest French brandy when I first met him and tried to tell me he had distilled it himself."

"Most of the goods were then taken by the Kitchins in their skiff and unloaded on a deserted part of the coast between Whitby and Scarborough and taken by agents of the ultimate recipient, a criminal who dominates the northern moors to his base in the hinterland where they were distributed across the north."

"I know that possible recipient very well, Kit Jagger. That route conveniently misses the excise men. There are very few north of Hull and those that are, concentrate on Newcastle, Whitby and Scarborough. They do not have the resources to monitor the intervening coastline. So, what has happened within our smuggling ring since your mother died and Martin disappeared?"

"Just before she died, mother discovered something amiss. Martin was very cagey when he warned me, I might be in danger, because of what my mother and he might have done. It more likely concerns what Martin did—and mother discovered."

"Did they say it involved the smuggling ring?"

"No, but if it did it provides a possible motive for mother's murder. Any member of the ring may be involved if they thought the Moore family had not distributed the profits according to whatever was agreed. Maybe Martin falsified the records in terms of what goods were brought in and sold some independently of the group."

"Or the Kitchen family received more than they claimed they were given by the recipient's agents?" suggested Luke.

"Little money was exchanged at the handover. The recipient paid for the whole cargo into an account held by my mother, and since her death by Martin."

"From what I have heard neither Martin nor your mother visited the mainland. Who carried out the high finances for the organization?"

"The only people who regularly visit the mainland from Nith are James Denholm and John Corby, but a member of the Bohm family could have acted for the group."

"And if it was a member of the family, who is the most likely?"

"Up until his death, Harry would certainly have helped for a cut of the profits, but if anybody did it as a service to their tenants, I would suspect the Marchioness."

Luke was astonished by such an assertion. "Why the Marchioness?"

"Such a ring could not flourish on the island without the knowledge if not approval of the Marquess. As he never left the island then any support, he might give to the network must have been channeled through his wife.

I doubt that he would not trust either of his two eldest sons in such an enterprise."

"But the Marchioness never left the island."

Ellen shrugged her shoulders.

Luke thanked Ellen for her much valued information, and immediately visited John Corby. "John, are you aware of a smuggling ring conducted by the islanders?"

"Yes."

"Then why as constable have you done nothing about it?"

"Until your arrival on the island my legal superior was the Marquess, as lord of the manor. I was forbidden by him to refer any matters to the mainland. He fully supports this smuggling enterprise."

"For personal gain?"

"Not at all—apart perhaps for a few bottles of French brandy. On the other hand, it brought a reasonable additional income to the smuggling families. The Bohms were not directly involved. The Marquess argued that this activity made his tenants happy and therefore they were less likely to disrupt the well-being of the island. Their improved financial security meant that the Bohm family was never called upon to supplement the income of their tenants and workers."

"I have heard that members of the family were involved at least in handling the finances of the operation, especially in receiving monies from the ultimate receiver of the goods."

"James Denholm handled that aspect of their operation when he went to the mainland on estate business," replied John.

"Who ran the operation?"

"Martin Moore and his niece Ann Bentley."

"One murdered, one missing—was their role in the smuggling ring relevant to these events?"

"A distinct possibility, especially as my wife told me her sister Ann was highly agitated just before her death by something, she had discovered possibly involving the ring."

"How did the system actually work?" asked Luke anxious to verify Ellen's description.

"Martin collected the goods off shore, Ann organized their disposal, the Kitchins transferred them to the mainland, James Denholm collected the petty cash that may have changed hands, but who had access to the major accounts by which the ring was paid by the recipient I do not know. These large sums were ultimately accessed by Ann to put aside for the next delivery, or to distribute among the ring's members as profit."

"If Ann was troubled before her death, she may have uncovered that someone in the chain was feathering his own nest at the expense of the gang at large."

"Possibly."

"That could only be a limited number of people—Martin in falsifying the goods he had received, the Kitchins in removing some of the goods before delivery to the agents of Kit Jagger, or James Denholm in his collection of the monied owed."

"Or Ann herself. My sister-in-law was not the most honest of women. She may have feared that her possible mismanagement of the books had been discovered," suggested John.

"If a member of the ring was so affronted by whatever wrongdoing had occurred who was most likely to take revenge against Ann or Martin?"

"My brother-in-law, James Denholm, or Sam Kitchen. Sam has an overdeveloped sense of entitlement—and a short and fiery temper. And his blacksmith physique would make it easy for him to enforce his will," replied John.

"Or they could be the guilty party and acted to stop their activities being revealed by Ann, and later by Martin to whom she probably confided her suspicions."

Luke decided to follow up the suggestion that the Marchioness was involved. He arrived at her apartments just when she was dressing for dinner. She received him in her undergarments which she made no attempt to cover up. Luke apologized for arriving at such an inconvenient time as Jane led him by the hand to an upholstered bench underneath her double sized window which overlooked the garden and maze. "Don't apologize Luke, I look forward to you visits. I hope this one is social and not part of your investigation."

Luke decided to adopt the risky course. He would play along with her obvious amorous intent in the hope of receiving the information he sought. "My lady, this is a social visit, but there are two questions you may be able to help me with. Were you aware of your tenants' smuggling ring? And do you play any part in it?"

As she squeezed his hand Jane replied, "Yes, to both questions. On the day of our arrival here, Felix was informed of the situation by the islanders in their attempt to save Martin Moore from expulsion from the island. Harry had recommended that given Martin's corrosive influence on the youth of the island, that Felix should immediately expel him. Samuel Kitchen, James Denholm and Martin's three nieces petitioned Felix to keep him on the island. Felix who was made quickly aware of the bleak living conditions on Nith, and the need for his new tenants and workers to supplement their income at every opportunity, accepted their advice. Martin would remain and continue his major role in the smuggling ring. Harry was furious and spent the rest of his life trying to destroy Martin."

"I have been given an outline of how the group worked but there seems to be some confusion as to any actual involvement of your family."

"We benefitted by obtaining goods imported by the ring at a much-discounted price. As the ultimate recipient, a North Yorkshire criminal with important political connections, wanted to conceal his transactions. He paid the monies due into my account which I then passed on to Ann, and following her death, directly to Martin."

"So, it is you, and not James Denholm who provides this vital link in the chain?"

"My name and account are used, but Denholm with a letter from me carries out the physical exchange of any monies or letters of credit."

"If Ann was murdered because she had been falsifying accounts, or had discovered felonious behavior in others, who would be your most likely suspect."

"Quite frankly in my two decades on this island only two men would be capable. One is dead, my stepson Harry and the other is also possibly deceased—the dead girl's own uncle, Martin Moore."

25

That evening Luke had retired immediately after supper. Sometime around midnight the silence of the night was suddenly punctuated by screams for assistance.

Luke reached the long corridor and quickly established that the cries for help were coming from the apartment of the Baron. By the time Luke reached the area both Michael and Alice in their night attire were in the corridor giving orders to their servants.

Alice was in shock. "She could have killed us," she shouted at Luke. "Send your men after the madwomen!"

"What happened?" Luke asked of the slightly calmer Michael.

"Unbelievable. It was like a dream. Alice and I had just retired when our bedchamber door opened. There was no light other than a pale beam of moonlight. I recognized it was a woman who strode to the bed and pulled off the coverings. Then she attempted to lift up my night shirt. She kept shouting at Alice, 'Does he have it? Does he have it?' We both recognized the voice. It was Margaret. I jumped out of bed to restrain her, but she fled."

"I will go straight to your father's quarters. Lady Margaret might have returned to her confinement there," said Luke.

It was a night-gowned Ellen who answered his frantic knocking. "Why disturb us so late at night. I heard screams coming from the Baron's chambers. What is going on?"

"That is why I am disturbing you. The Baron and his wife were assaulted by Lady Margaret."

"No way! Her ladyship is sound asleep in the next room. Have a look for yourself!"

Ellen opened the door and there tucked up in bed was Margaret her outline clearly revealed by the moonlight.

"Don't be too sure," said Luke. He strode across the room and pulled the bed covering off the apparently sleeping woman.

There was no woman. The shape had been created by a number of strategically placed pillows.

"I will alert my men and John Corby. We must find her before she harms somebody or herself. Did you talk to her today? Was she better or worse than she has been?"

"She was certainly better than the night before, but clearly not herself."

"What happened the night before?"

"She appears to have had a very sensual dream that turned into a nightmare. She claimed that her dead husband Harry came to her, and as she prepared to receive this very aroused man, he grabbed a belt from beside the bed and tried to strangle her. She claimed she just managed to release the pressure for a moment, and utter a single scream, which brought the nurse running into the room."

"Not an unexpected dream for an apparently sensual women who since the death of her husband has been deprived of male company," commented Luke coldly.

"Yes, but it was strange. The nurse woke me and we both attempted to placate her ladyship. She was certainly very aroused sexually, but this could have been self-created, but she did have a reddish mark around her throat."

"You're not suggesting that her dead husband came to her in the middle of the night, and tried to strangle her?"

"Don't mock me, Luke, but as part of her dream, could she have tried to strangle herself?" asked Ellen.

"Possibly, that is why we must find her. Next time she may complete the job. Did she refer to those activities in the cold light of the following day?"

"She was not with it today, but for a moment when she briefly recognized me, she squeezed my hand and said, 'Your mother was right' Any attempt to probe what she meant was met with a blank look."

"Remember we are not dealing with a sane woman. Who knows what dangerous thoughts are surging through her mind, and what strange ideas she may have constructed to explain her current circumstances? As she is Catholic, Felix must send her to a convent hospital in France or the Spanish Netherlands. She has to be confined for her own safety."

"I expect after this episode the Marquess has no other viable options," noted Ellen.

"Margaret was brought up on Nith. As a young girl who were her friends among the general population?" Luke asked.

"I don't know, but my aunts might."

Within minutes Luke was in the Denholm's apartment and questioning Isabel. "You have probably heard that Lady Margaret has caused an incident and has subsequently disappeared. She is in a highly disturbed state and must be found before she causes damage to others or herself. When she was growing up on the island was she particularly friendly with any of the islanders, whom she might now seek out in her current crisis?"

"She was so besotted with Harry that once she married him, she cut all ties with her schoolgirl friends."

"Who were?"

"My righteous sister, Hannah was close at one time."

"What about Ann and yourself?"

"The former Marquess hated our uncle, Martin Moore, and we were considered too wild to associate with his ward."

"Anyone else, apart from Hannah?"

"Yes, despite cutting her ties with the inferior classes after marrying Harry Bohm, she made one exception. This person remained close until the arrival of William Perry and that woman's conversion to Quakerism. Maybe with his death she may in her current state, turn back to her old friend, Ursula Keddy."

"I though Ursula Keddy was a mainlander."

"No, Vincent is a mainlander whom Ursula met while she was in service in Whitby, but she spent the first two decades of her life here. She was a Kitchin, Samuel's younger sister, and Tom's aunt."

Luke then moved to the Corbys and indicated to Hannah that he had a few questions with regard to Lady Margaret. "Your sister Isabel says that as a girl you were very close to Lady Margaret. Has she contacted you recently, or is there a safe hiding place as girls that you might have frequented, that she could conceivably return to now?"

"Lady Margaret and I have had no contact since the day she married Harry. Harry indulged in a vendetta against the Moore family, particularly Uncle Martin, but also against my sister Ann and myself. As schoolgirls we were very close. The old Marquess employed a tutor for his ward, Lady Margaret. Only two island girls were educated with her—Ursula Kitchen, now Keddy, and myself."

"What about hiding places?"

"Margaret knows every inch of this island, including the supposedly secret network of caves and tunnels that led up from the eastern shoreline to both this building and the parish church, and to many other parts of the island. She could be anywhere within that vast complex which I understand your men have still not fully explored."

"No favorite places?"

"As girls the three us liked to hide in a part of the network that had an opening high up on the cliff face. We could peer out into the turbulent sea and bitter blizzards from the warmth of our little cave. But that was over twenty years ago. Martin told me much of the old network of tunnels has caved in."

"But to search that complex would be worthwhile nevertheless?" asked Luke.

"Maybe."

Luke turned to John. "Make that your priority in the search. My men will join you in the eastern cavern and we should have enough men to follow every alternate passage that we come across. I will join you shortly."

Luke left and made his way to the Keddys. Ursula opened the door and remarked, "You have just missed Vince. He has gone to join the search for Lady Margaret."

"I have come to see you on that very issue. I gather that as schoolgirls, you were very close to her, even after her marriage to Harry Bohm?"

"Yes, we were educated together, and Margaret and I remained in close contact until the arrival of William Perry. After Harry's death Margaret needed the counsel of a priest, rather than that of an old school friend. Also, my acceptance of George Fox's Quaker teachings did not go well with Margaret's growing Catholic extremism."

"If she is in hiding, where given your schoolgirl adventures, would she be?"

"In the complex of caves and tunnels overlooking the sea at the eastern end of the island."

"Can you take me there?"

"There was more than one favorite spot. We probably had at least three little nests as we called them. After Harry's death she went to the one that had an opening onto the cliff face where he fell to his death. She told me during one of our last conversations that going there was proving too much for her, so she went to one of the others that did not remind her of her husband's death."

"These nests have openings wide enough for you to view the cliff face and ocean. Were any of these openings wide enough to climb through? In essence if we found Margaret in one of these places, could she could jump through the opening to her death on the rocks below?"

Ursula uttered a cry of alarm. "Not when we were schoolgirls, but I know in recent years Margaret has been enlarging the holes to gain a better view of the coastline. She is such a tiny woman escape through those openings is now a distinct possibility."

John Corby and his men, and all of Luke's troops under the command of Mark gathered in the cave to begin their intensive search of the tunnel system. Luke and two soldiers remained on the surface ready to follow Ursula's directions.

"The quickest way is to use the hidden entrance near where Martin Moore lived before the fire. I heard that there have been cave-ins, but I don't know on which side of these collapses is our schoolgirl nest."

They were in luck. Just before the first cave-in there was an incline leading upwards. Luke and Ursula wriggled up the incline into a small cave which had an opening to the elements—an opening that had been enlarged and capable of providing an exit from the nest. Also obvious was an extinguished candle. Fresh candle grease covered the floor. Someone had been there very recently.

Ursula and Luke looked at each other. Both were thinking the same thing—had it been Margaret? And had she jumped to her death through the opening?

Two days later John Corby and Mark reported that every inch of the network had been searched, and while the smugglers' store house had been found, there was no trace of Lady Margaret. The pessimistic view was that she had jumped to her death. Mark redirected the troops to search the base of the cliff and the surrounding sea.

Luke was more optimistic. "Margaret is on a mission. At this stage her suicide would be premature."

26

The discovery of the smugglers' storehouse forced Luke to act. As evidence indicated that the Denholm's may have taken the place of Ann Bentley and Martin Moore in its operations, he called on James.

"I can have you arrested for denying the King his rightful revenue from the duties on wine and spirits, but if you co-operate, we may be able to find some other solution."

"In what way can I co-operate?" asked a surprisingly amiable James.

"Has the death of Ann and the disappearance of Martin had more to do with problems within your smuggling ring than other issues? Were those two fiddling the books, or did they discover that someone else was feathering their own nest at the expense of the rest of the ring?"

James laughed in a manner that indicated these questions came as a great relief to a man who obviously anticipated a different line of questioning. "No, Sir Luke, everybody is happy within the smuggling ring and especially in the way that Martin and Ann ran the operation. Since Ann's death Martin has been re-organizing the network. Only a week before he disappeared, he called a meeting at which it was agreed that I become his deputy in general matters and Tom Kitchin replaced him in collecting the goods from the continental trawler, as well as continuing to transport them to the mainland. In addition, I was to train my niece Ellen to eventually follow her late mother as the pivot of the operation."

"Ann's murder and Martin's disappearance therefore can't be attributed to problems arising out of the smuggling operation?"

"Definitely not. Their role in the ring made them popular among the other members, and all those who benefitted from our activities. Ann's death was due to her extreme sensuality and overt immorality. She infuriated a lot of wives on the island. My wife Isabel tried to persuade her sister to cease her open adultery, but only succeeded at most in having Ann be slightly more discreet."

"I am inclined to believe you. For the moment what am I as a magistrate sworn to uphold the laws of land going to do about a clear breach of the excise regulations?"

"If one of our number confessed to be the ringleader and he paid a hefty fine that you might impose would that suffice, or must one or more of us be gaoled?"

"And your operation closed down," added Luke.

James was now very agitated. Luke moved quickly to quell his fears. "Don't worry! I have a solution that will enable you to continue your activity, and none of you will finish in gaol—but you will take a cut in revenue."

James waited on Luke's every word. "Many of the goods you import do not carry an excise or other forms of duty. In other words, much of your activity is legal. It is the importation of wines and spirits where you are defrauding the King of considerable income. Put an end to this by simply paying the excise required, and instead of being a smuggling ring, you become legal importers of continental goods. I have confiscated your books which were found in the storehouse and will levy the duties due on your last shipment. I will approach the Marchioness to arrange the transfer of the required amount into the government's coffers."

James was surprised that Luke knew of the Marchioness's role but was so relieved that their activity could continue with a substantial but not crippling loss of income.

"Do you think Martin is in hiding from a would-be killer, or has he already been murdered?" asked Luke changing the topic.

"I fear the worst. Your thorough search of the caves and their associated tunnels did not reveal his person or his body. Many foul deeds on this island escape detection, let alone punishment as it is easy to push victims, dead or alive, into the sea," confessed James.

Luke had just left James when he was accosted by a distressed Ellen.

"Sir, I have not told anybody, given her state. This morning we found Lady Margaret back in her bed, apparently suffering no major physical injuries from whatever adventure she had been on."

"What do you mean 'given her state'?"

"We found her pleasuring herself and making love to a non-existent Harry whom she believed was in the bed with her. You must have the Marquess make those arrangements for her to be taken to a continental convent. Her physical, mental and moral wellbeing are at stake," announced Ellen rather primly.

"Did she say anything that could explain her absence or condition?"

"She clearly now believes that Harry is alive and repeated several times that my mother Ann was right when she said, 'things were not as they seemed.'"

"This statement by your mother appears to have triggered Margaret's current state of mind, probably reinforced in her mind by Ann's murder. What was it in the few weeks before her death that led Ann to make such a claim? A similar comment to her uncle may have triggered his view that someone was out to get the Moores."

Luke suddenly shouted, "Eureka" and began hitting his head with a closed fist.

An alarmed Ellen enquired into his health.

He responded dramatically. "What if Margaret is right? What if Harry is still alive?"

"Not likely! Where has he been these five years? And what would be the point of his disappearance. His sins were already made known to the family, and he had been forgiven, at least by Felix."

Luke was silent for so long that Ellen began to feel uncomfortable. He then explained, "It is so simple, and it explains a lot. How could everybody miss such a simple substitution?"

"What do you mean?"

"Two brothers, identical twins hunt together. One falls to his death. How do we know which one fell? They were identical in appearance?"

"Yes, so much so that Felix ordered them to wear distinctive doublets, Harry wore green, and Michael red."

"But both of these were removed when they hunted," surmised Luke.

"What would be the point of Harry pretending to be Michael. If Michael had died, Harry would become heir and the Baron. There is no advantage for him pretending to be Michael."

"Unfortunately, you are right, but if Harry had substituted himself for Michael it could have helped explain why both your mother and possibly your great uncle were murdered."

"I don't see the connection."

"To the outside world the twins were identical, but what if they were different in the area of their private parts. One may have had a birth mark and other not. The only person who would have come across this subtle difference would be someone who had slept with both men."

"My mother!"

"According to your aunts your mother slept with both Harry and Michael in her younger days, and that Harry continued to seek her company up to her death."

"So, if your suggestion of a substitution is true Harry, now masquerading as Michael, missed my mother's company so much that he sought her affection in his new persona. She recognized something peculiar to Harry. But how did this lead to her death?"

"Your mother may have seen some advantage in threatening to expose the substitution."

"You mean she blackmailed the nominal Michael threatening to reveal his true identity as Harry?"

"To keep his secret Harry had Ann killed, and suspecting she told her uncle and maybe you, all three had to go. For your mother to tell Lady Margaret that Harry was still alive was a very cruel act. It would have been enough to set her off on her current mental downturn."

"Mother was not a nice woman."

"The only reason I cannot fully accept the scenario I have outlined is that I can see no advantage to Harry in such a pretense."

"And there are two other reasons to reject this link between the substitution of one brother for another, and the murder of my mother. There was no overriding reason to keep the secret. If Michael was declared dead, then Harry would take over and act as he had in his pretend role of Michael. His parading as his brother had brought him no advantage. The law would not see his actions as particularly in need of heavy punishment.

A second reason I question your hypothesis is that my mother and Harry were always very close. If she really loved anyone it was the Harry. She would never blackmail him."

"True, but it would be interesting to know if the brothers had distinguishing features in the private areas of their body. Are there other women on the island who have slept with both the Bohm brothers?"

"You can't go around asking respectable matrons on the island if in their wayward youth they had slept with both brothers, and if either one had a distinguishing mark," Ellen observed with a slight giggle of embarrassment.

"Nevertheless, I will ask your aunts. They are store of knowledge on the social life of this island."

"I think you have won them over. Aunt Isabel lusts after you, and I am sure Aunt Hannah has similar feelings, if only Uncle John let her express herself."

It was Luke's turn to blush.

At the Denholms, Isabel opened the door, and kissed Luke. "Thank you for not closing down our importing venture. James has not been in a better mood for years—but why are you here now?"

Luke explained his delicate mission, which did nothing to lessen Isabel's growing sensuality.

She confessed, "Like Ann I slept with both brothers, but it was before my marriage and before Harry married Lady Margaret. I did not notice any difference. Both reminded me of my father's stallion. Need I say more."

"Are there any other women on the island who slept with both brothers in more recent times?"

"I could name dozens who claim they have slept with Harry, but the married Michael led a fairly moral life. I can raise the question with my women friends, and if something relevant emerges I will let you know."

Three days later Ursula Keddy knocked on Luke's door. She seemed somewhat embarrassed, and said she had some information regarding the delicate matter he had raised with Isabel. Luke was surprised. Had this now conservative Quaker matron fallen victim in her youth to charms of both Bohm brothers?

Luke was quickly put right regarding such an unthinkable assumption.

"I never slept with either brother, but Harry did have a mark in his private areas that made him distinguishable from his brother."

"How then do you know this most intimate detail?"

"Harry's wife, Lady Margaret told me almost twenty years ago, just after their marriage. She was and is a very sensual woman. Her lovemaking was so passionate that just after their wedding Margaret bit Harry somewhere in that area during their lovemaking that caused a small wound that needed medical attention from the Marquess. It apparently healed, but it left a small scar."

"Why would Margaret reveal this to you?"

"She was proud of what she had done. She had put her mark on Harry forever. In some twisted way, she probably thought this might deter him from his womanizing ways."

"Thank you. Everything fits, if only I can find a motive for the substitution, and if this did happen, a motive for the subsequent murder of Ann."

"I can add another fact that will demolish your theory that Harry, as Michael, killed Ann. According to the in-servants of the Baron, Ann was a regular visitor to Michael's bedchamber up to her death. These servants were amazed that the conservative Michael had become besotted with the amoral Ann. Whether he is Harry or Michael, the Bohm heir, remained close to Ann," revealed Ursula.

Luke discussed with Mark his new obsession that it was Michael, and not Harry that had died.

Mark was skeptical. "What does Harry have to gain from such a substitution? There is no strong motive to do so. Harry's crime, if he did substitute himself for his brother, did not involve personal gain and would not be viewed too seriously by the law."

Luke was disappointed at this rebuttal of his hypothesis. He visited Jane for comfort and conversation. He explained his view that Harry still lived.

Jane's response was more positive than he could have expected. "I agree with you that the brother claiming to be Michael could well be Harry. It would explain a lot."

"Why do you agree with me when Mark has his doubts?"

"Two factors support your view. First—ever since Harry's alleged death, Michael has been a changed personality. He became more like his late brother—more efficient, more ruthless, better organized. If he were his late brother, these changes are automatically explained. Second—you are wrong to say that Harry had nothing to gain by this subterfuge. He had a major gain, and given his womanizing tendencies, it may have loomed the most important in his thinking at the time."

27

"Which was?"

"Given your own past, I thought it would have been obvious. He gained Alice, his longtime mistress. By pretending to be Michael, his mistress became his wife, and his long-estranged wife, Margaret, is relegated to a grieving widow."

Luke gave Jane a peck on the cheek. "How could I miss that? But this does not make the murder of Ann in any way explicable in terms of the deception. If our Ecclesiastical Courts are reinstated, they may find Harry guilty of sleeping with his sister-in-law, but the secular courts would have little to act on."

Jane chuckled. "Luke, you think like a male, and see the answers in terms of what males may or may not do. What I have told you opens up a new avenue for you pursue in terms of both motive for the substitution, and its relationship to the murder of Ann Bentley."

"In what way?"

"The mind behind both these developments—the substitution of the brothers and the subsequent murder of Ann, is surely a woman. And that has to be Alice."

Luke gave Jane a big hug which was returned in a flurry of passionate kisses. "My lady, you may have solved the murder in that simple statement. Alice had the most to gain by the subterfuge. She remains the Baroness, and the next Marchioness, and she has the man she lusted after as her husband. Conversely, she has the most to lose if the substitution is revealed. She loses everything—current position, future status and the man of her life. I can't wait to confront her."

"Be careful! Alice is a formidable woman. She will not submit to your charms nor your bullying."

"Before I see her, let me clarify the circumstances in which it was believed that Harry had died, and not Michael."

Luke asked James Denholm to outline the events of that fatal day.

"The two brothers left the rabbit warren and went to the cliff to shoot the seabirds that nest in the cliff face. I heard several shots and then after a long silence I heard a shout of alarm. I ran to the cliff top where Michael told me that Harry had fallen."

"How did you know that it was Michael you met on the cliff face?"

James suddenly looked flummoxed. The doubt that Luke had sown with this question, suddenly overwhelmed him. He whispered, "Because the man who met me said it was Harry who had fallen. If that was the case, then the man I met was Michael."

"There was no way you could independently confirm the survivor's identity?"

"No, and at the time I naturally believed what I was told. Why would either brother lie to me?"

"What happened next?"

"I procured Harry's body, and on the way back to Nith Hall handed Michael his distinguishing colored doublet."

"Did either Lady Alice or Lady Margaret see the body?"

"No, the Marquess thought that given the damage done to Harry's face as a result of smashing onto the rocks that it was not a fit thing for the women to see—even though Margaret complained bitterly."

Luke decided to give the usually aggressive Alice the discourtesy of simply appearing on her doorstep with a unit of soldiers—and not go through the formal and time-consuming ritual of seeking to make an appointment with his social superior.

The Baroness was rightly furious with this breach of protocol—a mood that Luke hoped would lead her to reveal more than a calmer interviewee might have done. He would begin with an outrageous statement, hoping the arrogance of the bluff would unsettle Alice.

"Baroness, I have only come here out of courtesy to your position. I wanted to let you know that I am about to reveal to the island the misrepresentation you and Harry have indulged in for the past five years, namely that it was Michael who died."

Alice was livid. She was literally lost for words.

Eventually she was able to splutter out, "Liar, you cannot possibly prove such a ridiculous claim."

Luke replied with a concentrated glare directly into Alice's face.

She reacted to this attempted intimidation defiantly, "If true, it is hardly a major crime. Harry is entitled to everything he enjoys as Michael, in his own right as Michael's heir."

"That is true for Harry, but not for you. The one thing he had legally as Michael, which he would not have as Harry, is you. And the only person who loses considerably if this deception is revealed, is you. You can see why I am here to arrest you."

"What exactly is my crime?"

Luke ignored the question and asked, "Did you plan Michael's murder and the substitution of Harry?"

"I refuse to answer such a ludicrous question."

After a period of silent confrontation Alice changed her approach. She would confess all.

"If it is Harry who lives, it was his brilliant on the spot decision made entirely without my knowledge. It was not so much that he could now have my favors as his wife which he had as his mistress—but that it was a way of ridding himself of the increasingly unstable and dangerous Margaret."

"You suggest that this deception on the islanders, and especially on Lady Margaret was an opportunistic move on the basis of an unfortunate accident. I could construct a more sinister background namely that you conspired with Harry to kill your husband and remove his wife by this clever and cruel misrepresentation."

"You can let your imagination run riot, but as a magistrate you know that you have no evidence to support any of this fantasy. In fact, you have no evidence to prove that the current Baron is Harry and not Michael."

"That is where you are wrong. I have irrefutable proof that the current baron is Harry."

"You are lying. And I will not fall for your bluff. Your methods of interrogation are well known."

"In that case you know I will not hesitate I will arrest the Baron, strip him naked and have several women point out to any gathered crowd why this is Harry and not Michael."

Alice's fury suddenly escalated.

She exclaimed, "I knew that bitch Ann would not remain quiet. Harry was stupid to renew his relationship with her."

"I would be cautious concerning what you say about Ann. I could build a case that you had her killed to prevent her spreading news of her discovery. But let's stop playing games! My only interests in this matter are whether Michael was murdered, or had an unfortunate accident, and who killed Ann. You can see from my point of view that you and Harry had motives for both murders"

"But our motives are not that strong. In terms of possessions and power Harry has obtained what would be his right as heir, and in terms of having me as a wife is not a big issue. Harry is a womanizer, and being his wife has more disadvantages than being one of his several mistresses."

"Despite everything the one person who did gain substantially from the current misrepresentation is yourself."

"In what way?"

"If Harry had not concealed Michaels's death, he would have become Baron and Lady Margaret the Baroness. Margaret, and not you would eventually have become marchioness. And I know how much you desire that title and position. When I reveal all this to island, you lose your current position, and any chance of becoming marchioness."

"Don't be too sure of that you arrogant Roundhead. Harry will have his marriage to Margaret annulled on the grounds of her madness and marry me."

"I am no Catholic, but I understand such a development is much more difficult to achieve than if you were within our more tolerant Anglican church."

"What are you going to do with your mixed bag of facts, guesswork and pure fantasy?" asked Alice attempting to get back on the front foot.

Luke was saved from having to answer by the arrival of the Baron.

Luke struck, hoping to catch him off guard. "Harry, I am here to discuss your future."

"Are you mad, I am Michael."

"Don't go on, my love! This busybody has evidence to prove who you are. If you had not been such a womanizer, there would have been no evidence to disprove that you were Michael. If you had not renewed your acquaintance with Ann Bentley, none of this would have happened," said an Alice oscillating between distraction and rage.

She then strode from the room.

"What do you intend to do about all this?" asked Harry.

"Nothing for the moment. I have Ann's murder to solve and your father's potential murder to forestall—and the urgent need to find Martin Moore. That will give you time to sort out the situation with the family. I am intrigued with the origins of this substitution. Lady Alice said it was purely opportunist."

"Absolutely! The one thought I had as Michael fell, and I saw his crumpled body motionless on the rocks, was Alice. At the time I was particularly besotted with her, and our regular meetings were becoming more difficult to conceal. If I pretended to be Michael, and claim that it was Harry who fell, paradise would be mine."

"Lady Alice was not aware of anything until after it happened?"

"No, the first thing she knew was when we went to bed that night. I have never been with anybody so deliriously happy."

"You had no thought for poor Margaret who as a result of your trickery has become insane."

"Have no pity for that woman. She is not the innocent victim she pretends to be. She is an evil, malevolent woman, whose current mental condition was always there, but cleverly concealed."

"Most adulterous husbands blame their wives. Have you any evidence for what you say?"

"Yes, and I hope you find Martin Moore, because he can verify what I say. When I came to Nith before father became Marquess, I spent most of my time with Martin. He organized the most outrageous of gatherings where I first met Ann, then just out of girlhood. The one person, given her rank as a ward of the Marquess, and a distant relative, not invited to these orgies was Margaret Neale. Unknown to me at the time was that the girl was a seething cauldron of barely controlled sexual urges, far in advance of even the promiscuous Ann. I discovered this animalistic passion on our wedding night leading to the serious bite that left the permanent scar—your evidence that I am not Michael."

"Her extreme sensuality does not make her malevolent or evil. On that criteria a large number of this island's women would be found to be so."

"True, but what she did to Martin certainly did. She told her guardian that he had raped her. Although her story was not supported by anybody else Peregrine informed the ecclesiastical authorities that Martin was not a fit person to be rector here. The diocesan authority that decided the case was one of Peregrine's relatives. Aware that the old man did not have long to live, the defrocking was expedited. Peregrine ordered Martin off the island but died before that injustice could be effected."

"And your father never implemented it?"

"No, I told him what I knew about the incident, but I suggested he should still exile Martin as a bad influence on the island's youth. He ignored me. He allowed Martin to stay, and in fact assisted him to develop a new life here. Even though Martin had been unfairly treated I thought his removal would be in everybody's interests."

"Given your knowledge of Margaret's role in this affair why did you marry her?"

"Father. In his various roles as alchemist and Anglican priest he assessed Margaret as a normal, if sexually obsessed young woman, and that marriage to a lusty young male such as myself was all that was needed for her to settle down."

"You went along with it."

"I had no choice but from that point on, I was never close to my father. Forcing such a marriage on me, made me determined to go my own way. Developing an independent future funded by property acquisitions independent of the family became my immediate aim."

<h1 style="text-align:center">28</h1>

"Why did you renew your relationship with Ann? If you hadn't, your substitution would never have been uncovered," asked Luke with some degree of sympathy which surprised him.

"From that fateful day in 1642 until my presumed death, Ann and I were regular partners. She was an astonishing woman. After a few years of 'marriage' to Alice I became obsessed with renewing my relationship with Ann. In my guise as Michael I invited her to my apartment. As soon as we were in each other's arms, she realized that I was Harry. I was in heaven and knew I could not be without her company. I saw her most days leading up to her death. She became the only women of all those I have slept with that I showered with presents, including a piece of family jewelry—a small sapphire pendant that belonged to my grandmother."

"I initially thought you murdered Ann because she had discovered your real identity and was blackmailing you to maintain her silence. You now confess that Ann and you had resumed a close relationship in which both of you were sublimely happy. Was Alice aware of this renewed relationship?"

"That it occurred, but not to its depth and frequency."

"Did she have Ann murdered?"

"I can't see why? She has long accepted that I am a womanizer. What is important to Alice is that she is the Baroness, and eventually the Marchioness."

"Lady Alice is my prime suspect. She has the strongest of motives. She may not care less about your sexual adventures, but she as you have just admitted had to protect the falsehood that she is the legitimate wife of the current Baron to preserve her future."

"I don't believe that Alice would have murdered Ann but even if she had, you cannot prove it. Your evidence is circumstantial," concluded Harry.

Three days later Luke was summoned by the Marquess. "Well, Luke you have certainly caused a family upheaval. I appreciate that for the moment you have considered the situation a family matter—and not taken it to the legal authorities."

"I won't be able to conceal it much longer," Luke confessed.

"We have taken steps to put things right, and to legitimize those aspects of the false scenario that were illegal. Harry is having his marriage to Margaret annulled on the grounds that she was insane at the time of the marriage—a state of mind that he was aware of, but which I blindly ignored. She is in no position to contest it. She is currently on her way to a convent in Normandy. John Corby has escorted her to a friend of Lord Stokey in Hull, who will see her safely to her ultimate destination."

"All this may be to the good, but I am now investigating Michael's death. If I discover that he was pushed, and did not fall, all of this will come tumbling down, as the only person on the spot when Michael lost his footing, was Harry. In addition, I strongly suspect Lady Alice of murdering Ann Bentley. You need a fallback position regarding the succession. Ralph and Felicity should be made aware of the possibility that they may succeed you and Jane."

"You are wrong Luke, Michael's death was accidental, but Alice does have the strength of character to commit such an act, if she had the motivation."

"And she did—the loss of her future as the next Marchioness."

Luke could see that Felix did not reject the suggestion outright.

Next day Luke discussed with Mark his new priority. "I am convinced that Alice murdered Ann so that she would maintain her current and future positions."

"I still don't think that is strong enough motive for an aristocratic woman to murder a servant," replied an unconvinced Mark. "It is more likely to be one of the sexually deprived women on the island whose husband or lover was dallying with Ann."

"If you look at Alice's position logically, she was in danger of losing everything. Her husband is dead, and her lover beginning to stray into the arms of a woman who could destroy the one thing she had left—her position."

"How do we progress from here?" asked Mark.

"Probe more deeply into Ann's situation just before her death. Isabel and Ellen must be able to tell me more."

Isabel was in a friendly co-operative mood, probably provoked by Luke's lenient attitude towards the smuggling ring, now run by her husband.

Luke asked, "Was there any great change in Ann's demeanor in the six or seven weeks before her murder?"

"There was a major change compared with the months before, but that was the pattern of Ann's life. She had weeks when she was on a high, boasting of her achievements and predicting an even better future. This was usually followed by deep depression when life was not worth living, and a strong belief that she had been betrayed by her friends, relatives and especially her lovers."

"So, before her death she was on a high?"

"Yes, and for the same old reason. She had resumed an affair with an old lover who not only returned her passion, but in this case showered her with presents."

"And that old lover?"

"It could only have been the Baron himself although he had no great reputation as a lover. However, since Harry's death, he has put himself about a bit more. Lady Alice failed to keep a tight rein on him."

"Did you see any of these presents?"

"Ann tended to exaggerate and make things appear more important than they were. She probably received a mere trinket, but in her mind, this was the beginning of a flow of precious jewelry. She may have told Ellen what she received. In that last week she did seek a rapprochement with her daughter."

Luke next visited that daughter. "I'll get straight to the point, Ellen. Did you mother receive any jewelry in the weeks before her murder?" Luke then noted that Ellen appeared distracted and he asked, "Are you alright?"

"I am sorry Luke. I am just recovering from the shock announcement the Marquess has just made. He says that the Baron is in fact Harry, and that it was Michael who fell to his death."

"Yes, I know but I am surprised his lordship has told you. The family was to keep it a secret until they had tied up a few loose ends."

Ellen regained her composure. "In response to your question. Mother did receive a present from the person we now know to be Harry. It now makes more sense because she and Harry had a regular liaison for a decade or more before his apparent death. I always thought mother sleeping with Michael was a strange aberration, but now her contentment in those last few weeks is understandable. Mother not only enjoyed her immoral life but was also very venal. She hoped her lovers would add to her assets."

"What did she get from Harry?"

"It was pathetic really!—a minute sapphire and silver pendant attached to a thick silver chain."

"Did you see it?"

"Only glimpses of the silver chain. She wore it next to her skin under her clothes. I joked that she would have to remove it when confronting her next lover. She then made a remarkable statement for her, which I did not believe, that there would be no more lovers."

Luke's mind was racing. He concentrated on 'a thick silver chain'.

Ann was probably strangled by this very chain. It was not on her body. Where was it?

Luke returned to Harry. "My lord, you said you bestowed on Ann Bentley a sapphire and silver ornament."

"Yes, it was a token that our relationship was to be enduring. It was a trinket from the family treasure chest."

"Was it attached to a strong silver chain?"

"Yes, Felix made it himself."

"Did Ann have an expectation of you annulling your marriage and wedding her?"

"Don't be ridiculous! I would not marry beneath myself. Ann was after all a servant. Her highest expectation was to be my mistress—my sole mistress. I did at one point rashly promise her that I would restrict myself to Alice and herself."

"Was the pendant very valuable?"

"Compared with what? As a small item in the family jewel collection it was not that valuable, as a present to Ann it would be invaluable. Why do you ask?"

"It gives us another possible motive for her murder. She could have been killed for the pendant. I gather she wore it all the time, but it was not found on her body. In addition, it may have been the item that killed her. She was probably garroted by the silver chain."

Harry was visibly upset. He put his head in his hand and muttered,

"Good God, my gift killed her."

"You mention a family jewel collection. Do the islanders know of its existence? Having obtained a small part of it, a professional criminal might have designs on the rest."

"No, not even all members of the family know about it. It was a dowry that my mother provided on her marriage to Felix. It had been in her family for generations and was known as the Strange Sapphires, incorporating my grandmother's family name. It would be incredibly valuable. Large and small sapphires have been worked in both silver and gold into almost every type of jewelry—rings, pendants, brooches, necklaces, bracelets, and earrings."

"Had Ann seen any of this collection?"

"Yes, I showed her several of the pieces."

"With the indication that she might receive some of them?"

"Yes, but I made it clear that it would have to wait until I became Marquess. Only the Marquess could legally dispose of any of it."

"What is the future of the Smart Sapphire collection now?"

"It remains in the Marquess's possession until we fall on hard times, or when all or part of it is needed as a dowry for some female descendant. Poor Alice was looking forward to wearing the contents of this treasure chest when she became Marchioness."

"So, Alice had a particular possessive interest in the sapphires?"

"Yes, almost an obsession."

Three days later the whole island crammed into the parish church having been summoned by the Marquess to hear some astounding news.

By the time they had gathered in the church most were already aware of the Marquess's imminent revelations. Harry, not Michael was the

Baron, and was Felix's successor. Unfortunately, there was no Baroness, as Margaret had had a mental breakdown, and was in confinement on the continent with little prospect of recovery. The Baron was seeking an annulment of his marriage.

It was the news of Alice that shocked and infuriated Luke.

"Lady Alice, in these trying and humiliating circumstances has left the island. Her return will depend on any new relationship being developed between her and the Baron. In the interim my wife, Lady Jane, and my daughter-in-law Lady Felicity will act as Baroness on the social occasions where such a presence is expected," decreed Felix.

Luke was seething. Alice had left the island before his investigation into her as the possible murderer of Ann had been completed. He had been tricked and ignored by the Bohm family. Family interest, even in this dysfunctional family, came first. A Royal investigation clearly meant nothing.

As soon as possible he confronted Harry. "Why was Lady Alice allowed to leave the island. You knew I suspected her as Ann's murderer."

"I thought you now favored the theory she had been killed by a thief who stole her necklace. Also, father felt that Alice was left in an impossible situation. To avoid her utter humiliation, it was decided that she should leave the island. Rest assured Luke, if you find evidence of her guilt, I know where she will be for the next few months."

"In the meantime, have I permission now to search the rooms that were occupied by Alice in her role as Baroness?"

"Yes, nothing has been touched. Alice only left last night."

Luke fantasized that he would find the missing silver sapphire necklace hopefully with a broken chain caused by the pressure exerted to strangle Ann.

He and his men found nothing.

29

Mark was very relaxed when he and Luke discussed progress. "At least the possible murderers of Felix on coronation day have been reduced. Ann is dead, Margaret in a continental convent and Alice hiding somewhere on the mainland."

"In addition, we now know why Ann and her uncle fell out just before her death," added Luke.

"And why was that?"

"Ann told Martin of Harry's survival. She wanted to keep it a secret, but Martin could see that Harry could be his main witness to have the case of corrupting the youths of Nith, and his alleged attack on Margaret Neale reopened, and his defrocking reversed."

Mark changed the topic and asked, "Was nothing at all incriminating found in Alice's apartment?"

"No, Harry and Alice have removed or destroyed anything that would have compromised them in our eyes. They had days to do this before we were informed that Alice had left the island."

"Don't be taken in by Harry's friendly demeanor! Given his ruthless career I would not believe a word he says," added Mark.

"What I did find interesting in our search was that Alice took none of her possessions with her," commented Luke. "I raised that point with Harry who said she had to leave in a hurry before we stopped her departure. He will send her possessions on to her. He also said he will not do this immediately because he hoped she would soon return to him as his wife."

"He cannot be overconfident that the Roman Church would agree to this."

"He isn't, and the role of William Perry in this may have been crucial. It may have provided a motive for Harry to have Perry murdered."

"Why? Perry and Harry were the closest of allies!"

"Not towards the end. Harry made an interesting comment about Perry, implying the priest had betrayed him. He had persuaded Perry to return and as Harry's relationship with Margaret deteriorated and that with Alice intensified, he was delighted to have found that Perry was trained at a college whose principal had been made a cardinal. Apparently, Harry took steps with Perry to put his case for annulment to the church authorities through that prince of the church."

"Why then suggest Harry could have murdered Perry?"

"Because after commencing proceedings Perry became closer to Margaret and estranged from Harry. Then with Harry's supposed death such proceedings ceased. As our men searched Alice's room, Harry confided in me that he was worried that in the past few years, Perry may have poisoned the mind of the Catholic establishment against him, and that his recommened plea for an annulment might fall on hostile ears."

"You clearly had an intriguing discussion with the new Baron, but it does nothing to clarify the remaining problems that confront us, although the new lead regarding the silver necklace might."

"I agree. I want our men to find out who possesses silver of whatever form on the island, and where they obtained it. You take two or three men, and methodically go through every household on the island. I will interview the Bohms."

Luke visited Jane. She was not surprised that Alice had left the island. "I never liked the woman, but to have her sole obsession to become Marchioness removed from her must have been devastating. From controlling this island to becoming a powerless adulterous widow would have been almost impossible for our haughty Alice to bear. Why are you here?"

"I want to see your silver," he half-jokingly demanded.

"You can't burst into a lady's boudoir, and demand to see her silver. Is this a new obsession? It sounds like the actions of a military dictatorship, not of a relaxed monarchy," continued the bantering Jane.

Luke smiled, "If I find what I am looking for, it will solve Ann's murder."

Luke explained the possible role of the silver and sapphire necklace.

"Stupid Harry! If he had not given that woman a trinket from the family's vast sapphire collection he would still be seen as Michael, Alice would still be flaunting it as the Baroness, and Ann would be alive," was Jane's reply.

"May I see your silver jewelry?" Luke persisted.

"Yes, but to what end. How will you know what I show you is my total collection? I, or any other woman on the island could conceal part or all of her silver items. You do not have the manpower to search every inch of every possible hiding place for such a minute piece of jewelry. In any case a thief worth his salt would have it melted down, and maybe remodeled into an entirely different piece of jewelry."

Luke thought for a while and taking Jane's hand said, "You are right. If it was the murder weapon, the killer may have even disposed of it completely. It could be at the bottom of the North Sea."

A dispirited Luke was about to leave when Jane gave him a big hug,

"Do not despair! There is a way to winkle out the island silver. What I have learnt about Nith is that its inhabitants are a mean and greedy bunch who are after every penny they can obtain. My assistance in their smuggling ring has highlighted that they are also canny businesspeople."

"Well how can we separate such astute people from their silver?"

"Trickery!"

"Trickery?"

"Yes, I shall have Felix ask for as much silver as the islanders can put together, which he will turn into gold. Felix can say that it will be his last attempt to achieve this magical transformation."

"But he can't do it, can he?"

"Most of the islanders believe that he can—and greed is an overwhelming motive."

"What happens when he fails?"

"Nothing, we return the silver, explaining that Felix has lost his powers to do the transformation."

"You suggested that some islanders might have received the necklace and melted it down, and even recrafted it. Who on the island could do so?"

"Only two men, Felix as an alchemist, and the blacksmith Samuel Kitchen. Sam may not have the skill to recreate fine items of silver jewelry, but he can certainly melt down any silver given to him."

Luke called off his search of the islanders' homes, and with Jane put their plan to the Marquess.

"Luke, I hope your imminent child does not cause you the grief that Harry has caused over his lifetime. Perhaps I treated him too lightly on three occasions—when he faked his kidnapping and received a fortune as ransom, when he built up independent property worth as much as was then in the family portfolio, and now after pretending to be Michael for several years and the traumas he created for poor Margaret by such a pretense. Would Harry's record give me any chance before the law to disinherit him in favor of Ralph?"

"I am no expert in the law, but it may be easier for the King to take the marquisate from him for crimes against the state, and to re-issue the title and lands to Ralph. If you go down the legal path you would be long dead before the case reaches a conclusion, and most of the family fortune would be lost in legal fees."

"Well I may have to call on your closeness to the King after you leave here to put my case to His Majesty."

"A case that will be much stronger, if you take back the administration of your properties and sell back those you obtained from Royalists leaving the country to go into exile, at the same price you paid—or even less. It will not seriously affect your income."

"I am too old and lack the energy to be engaged in such a business."

"Hand the daily running of such activity over to Ralph."

"That would be a major humiliation to Harry, especially if Ralph involved his capable wife Felicity in the enterprise."

"Then let your wife take charge. During my investigations I have discovered she has capably assisted the islanders in their economic adventures."

Felix nodded his approval and went on muttering that Harry was the most able, but somewhere along the line he lacked moral fiber.

Luke bowed and was almost through the door when Felix called out. "I have some good news for you. The silver in the Smart Sapphires is of a slightly different composition to most English and continental silver. If someone has melted down the item Harry gave to Ann, I will still be able to identify it."

Over the next week James Denholm and his men had the task of receiving the silver from the islanders, recording its owner and passing it on to Felix who in unison with Luke and Mark carefully examined each item.

After ten days Felix claimed he had received enough silver for his purposes. Felix's plea for silver met with a remarkable response. The canny islanders had estimated that their assets would increase dramatically, if the silver goods provided were changed into gold.

The examination of the silver items was delayed frequently as Felix was not well enough, or not sufficiently alert, to assess what could have been obtained from the necklace. Luke's patience was running out.

Then in the middle of the night there was a knock on his door. There in his night shirt was Felix. "Luke, I could not sleep and looked over more of the silver items. There is one of the same composition as the missing necklace. I have found your murderer."

What form does it take?"

"It is a simple small silver dish with the same amount of silver that would have been in the necklace chain. It is a crude production lacking the skills of a trained silversmith."

"Who submitted the silver?

"Tom Kitchen."

Luke was crest fallen.

"What is wrong Luke? I thought you would be ecstatic?"

"Given the source of the melted down necklace, it raises a completely new scenario that may have nothing to do with the murder. Ann may have given the necklace to her daughter Ellen who in turn gave it to her sweetheart, Tom Kitchen, who had his father melt it down maybe to give back to Ellen."

"I see your problem, but it is easily solved. Ask Ellen first thing in the morning! I am now going to bed."

Ellen repeated what she had told Luke previously. Her mother wore the necklace close to her body and it disappeared at the time of the murder. She had neither given to, nor received any silver from the Kitchens.

Within the hour a dozen soldiers descended on the Kitchen home and Sam's forge. They were in search of a tiny object—the sapphire that had been removed from the necklace. To Luke's frustration neither Sam nor Tom were at home. Their aged servant said that young Tom was off sailing as he did quite often in recent weeks, and his father had gone with him.

"Is that usual?" asked Luke of the aged retainer.

"No, I have never known master Samuel to go to sea before with his son. He has excused himself in the past because he used to get seasick as a child."

Mark was alarmed. "Have they fled?"

"Why would they? They do not know of our search for that necklace."

"Don't be so naïve, Luke. Nothing is a secret on this island. All your private discussions with the Marquess and Marchioness were probably overheard by a servant. News of our activities spreads fast, especially given all the recent developments."

"I'll check on what Tom is supposed to be up to."

30

Luke called on James Denholm. "Is Tom currently working for your importing operation?"

"Yes, we are expecting a large consignment. Tom has taken Martin's old boat with two attached dinghies. As he is a sailor rather than a rower, I suggested he take someone with him. Two rowers would have no trouble, dealing with the current troublesome seas, but one might find it difficult."

"Would he have taken his father?"

"It would be a good choice. Sam has the strength of two ordinary men, but as a boy he always got seasick, and he has refused to help in the past."

"This time he may have consented. Their servant tells me both men have gone to sea. I am just checking that such an enterprise was part of your importing activity, and not a sudden and unexplained adventure. When do you expect them back?"

"They should land just after dark."

The following morning Luke revisited the Kitchin premises. Neither men had returned home, a fact verified by James, who was now alarmed for the safety of the men. "A major squall blew across the island overnight and the sea was creating massive waves. Now that our operations are deemed legitimate by yourself as a magistrate, could you persuade the frigate to search for the missing men, and the trawler they were supposed to meet."

Within the hour the *Deadly Arrow* with Luke, Mark and James aboard began the search. The seas were calmer than the previous night, and the searchers were happy not to find any relevant wreckage.

Luke was in two minds. Had the Kitchins gone missing on a legitimate importing mission, or had they fled because of their complicity in Ann Bentley's murder which was about to be revealed by the reuse of the silver from the likely murder weapon.

Then the mood on board changed. Two empty dinghies were sighted, and James identified them as belonging to the smuggling ring. Luke turned to James. "The name of the trawler your men were to meet?"

"*La Marie de Rouen.*"

"There are a large number of trawlers just ahead of us. Maybe after delivering its cargo, *La Marie de Rouen,* has rejoined the main fishing fleet," observed Mark.

Peter Hutton intervened, "An English warship cannot sail too close to those fishing trawlers. They have protection. Look at that French man of war bearing down on us!"

Luke suggested that Hutton raise a white flag indicting that he wished to talk to the French.

To Luke's surprise the French were very obliging. They lowered a longboat which was soon alongside the English frigate. Its commanding officer asked the English why they were harassing a fleet of French fishermen.

Mark replied in perfect French that they were looking for two missing English fishermen that had been scheduled to meet *La Marie de Rouen* the previous day. The very accommodating French officer replied that as that trawler was one of the nearest, his men could row an English officer to it to question its captain.

Luke regretted his lack of fluency in French and answered, "My deputy Colonel Cowper will accompany you." Mark scrambled down a swaying ladder, and literally fell into the French long boat.

Two hours later Mark re-boarded the English frigate, and reported to Peter, Luke and James. "A mixed bag. The good news is that when last seen by the trawler captain, the two English fishermen were safe. He was very cagey in front of the French naval officer and admitted to nothing except trawling during which they came across two Englishmen in a small boat in danger of sinking."

"Were they aboard the trawler at any time?" asked James.

"Yes, the captain claimed he attached their boat to his and sailed close to the English coast where they reclaimed their boat, disembarked, and landed somewhere between Scarborough and Whitby."

"Sounds like Tom used his initiative. Unable to transfer the goods out to sea, he carried out the operation close to shore, and then took the cargo directly to its mainland reception point," said James.

"In other words, he carried out the normal operation, but omitted the Nith island section of it," summarized Mark.

"But surely an essential part?" asked Luke.

"Yes, Tom will have some explaining to do. At least we can call off the search, and return to Nith and await his return," concluded James.

"After he reports to you, ask him to come with his father to see me. It is fairly urgent," added Luke.

Late the next afternoon Tom Kitchen reported to Luke. "Mr Denholm said you wanted urgently to see my father and me. Unfortunately, father is not here."

Luke was alarmed, "Where is he?"

"Still on the mainland. Given the conditions at sea and our rescue by the trawler, I persuaded the French captain to complete our transaction by taking us almost ashore near Scarborough, where I always take the goods for distribution. The trawler refused to come closer to Nith which was my first suggestion because of the frigate. It did not want to be caught in English waters, as it would then have to explain both to the English and the French authorities why it had left the Rouen trawling fleet for the English mainland. You may have made our part of the importing, legal, but I'm not sure that the French authorities see the activity in the same light."

"Why is your father still on the mainland?"

"Awaiting my return and protecting our goods. The designated recipients would not take the goods because I did not have the usual paperwork provided by Mr. Denholm or the Marchioness. They suggested we may have stolen the goods and were bypassing major elements in the chain. Why did you want to see us?"

"It is rather bad news. Evidence has emerged that incriminates you or your father in the murder of Ann Bentley."

"Rubbish! Ann was very kind to me. When she ran our trading network, it was she that asked me to take the allocated goods to the mainland and increased what I was paid for that service on at least three occasions. Martin Moore and James Denholm have not been as generous since they replaced her. And father was one of Ann's long-term lovers, ever since mother died. What is this spurious evidence that you claim to have?" asked an angry Tom.

"Ann was strangled, or rather garroted by a silver chain that was part of her necklace, which was then taken by the murderer. We have obtained part or all of that silver necklace, now melted down and made into a small silver plate. It was offered to the Marquess to be transformed into gold. It was submitted by you."

"I don't know how you know that it was made of silver from that necklace, but you are right. But why do you assume it had anything to do with Ann's murder."

"How did your father, or you obtain the necklace?"

"Ann gave it to father. He told me weeks after her death that it was a token of their long-term friendship, and of her undying love for him. When she was murdered, he could not bear to have it in the house and decided that it would be a nice gesture to turn it into a silver plate, which I could give to my sweetheart, Ann's daughter Ellen. The offer of the Marquess to double its value was too much of a temptation. I never told father that I had sent it to the Marquess. How does it incriminate father, or myself in the murder?"

"I am afraid your father lied to you. In the last few months before her death, Ann restarted an old relationship that developed so passionately for both parties that her current lover gave Ann a silver and sapphire necklace, and Ann for the first time in her life declared herself a one-man woman. She cut off all her other relationships. Her favors would no longer be available to any of them. Your father, one of her most longstanding and frequent partners, was shattered. I assume he went to remonstrate with her, saw the offending necklace, and maybe simply tugged at it a bit, which cut her skin. She may have responded with cruel words, and he strangled her. He then brutally ripped the chain from around her neck."

"But all that is only conjecture?"

"I prefer to call it circumstantial evidence. At least your father has a case to answer."

"I will tell him to see you when I return to the mainland to finalize our transactions."

"No Tom, you will stay here. Mr Corby will keep an eye on you, until this matter is solved. You are not under arrest, as I do not believe you had anything to do with the murder, but you might try to warn your father. Mr Denholm will complete the transactions, and I will arrest your father."

When the Nith contingent consisting of James, Luke, Mark and twelve soldiers came ashore, they were greeted by a relaxed and jovial Sam. "No need for all that protection, the mainlanders have not stolen our goods or attempted to assault me. James, you will find all the cargo that Tom and I landed is intact."

"Unfortunately, Sam the troops are not here to protect you, but to ensure that you do abscond," replied James.

Luke immediately clarified the situation. "In the name of His Majesty King Charles II, Samuel Kitchen, you are under arrest for the murder of Ann Bentley. You will be taken from here to York Castle where you will remain until your trial at the next Assizes."

"Your reputation is not misplaced. How could you possibly have reached such a conclusion," asked an apparently relieved Samuel.

Luke was surprised that there was no attempt at denial, but rather surprise that he had been found out. "Taking that silver and sapphire necklace was your big mistake. It gave us a murder weapon and an object to look for," replied Luke.

"But I melted it down, and surely no one could tell the silver apart from that which I used in crafting other items for the islanders. In addition, I kept a small dish made from the offending necklace in the family. Tom was to give it to Ellen."

"Unfortunately, neither of those conditions were maintained. The Marquess could tell it apart from all other silver on the island as it was of oriental origin and of a different composition to English silver—and it was not kept private. You son sent it to the Marquess to be turned into gold."

Six of Luke's men escorted Sam to York Castle.

As they marched off Mark confided to Luke. "You will still need more evidence to get the verdict you desire!"

"Precisely, but a few months in York Castle may turn Samuel into an even more co-operative witness, and during that time I hope to unearth further damning evidence."

31

Luke and Mark exhibited an air of mutual self-satisfaction as they slowly imbibed the finest French red wine, courtesy of the now legal trading operation of the islanders. "The King should be well contented with our achievements. The smuggling ring that cheated him of his duties, miniscule though they were, has been brought under control, the selling back of exiled Royalist properties that were being used to exhort unreasonable sums from these exiles is now under the control of Jane and Felicity, who will sell them back at cost price. This will entail a loss for the Bohms, but one they can easily afford. This gesture will certainly assist the King in re-establishing those loyal supporters who fled England during the war," declared Luke.

"And we have solved two murders, that of William Perry and Ann Bentley," added Mark.

"There are still many loose ends to tie together. Was Michael's death accident, suicide or murder? So far, all the evidence suggests that Harry consumed with lust for Alice, simply took advantage of an accident. Who shot at Ellen, and killed Richard Banks? Are Michael Moore and Jerome Tighe alive or dead? And is the Marquess still in danger of being killed on the King's coronation day?"

This euphoria did not last long. Early the next morning a servant aroused Luke and took him to the quarters of the Marquess. Lady Jane and Ellen received him. Jane gave him a hug and declared, "Felix is dead." Ellen added, "I came to give him his early morning drink. He was icy cold. He must have died soon after he retired last night."

Luke examined the body. He noted that death had not come as a peaceful extension of sleep. He had vomited, and by the dominant odor had had an attack of diarrhea. His pillow was soaked with excessive saliva. As he moved Felix's head masses of hair came away. He had seen these symptoms several times before. While not irrefutable, it suggested arsenic poisoning.

He would not upset the ladies any further with this tentative conclusion. He would seek a second opinion from the doctor aboard the frigate. He turned to Jane and explained what he would do. "I don't think his body should be moved until the doctor has had a look at it. Will you send for a clergyman to conduct the funeral service?"

"I can do nothing. Harry is now the Marquess, and it is his prerogative to make all arrangements regarding his father. Ellen, you will immediately return to my service. I will inform Harry of his father's death, and Ralph and Felicity that they are now Harry's heirs as Baron and Baroness Nith. Luke, stay here until Harry arrives, and you can make any suggestions to him."

The women left the room. Within minutes Harry arrived. "What happened?"

"Your father died in his sleep many hours ago. I have sent for the nearest doctor to examine the body. Luckily there is one aboard the frigate. He should be here within a few hours. Until then, the body should not be moved."

"Why the second opinion? You have seen more deaths in your career than most physicians and surgeons. Do you suspect foul play?"

"It is a possibility."

"Any solid evidence?"

"Given the claim that your father would be murdered on the day of the King's coronation, and the current state of the body, which might reflect arsenic poisoning, I cannot assume natural causes."

Later that day Luke, Mark and the ship's doctor discussed the situation.

The doctor was explicit. "Death may have been due to arsenic poisoning, but in my experience, it was not a sudden ingestion of the poison. It was something that built up over time. Find out if the Marquess showed signs of such poisoning over recent months if not years."

Luke was disturbed by this diagnosis. The only people who were close enough to the Marquess over that period, and basically controlled what he ate and drank, were Jane and latterly Ellen. These two had every opportunity, but no obvious motive. On the other hand, who did have a motive?

To Luke it was Harry. He may have heard that Felix was about to put in place procedures to disinherit him in favor of his youngest brother Ralph. Felix had already removed him from administering the family properties a task handed over Jane and Felicity. Harry may have found such a move intensely humiliating. In addition, Felix was now more active in running the Nith estates than he had been for years.

Next day Luke sought out Ellen. "Did the late Marquess vomit or have trouble with his bowels in recent weeks?"

Ellen asked, "Why do you ask?"

"The ship's doctor thinks there is a possibility of arsenic poisoning, but that it was a long-term program of ingestion. A sudden ingestion of arsenic would have led to a more violent death. If Felix has been poisoned it is a medically professional job—although everything that the doctor has emphasized could have resulted from natural causes."

Ellen began to shake, and her trembling continued. Luke took her hand.

"What is it?"

"If Felix was poisoned, I will be blamed. In recent weeks I alone controlled everything he ate and drank. I also monitored who had access to him."

"Yes, there is no doubt that if he was poisoned, you would be the first and, in some eyes, the only suspect. Did he show the signs I asked about?"

"In part. He did vomit a little more than usual, which I put down to the rich food he constantly craved, and which from time to time in consultation with Lady Jane, I did provide."

"Your security over food was not as tight as it might have been as Lady Jane occasionally brought in additional snacks for her husband. And any visitors around mealtime could have added things to his meal—and an area over which you had no control, Felix could have added things to his own meal in the seclusion of his laboratory."

"He did add vast amounts of salt and sugar to his food from the so-called chemical supplies he had in his laboratory."

"And he may have added arsenic as well."

"To what end?"

"I don't know. I am interested in who had access to Felix. You controlled the main door to his apartment, and Jane had control of an interjoining room from her part of the complex. Did you ever see Felix in his laboratory with someone that you had not admitted?"

Ellen did not need to think. "Two people were with Felix on numerous occasions in recent times. They both pretended they had slipped past me or Jane."

"Who were they?"

"The then Baron who we thought was Michael, but now know was Harry, and Lady Felicity."

Luke was delighted. The man who had most to gain, and the woman who had threatened Felix with death on the day of King's coronation were now possible poisoners. The problem, given the doctor's hypothesis was that this was administered regularly over a long period, was that neither appeared to be regular and consistent visitors—unless there was a secret entrance to the Felix's quarters.

Luke had been told of secret passages throughout Nith Hall. Felix who knew of their whereabouts could no longer help, but maybe the now dowager Marchioness Jane, had some knowledge?

Jane confirmed Ellen's view that the two most common visitors that neither women had admitted were Harry and Felicity. Yes, there was a secret passage that led to Felix's laboratory, but she did not know from where it came. The main secret passage from the Marquess's apartment was connected to the network of caves and tunnels that led to both the eastern coast, and to the parish church.

Luke summoned his men to search every inch of Felix's laboratory for the secret passage. It took little time. A bookshelf moved aside and opened up on what was clearly well used tunnel. Luke took a taper and accompanied by Mark and two soldiers began to explore. The men had to bend considerately. It was not very tall or wide, and Mark conjectured that it ran between two levels of Nith Hall. This was verified when the first outlet they came across was a grill on the floor of the long passage that ran from one end of Nith Hall to another—a grill that anybody could use to get access to Felix.

They continued and the next exit required climbing a small ladder at the top of which was a small door. Pushing it open Luke realized where he was. It was the library of the former Baron. Harry had secret and direct access to his father.

Mark and Luke returned to Felix's quarters while the soldiers continued their journey along the secret tunnels. The men who had remained in the laboratory searching for whatever could be relevant pointed out to Luke several containers labelled as various compounds of arsenic.

The soldiers who had followed the secret passage reported back to Luke. It did join up with the network of caves and tunnels that eventually led to the sea. There was only one diversion. A newly dug tunnel not far from the entrance to the Baron's quarters led to the Catholic chapel. Could Jerome Tighe have used it to surprise Father Perry?

Luke and Mark discussed how to progress. They decided to play their suspects off against each other. Luke tackled Harry. "My lord, I understand that you used the secret passage between your residence and that of the late Marquess quite frequently. Are you aware of anyone else on the island who used such access over the years?"

"Yes, my sister-in-law Felicity. In recent times father treated her as his assistant, and she was often there when I arrived."

"To be frank, if your father was murdered through poisoning, you and Lady Felicity are now my prime suspects. As you have the stronger motive, you can see why you currently top my list."

"Come Sir Luke, I am not an ignorant peasant whom you can trick and bully into submission. I have noted how you work. Pretend that you know more than you do, and have more solid evidence than you have, and hope the suspect will confess. You have nothing. You cannot tell whether father died of natural causes or was murdered. If he was murdered how could you ascertain whether it was Felicity or me. As to opportunity a number of people knew of the corridor grill entrance to the passage that led to father's laboratory. It could have been anybody. And as far as motive was concerned, there was no need to murder father to gain the marquisate. Father was dying and on my last visit to him, looking back, he was saying goodbye. He was struggling to stay alive until the King's coronation so that he could go out in full glory, proving the validity of his magical powers of prediction."

"How would he have fulfilled the condition that he was murdered by a woman?"

"Obvious, at least to my devious mind. He was setting up Felicity to deliver the final blow, either overtly or indirectly. The new Baroness has to be questioned. I must get on with the funeral arrangements for father."

32

Felicity was blunt when accosted by Luke. "Jane said that when you discovered that the new Marquess and I had regular, if secret access to Felix, you put us at the top of your list as murder suspects."

"True, and Harry has done an excellent job in implicating you," exaggerated Luke.

"Why would I murder Felix?"

"Because you sent a letter threatening as much. What I cannot understand is how a person with a desire to kill Felix is suddenly accepted as his assistant—and I imagine confidante?"

"Simple. My initial hatred was based on lies. After I sent the letter to Felix, he summoned me to his quarters. He asked me why I had sent the note, and why I bore such antagonism towards him. I explained that it was the result of his trickery that my father lost the family fortune, and committed suicide, quickly followed by the death of my heart broken mother. This subjected me to a life with a horrible uncle and aunt from whom I escaped when little more than a schoolgirl, by marrying an obscure French diplomat. During the period when I was living with my uncle, I dreamed up all sorts of revenge, I would take out on Felix Bohm. One of the reasons that Ralph did not come to Nith until the supposed death of his brother Harry, was because I refused to leave London, given my depth of hatred for his family."

"Felix defended himself against what you claimed?"

"Yes, so well that I was convinced that he told the truth and the lies lay elsewhere."

"What was his explanation?"

"He and my father were very close friends and that when father approached him explaining his difficulties, Felix not only returned the silver father had invested in alchemist's scheme but lent him quite a considerable sum to get him out of the trouble."

"What trouble?"

"Father owed my uncle thousands of pounds. It was uncle's decision to foreclose on all my father's debts, a major humiliation, that led to the suicide, not Felix's scheme."

"So, as some sort of expiation for your falsely based thoughts of revenge, you agreed to help Felix in his experiments?"

"It was not quite like that. In discussing my life before I met Ralph, Felix was very interested in my life at the French Court. He was fascinated by my tales of aristocratic poisonings, and the presence at court of a number of highly placed women who specialized in providing poisons for discontented ladies. I told him the poison of choice was *la poudre de succession*. It changed the fortunes of so many noble houses. I knew several ladies who provided this poison, and I was made privy to some of their secrets."

"To us laymen, what is this *la poudre de succession*?"

"Arsenic."

"The very poison that was administered to Felix."

"Yes."

"Why was Felix so interested in arsenic?"

"He had been experimenting with it for years and was using his own body to experiment with it."

"To what end?"

"When I became Felix's confidante, I learnt that he was dying. He believed that small doses of arsenic would delay the end. He systematically added arsenic to his food, in ever increasing amounts. He believed that while small amounts of it was beneficial, an excessive amount would kill him. That is what happened."

"Felix poisoned himself—committed suicide?"

"Not suicide. It was accidental poisoning. He was determined to last until the King's coronation, when he would then have taken a deliberate overdose to prove that his predictive powers were intact. As he said, why put up with the pain and the growing weaknesses brought on by his illness, without gaining something from it."

"You did not administer his last dose?"

"Even if I did, you could never prove it," said Felicity provocatively.

Luke ignored the comment and asked, "In what ways did you assist him?"

"Actually, I had nothing to do with the arsenic. Felix was in great pain and he read in an Islamic treatise that an extract from the hemp plant relieved pain. My task was extracting the juice from this plant, cannabis, which he found worked exceedingly well. Without it he could not have hidden the seriousness of his illness. The pain would have confined him to his bed."

"So, if you are to be believed, Felix accidently poisoned himself, and neither you nor Harry had any part to play in the event?"

"Absolutely!"

"Can you prove it?"

"If I can't, you equally, cannot prove the opposite."

"Then we are at a stalemate."

"Not at all. Felix wrote up all his experiments involving arsenic and cannabis down to the precise amount he administered to himself. He included a letter explaining my role in the affair. The letter will exonerate me."

"Where is the letter?"

"In the laboratory."

"We found no letter."

"Then you better search again with my guidance."

Luke and Felicity returned to the laboratory and assisted by Mark and half a dozen troops re-searched the room.

"Felix's personal letters are in the top left-hand draw of his desk. The key to it is in a secret compartment at the back of the unlocked bottom right hand draw," explained Felicity.

Luke was alarmed. The top draw was not locked, and the secret compartment was empty. Someone had stolen Felix's personal correspondence, including the letter that would exonerate Felicity.

The situation worsened for Felicity when she announced, "This is not right. Felix's work diary in which he recorded every scientific move he made, is missing. It was three inches thick. It could not have blown away or be missed by even the most stupid of searchers. And even worse, the phials of arsenic that were contained on the upper shelf against the wall are missing. Someone has ransacked this room to obtain Felix's secrets—and a supply of arsenic sufficient to kill off the whole island."

"Who could have done this?" asked Mark.

"The obvious culprit is Harry—and we can do nothing about it. The minute Felix died all this became Harry's. To remove his own arsenic, and documents is no crime," complained Felicity.

"Let's assume for the moment that it was not Harry, nor you Felicity. Whom else might it have been?" asked Luke of Mark.

"Possibly Jane. She never liked Harry and there are probably things in Felix's private papers that she does not want Harry to see," he replied.

"I can see Jane taking the private papers to protect herself or her late husband, but not his work diary nor the arsenic," commented Felicity.

"Who else knew of the secret passages and was a regular visitor to Felix? continued Luke.

"The person who knew all of the secret passages and was treated as a special friend by Felix was Martin Moore," said Felicity.

"A possible suspect—if he is still alive," Luke replied.

Mark added, "In reference to whether people are alive or not, would Jerome Tighe have known of the secret passages?"

"Heaven forbid! If Tighe is alive and in possession of dozens of phials of arsenic, we could all be poisoned," said an obviously alarmed Felicity.

"A much more optimistic conclusion is that the arsenic was stolen by our smugglers to add to their assets. Phials of arsenic would bring a good price. Jane might have aided them in that entrepreneurial enterprise," suggested Luke. "I will talk to Jane, Harry and James Denholm."

He received satisfying news from Jane and Harry. Jane had taken the private correspondence but had not looked through it. With help from Luke, she soon found the letter which set out Felix's medication, and the role of Felicity in his last days. It verified her account of events. Harry took the diary and work notes. He felt his father's life work must have some commercial value, which he was keen to exploit.

The information from James Denholm however was disturbing.

James confirmed that before the Bohm's arrived on Nith most of the youths knew of all the secret tunnels and passages. "This knowledge became such a danger to the security and privacy of those living in Nith

Hall, that the then Marquess had all exits from the passages either sealed up, or locked. Since then one can only exit the secret passages into Nith Hall, if the people in the room you want to visit unlock the exit door. Jerome Tighe would certainly have known of these secret passages."

Luke then asked, "Did Felix leave your trading network any of his possessions."

"No! Although he knew of the existence of our smuggling ring, officially he always denied it. All dealings we had with the family was through the Marchioness. Anyhow I doubt if he had any possessions that we could sell on."

"Unfortunately phials of a deadly poison have gone missing. I would have been delighted if you had told me someone had stolen them on behalf of the trading syndicate."

"You have ruled out the more obvious suspects?"

"Yes, what remains are two men both of whom may be dead—Jerome Tighe and Martin Moore."

"A possible catastrophe looms. Martin would not embark in wide scale poisoning but given Jerome's hatred of those that participated in his rape and humiliation years ago, he might wipe out the whole island," replied a worried James.

"Yes, a warning must be given that poison phials have gone missing, and that if any food has a slight metallic taste it should be discarded. Those who were part of Martin Moore's close acquaintances in 1642 should be especially concerned."

The only person who was very close to Felix in his last days and with whom Luke had not have an extensive conversation was Ellen. He found her in Felix's laboratory cleaning out what Harry did not wish to retain. Despite Felicity's pleading he would not retain the room as a laboratory.

"Ellen, can you confirm the truth or otherwise of what I have been told concerning Felix's death? Felix was dying and had little time left. He had been experimenting with arsenic in an endeavor to prolong his life. He accidentally took an overdose, which killed him. Lady Felicity was his assistant and was well aware of his medical condition, and through her extraction of a juice from the hemp plant relieved his pain. He deliberately highlighted the story of his death at the hands of a woman on the day of the King's coronation to emphasize the validity of his predictive powers."

"I can confirm all of that, except the most important. Did the Marquess accidentally take an overdose, or did his illness so overwhelm him that he deliberately took it. It would be useless of you to pursue that line of enquiry because the family would never admit that Felix committed suicide. And did he act alone? Did Felicity administer that last dose? Is it murder, if you fulfil the wishes of the victim? Felicity and Felix became quite close over the last few months. She became the daughter he never had. He never liked Alice or Margaret. She saw in Felix the father that she had been deprived of. We often had a conversation whether it was better to lose a father at a very young age, or as in my case, not know who he was."

Luke and Ellen left the one-time laboratory together. As Ellen locked the door for the last time, a tear ran down her face.

Five days later Harry as the new Marquess summoned Luke. He was blunt. "I expect you and your men to leave Nith within the week."

"Why, my lord, would you expect that?" asked a surprised and irritated Luke.

"Your mission, including some of its more secretive aspects must be complete. Father's sudden death has rendered your prime mission of preventing his murder on the day of the King's coronation null and void. Your attempt to improve the King's coffers by unravelling the island's smuggling network, of which I was not aware, was successful, and you have solved the murders of Ann Bentley and William Perry. What more is there to do?"

"I am obliged to assist the King in his reconciliation of ardent Royalists who went into exile at the beginning of the war and sold their estates to the Bohms to escape confiscation by the Parliament, by having those properties sold back at cost price or below. I have just learnt that you have removed the dowager Marchioness Jane and the new Baroness Felicity from that responsibility and resumed complete control of the sell-back to yourself."

"Absolutely correct. Land development and speculation is not a charity. Nor is it the work for aristocratic women. Our family saved those people from the complete loss of their property. In holding these lands for almost two decades we have incurred costs. Sentimentality will not interfere with profit."

"May I beg to differ my lord. A little generosity in this area would be seen as a great contribution to the reuniting of the country after the divisions of the wars. It could be argued that your greed is not in the national interest. Do not make an enemy of the King! As a high aristocrat your position depends to some extent on his goodwill. History records many a nobleman brought to his knees, or even executed for getting in the way of royal policy. My report could raise such issues and His Majesty may feel inclined to investigate further."

"There is nothing on Nith, or in my past, that interests the King."

"Come! A fraudulent ransom, the possible murder of your brother, your impersonation of him, your continued adultery with his wife, and now your exploitation of impoverished Royalist exiles. I could make a strong case that Henry Bohm is not a fit person to be Marquess of Nith."

"Are you attempting to blackmail me?"

"No, I am giving you sound advice, and suggesting what is in your long-term interests. In the short term do not obstruct my continuing efforts on the island, namely, to find Martin Moore and Jerome Tighe, dead or alive, and recover a dozen phials of arsenic."

Harry did not back off. "Luke, you must accept that I am now the Marquess with absolute authority on the island. You are only here because, for the moment you exercise the authority of the King. As you see from my current location, I have already moved the family around. I am occupying the apartments that father and Jane occupied. Jane has been moved to the area previously occupied by Ralph and Felicity who in turn have moved into the quarters that have been vacated by Alice and myself. I have also informed James Denholm that I will take over his organization, the former smuggling ring."

"That will not be a popular decision," said Luke.

"Maybe not initially, but as I pointed out now that these activities are a legitimate trading enterprise, it needs an injection of capital and an expansion of its area of operation. Every member of the group will in the end be better off. Opposition to my leadership will quickly fade as profits increase."

Luke took his leave but his attempts to see Jane and Felicity came to nothing. Both were absent from Nith Hall. That evening Mark and he had supper with the new Marquess and his leading servants. No other family members were present. Alice and Margaret had left the island, Felicity and Jane did not appear, and Ralph had been sent to London to tidy up the legal aspects of Harry's accession.

Luke asked whether Jane and Felicity were unwell.

Harry replied, "No. I was told that they had gone sailing with young Tom Kitchen. The weather has deteriorated. They may have put ashore until the storm passes."

The senior servants James Denholm and Vincent Keddy were taciturn, if not sulky. Luke put it down to their dismay and resentment at Harry taking over their trading network.

Corby revealed that as parish constable he had just received notification that a prisoner sent from Nith, Samuel Kitchen, had been killed during a prison riot at York Castle. Whether his assailant had been a prison officer, or a fellow prisoner was not revealed.

"Does Tom know of his father's death?" asked Luke.

"No, I will inform him as soon as he returns with their ladyships," answered Corby.

"It saves you the cost and trouble of a trial, Sir Luke," observed Harry gleefully.

Isabel Denholm made an unexpected intervention. She turned on Luke, "Does it ever play on your conscience that that man may have been innocent—and now he has no chance of proving it?"

"Yes, it does," answered a contrite Luke. "Although in the interests of the state, I have been known to adopt extra-legal solutions in the case of Samuel Kitchin the evidence against him was circumstantial, and I was anxious that it be tested before judge and jury."

Mark intervened, addressing Isabel, "I am surprised by your comments. This man most likely murdered your own sister."

"My sister created a multitude of enemies in her lifetime. I could name a dozen people who hated her more than Samuel Kitchin ever could. He loved her for most of his adult life. If he was guilty, Ann drove him to it."

The discussion clearly upset Harry. "Enough, I was close to Ann. Let's remember her finer points and not dwell of her frailties." With that he crossed himself and left the table. The group rose to their feet as the new Marquess exited the room.

Resuming their seats, the former reticent group suddenly broke out into a babble of competing conversations. James turned to Luke, "You have heard that the Marquess has taken over our trading enterprise. Can he do that?"

"Yes, the Marquess of Nith is an absolute ruler on this island. His powers on estates elsewhere is constrained by a range of factors, but here he can do what he likes. How are the members of your group reacting to the news?"

"Mixed. Some want to oppose it in every way possible, even to sabotaging our operations. Others see the introduction of the Marquess's wealth, and his ruthless operating methods as an advantage that will increase their profits."

"What are you personally going to do?"

"I am more concerned with whether the Marquess re-appoints me as the steward of this estate, than my role in the importing network. I certainly will not openly oppose his plans."

Next morning around ten o'clock Ellen confronted Luke, when once again he tried to communicate unsuccessfully with Jane.

"Luke, I am worried. Her ladyship and Lady Felicity should be back by now. I am also very concerned about Tom's safety. There was a powerful storm last night. What if they had no time to take shelter? At the worst the boat may have capsized, and the three of them drowned."

"My men will search the coastline and I will have the frigate circumnavigate the island in ever expanding circles to pick up any wreckage. Do you know where they were going?"

"Not their full itinerary, but they were going to visit Resurrection Isle."

"Resurrection Isle, I have never heard of it. Where is it?"

"It's hardly an isle. It is large rock just above the water line with one tree and a crumbled ruin of a small chapel. The whole isle is no bigger than this room. Centuries ago it was the home of a hermit monk. At high tides, apart from the top of the lone tree, it is under water."

"I will direct the frigate to go there first. Tom may have wrecked his boat in approaching or leaving it. Hopefully the three of them will be found sheltering on it. Why would their ladyships have gone there? Have they been there before?"

"I can only speak for Lady Jane. In all the time I have worked for her and her late husband, she never mentioned the isle, let alone visited it."

"How do you know about it then?"

"I've been there many times. It was a favorite fishing spot for great Uncle Martin—and I have since discovered a place where he waited if the French trawler loaded with contraband was delayed."

A sudden thought hit Luke "Could Martin hide there, and their ladyships have gone to rescue him, or at least resupply him?"

"It is a possibility, but he would get very wet."

"I will join the frigate and direct their operations. Let's hope we find the missing trio alive."

The *Deadly Arrow* had difficulty finding the isle. It was so low in the water that its location was obscured by even the small waves that now dominated the sea. The lookout eventually sighted the single tree.

The ship's longboat took Luke to the rock. There was no wreckage. He ordered the rowers to circumnavigate the rock.

There was an almost immediate gasp of horror from one of oarsman who shouted out, "To the port side, sir! My oar hit the top of a mast just under the surface." Closer inspection after the sailors managed to partly raise the boat to which the mast was attached indicated that it was Tom's skiff. An intensified search of the surrounding waters failed to find any bodies.

Luke returned to Nith Island with a heavy heart. Lady Jane, Lady Felicity and Tom Kitchin had probably drowned.

Luke informed Harry.

Luke was disgusted by his response. Not a word about the deceased. He had sighed and bemoaned the fact that his re-organization of the estate would now be little more complex. "It is now imperative that Ralph remarries quickly and produces an heir—in case I fail to do so."

Luke could not help thinking that the end of the Bohm family might not be a bad result.

Isabel Denholm as the most senior woman remaining on the island discussed with John Corby what arrangements should be made. Both deceased women were Catholic and there was no Catholic cleric immediately available, nor was there an Anglican rector who could in the dire circumstances play some role in a memorial service. An alternative solution had to be found.

The gloom that engulfed the island did not last long. Early next morning the frigate came close to shore, fired its cannons in rapid succession, and launched its long boat. From the tower of Nith Hall three familiar figures were visible as the boat approached the island.

Their ladyships and Tom Kitchin were safe.

What had happened to them was a question the whole island wanted answered. While their ladyships disappeared into Nith Hall, Tom explained to a gathering of islanders which included Luke and Mark, "There was no secure place on Resurrection Isle to moor my boat. A sudden and unexpected gust of wind pushed it from its moorings, it capsized and before I could reach it, it sank. There was no way I could raise it."

"How were you rescued?"

"A fishing boat captained by an old identity Red suddenly appeared. He took us to Whitby, and this morning headed for Nith where he was intercepted by the *Deadly Arrow* that eventually brought us home."

Luke then asked, "Why did you go to Resurrection Isle in the first place?"

"I cannot answer that. Ask their ladyships!"

34

Next morning Luke did. Jane and Felicity received him together. "You have some questions for us?" purred Jane.

"Yes. Why did you have young Tom sail you to a partially submerged rock well out into the North Sea?" he asked.

Jane replied. "I asked Felicity to help me to go through Felix's personal papers that I had rescued from his laboratory. We found a note explaining that given Harry's new weakness of giving away family heirlooms, Felix had asked Martin Moore to take the Smart Sapphires and the rest of the Bohm treasures, and hide them in a safe place. Moore later informed Felix he had hidden them under the altar top on Resurrection Isle. There they could not be washed away by the sea, and any occasional visitor would have no incentive nor the ability to lift the heavy stone. As Martin regularly visited the area to fish, no one would give his trips there a second thought."

Felicity interrupted, "We were not as confident as Martin as to their security, so immediately on reading the letter, we decided to recover them and place them in a more secure place."

"Did Tom know what you were up to?"

"Not completely! We told him that Martin, when he ran the smuggling ring had left some valuable items on the isle, and as we were not sure when he would reappear, it was better to place them elsewhere," answered Felicity.

"Did you tell Harry what you were doing?"

"Of course not. Felix's original decision, and our rescue attempt were basically designed to thwart Harry," explained Felicity with a tinge of bitterness.

"Your ladyships must realize that with the death of Felix, these jewels belong to Harry. Your possession of them could be considered theft."

"Harry does not own them. He fails to understand the aristocratic ethos that everything he currently has is held in trust for future generations. It really is not his to give away. It is also a base on which he could build up further assets," added the dowager Marchioness.

"So where are the jewels now?"

"We don't know. They were not on the rock. Martin either never put them on the isle, or they have been removed since."

"Theft by an unknown party is possible, but it is more likely that Martin never put the treasure on the isle and has now absconded with it. This may explain his disappearance. He comes into contact with vast wealth, steals it, disappears and heads for London where he could dispose of it without too much risk of detection. He could start a very prosperous new life," summarized Luke.

"Regrettably Luke I have to agree with you," explained Jane. "With the approaching death of his friend Felix, the burning of his cottage, your interference in his smuggling empire, the imminent succession of Harry, the murder of his niece Ann, and threats to his own life, escape from Nith with the means to survive probably proved a temptation too great to resist for a flawed character like Martin."

"You will have to tell Harry?"

"Only part of it—that having discovered the letter, we sought immediately to recover the jewels, but found they were not on the isle. That will make him responsible for their recovery," said Felicity with a twinkle in her eye.

Luke was making his way back to his apartment when Tom Kitchin accosted him. Luke was dreading such a meeting as the young man may bear him an understandable grudge. Luke had imprisoned his father which led this innocent man, at least in his son's eyes, to his untimely death.

Luke intuitively felt for his dagger should the confrontation turn violent.

Surprisingly Tom was convivial, if not jovial. "Sir Luke, do you want to question me further on my adventures with their ladyships. I cannot add to what I told the islanders last night. Their ladyships told me they needed to recover goods left there by Martin Moore as organizer of the old smuggling ring. It did not ring true. Why would anybody leave anything on that half-submerged rock? Goods would not be safe there. If not damaged by the water, or washed away by the tides, the many fishermen who frequent the area could have stolen them."

Luke came to the defense of two of his favorite women. "Their ladyships were lied to. I am sure that Martin Moore never left anything on the rock."

Luke broached the more difficult issue, but one that could not be avoided. "I am sorry to hear of your father's death. I would much have preferred his case to have come to trial, where he could have defended himself from the charges I had made."

"Do not fret or blame yourself for father's death. It has saved me from a moral dilemma—whether to tell the truth or continue to protect him. I did not tell you all I knew when you questioned me."

Luke listened to Tom's confession. "In the weeks leading up to Ann's murder, father's love for her turned into bitter hatred. He, a faithful lover for decades, was cast aside for the trinkets of the nobility in the person whom we thought was Michael. Ann cut dead any further relationship with father. It was the necklace that turned father's disappointment into a revengeful obsession. On the day of the murder he told me he would visit Ann and have it out with her. Later that night he returned from such a visit absolutely distraught. I filled him up with strong liquor, but it did little to relax him. He was in a mess. One minute he hated Ellen and vowed to destroy all the Moores yet next morning, he brought me that little silver plate that he suggested I give to Ellen. Days later I found on the floor of the forge, ground into the dust, amid much other refuse, a small sapphire that I now know belonged with the necklace."

Tom withdrew from his doublet a little blue stone and gave it to Luke. "Convincing proof of father's guilt?"

Luke gave Tom a hug.

Tom responded with a half-articulated plea, "Sir, in return I need your help."

"What's troubling you?"

"When father had had too much to drink, especially in the weeks after Ann had stopped their relationship, he said contradictory things about the Moore girls especially Ann and Ellen. He demanded that I end my relationship with Ellen because we were half siblings. Yet later he gave me the silver dish to give her."

"After Ann's death he was completely confused as how to relate to Ellen?"

"Yes, on the one hand he claimed he was Ellen's father, and obviously had some paternal concern for her, yet on the other hand she was also Ann's daughter and obviously reminded him of her now hated mother."

"Have you told Ellen that Sam Kitchen was her father?"

"No. I hope that you can raise that possibility with her and assess her response."

Luke agreed, and next day he began his sensitive conversation with Ellen. "I have to raise the vexed question of your parentage. Recent events have highlighted two, equally unfortunate possibilities. Given the length and frequency of your mother's relationship with both Samuel Kitchin and Harry Bohm, one of them, in all probability, is your father."

"Yes, and if it is Sam then Tom is my half-brother," was Ellen's surprise response.

"Both church and state forbid marriage between siblings, and any sexual act is legally incest," declaimed a moralistic, if not pompous Luke.

"Since mother's death I have constantly thought of such a possibility. I do not know why society holds such a view. In the breeding of cattle such relationships can produce the finest of animals."

"And also, the most deformed and underdeveloped."

"In other words, Sir Luke, the law is essentially to prevent such a couple producing children. If the couple did not have any children, the worst aspects of such a relationship would be avoided."

"Yes."

"If I did not know that Tom was my brother, and we did not have children, we could lead a normal married life together, in time adopting one of the many foundlings that need a home."

"But could you ensure that you do not give birth?"

"After my miscarriage some years ago the damage done to me was so great that I probably cannot have any more children. But would Tom want a barren woman?"

"Talk to him!"

Luke reported to Tom and advised him not to tell Ellen what his father had said but admit that sharing the same father was nevertheless a possibility. As it was not certain however he suggested that Tom could propose marriage and given Ellen's damaged reproductive organs they might adopt a child. The spirit of the law, if not its letter could be kept.

Tom was jubilant. As he was leaving, he turned to Luke, "I almost forgot a second time. When we had our discussion a day or so ago, I forgot to pass on to you a vital piece of information regarding Martin Moore. He is alive and well—at least he was in Whitby a week ago."

It was Luke's turn to be jubilant. "How do you know?"

"Red, the trawlerman who rescued us from Resurrection Isle said he had seen Martin several times around Whitby, and especially in The Three Crowns, where he was obviously conducting business of same sort."

This information gave weight to the theory that Martin had stolen the jewels and was trying to unload them to buyers in Whitby. When Luke passed this information on to Jane, she was skeptical. "Martin has more common sense than to try to unload such gems in the local area, unless he was dealing with London buyers."

"Nevertheless, I will stay at The Three Crowns for several nights. With a lot of luck, I might entrap Martin. Is there an inventory of the Bohm treasures? It would help me to know whether particular items I might come across belong to the collection."

"You are in luck, Luke. Pinned to Felix's document regarding his request to Martin to place the treasures in a secure place was the very inventory that you seek."

After three days without any contact Luke was tiring of the sickly black licorice ale. Finally, there was a ray of hope. Red the trawlerman entered the inn. "Finished your work on the island? From what I hear there have been a few deaths and disappearances since you arrived," he commented.

"True, and that is why I am here. I had hoped to find the missing Martin Moore."

"You are three days too late. Last week he was here every day."

"What happened to him?"

"Three days ago, he boarded a collier bound for London."

"Damnation, he has got away."

"I am not sure it was through choice. One of my crew reported that he did not seem to be a happy passenger when he was dragged aboard the collier by two burly seamen."

"He is too old to be press ganged. Why would anybody kidnap an old defrocked cleric?"

"Because he spent days here trying to sell valuable gems. Someone probably wanted the whole collection that he referred to, not just the few trinkets he made available to potential buyers in the snug. He is probably being tortured as we speak to reveal the location of his total cache," said Red with relish.

Luke bought Red another beer and sought out the landlord. "Has the room occupied by Martin Moore been re-let?"

"No, Mr Moore booked it for two weeks."

Luke explained he was a magistrate and needed to search the room. Someone else had already done so—but not effectively.

Luke found a few places that had been missed, but he found no jewels.

Just as he was leaving the landlord asked, "Did you find what you were looking for?"

"No, replied a depressed Luke.

"Perhaps you should look in the second room that Mr Moore paid for. It was for a Mr Young, who as far as I know never appeared."

Under a loose floorboard in Young's room Luke eventually found the Bohm jewel boxes. He checked the items against the inventory and was surprised to find that most items, and all the very valuable ones were still there. The few that had gone were the least valuable. Lady Jane would be delighted, —but would they inform the Marquess?

As he left the inn, Luke ran into Red, and directed a few more questions at the trawlerman. "Do you know the name of the boat whose crew kidnapped Martin Moore?"

"The *White Rose.*"

"When did it leave here, and what was its next destination?"

"Two days ago, and Scarborough. It might be delayed there some time. The cargo it has to pick up could be delayed in reaching the port because of poor weather. Your frigate could catch it before it gets far in any case. The *White Rose* is old and built to transport heavy items. It was not built for speed."

Five hours later Luke was aboard the frigate and explaining to Peter Hutton, his new mission. It was now dark, and Peter decided to stay out to sea and sail directly to Scarborough. There was no hope of tracking any vessel at night. Hopefully when they arrived at Scarborough, the *White Rose* would still be there. If not, they would sail south until she was sighted.

Peter told Luke that they had seen the *White Rose* two days earlier, because unlike most merchant shipping, it was well out to sea and came very close to Nith Island—so close that he ordered his men to action stations. He monitored it until it was well away from the island. He gained the impression that the ship was heading to Nith but changed course when it sighted his ship.

Luke agreed, "A distinct possibility. Martin probably told his kidnappers that the missing gems were still on the island, but the *White Rose* did not want to confront a government warship."

The *Deadly Arrow* was off Scarborough before dawn, and a longboat from the ship landed Luke and five soldiers there before the sun was up.

They ascertained that the *White Rose* had left the previous evening. The harbor master recalled that it was heavily overloaded, being very low in the water. It had every part of ship overfilled with coal.

As the frigate sailed south it passed two merchantmen that from a distance were initially identified as the *White Rose*. To the frigate's inexperienced lookout, all cargo ships appeared the same. Luke reflected on his brief naval career in the Mediterranean where many merchantmen were low in the water because they were heavily armed and when challenged could answer with a full deck or two of cannon fire. At least an overladen, almost derelict collier out of Whitby had no such retaliatory capability.

The frigate eventually caught up with the *White Rose* and moved alongside it. Hutton shouted for it to slow down and be ready to receive a boarding party of a magistrate and Royal troops. The collier's response was evasive, but not unexpected.

"How do I know you are not pirates who have seized one of the King's ships, or a renegade vessel still loyal to the defunct republic, out for spoils?" asked its master.

"Whether we are a Royal ship or a pirate, I will have you de-masted with a single cannonade, if you do not slow to allow our longboat to come aside."

As evidence of his intention a shot was fired across the bow of the already lumbering ship. The collier master remained dubious. "Why would a Royal ship want to board this old collier? What are you after?"

It was Luke who replied, "I am a magistrate, anxious to find a man who was kidnapped and forced aboard this ship at Whitby."

The collier reduced sail and now progressed so slowly that the oarsmen on the *Deadly Arrow*'s longboat could outpace it.

Luke was soon aboard the old ship and explaining to the master that his men would begin a detailed search, which might reveal other secrets that he might not want to be known. If he produced Martin Moore immediately, Luke and his men would withdraw with the victim, and not proceed with any further examination.

Luke sensed a rising atmosphere of resentment. He immediately took precautions. "Master, order all your men to assemble on the quarter deck!"

Luke had his troops prime their muskets and point them provocatively at the assembled merchant seamen.

Luke drew the master aside, "Lead me to your brig! Is it occupied?"

The master relaxed. "Yes, sir. Six prisoners."

What! Did you subdue a mini-mutiny?" asked Luke.

"No. Their detention is legitimate, and as a magistrate you are duty bound to uphold the incarceration of these men. A local press gang acting in the King's name rounded up these six men for service in your navy. I am transporting them to London to serve in the undermanned Royal fleet following the desertion of many republican sailors. I am quite happy to transfer them all to you if you wish to complete that assignment."

Luke ignored the offer and questioned each of men. Martin Moore was not amongst them. He about to leave when he sensed that one of the prisoners wanted to talk to him, but not in the presence of the master. Luke requested that the master join his men on deck, so that he could question the prisoners alone.

With the master gone, one prisoner immediately asked, "Was the man you are looking for rather old, with a mop of white unruly hair, yet surprisingly mobile for his advanced years?"

"Yes, when did you see him?"

"Just before we left Whitby, we thought we were the last people forced on board. Before we were dragged down into the brig, two of the crew carried the person I have described up the gangplank, literally as it was drawn up after them."

"Can you describe the sailors who did this?"

"One was the boatswain."

Luke returned to the deck and addressed the assembled seamen. "Would the boatswain step forward?" A tall solidly built man did so.

Luke turned to his own men. "Escort this sailor into the longboat. He is being arrested for the kidnapping of Martin Moore."

The master intervened, "Sir, could we come to an agreement. My crew is very inexperienced, and without the services of the boatswain, I will be in serious difficulties making it to London. If we could find this missing Moore aboard, no worse for wear, and further enhance your successful recovery of the gentleman with a case of the finest French brandy, would you release my boatswain?"

Luke responded in a non-committal manner. "I am not open to bribery, master, but the prime purpose of my mission is to recover Mr Moore, not to punish his abductors."

"Come with me! The boatswain told me this man was a notorious criminal who had robbed wealthy households of their jewelry, the whereabouts of which we should ascertain, before handing him over to the authorities."

Luke asked, "When did you last see him?"

"I've never seen him, but the boatswain took him breakfast this morning just before we left Scarborough."

As they approached a door of a small cabin Luke called out, "Move away from the door Martin. It is Luke Tremayne here to rescue you."

He turned to the master, "A necessary precaution. Knowing Martin, he could be ready to smash our heads in with whatever he could lay his hands on."

"It would be difficult. He had his hands cuffed," replied the master.

Luke took the key from the master and unlocked the door. Luke was furious. The cabin was empty. "You will pay dearly, master, for this charade. What is the point of this delaying action?"

"Sir, my boatswain assured me Moore was here this morning."

"Then where is he now?"

"I do not know."

"I will be changing my charge against the boatswain and now will charge you both with murder."

"It was never anybody's intention to kill the man. We only wanted to elicit from him the location of his cache of gems. I was not directly involved in this, but I was to receive a small amount from what the boatswain and his partner could obtain, for my silence in permitting the interrogation to occur aboard the *White Rose*. If Moore has been murdered or died accidentally while being questioned, it had nothing to do with me. I am innocent," argued a very worried master.

Luke carefully examined every inch of the cabin. The porthole was open.

On the floor were most of Martin's clothes. Luke turned to the master. "You are lucky. Although that porthole is small, Martin was a thin and agile man. Either he escaped by removing most of his clothes and squeezing through the porthole and jumping into the sea, or he was murdered, and his body stuffed through the porthole. By the way, if you have managed to conceal Moore somewhere else on this ship, any torturing of him to find the jewels will get you nowhere. His cache was found in a Whitby inn, and returned to the rightful owners."

The master gave an exaggerated sigh.

Luke considered his options. He had little choice but to make the search for Martin his priority.

Once back on deck he announced, "Evidence for abduction and possible murder is strong, but largely circumstantial. When we recover Martin Moore dead or alive, our case will be enhanced. Consequently, I will take no action against the crew of the *White Rose* at this time, but in the future do not be surprised if a writ for your arrest is executed at any port in Yorkshire in the future."

He called down to his men in the long boat to send the boatswain back up the ladder.

On the *Deadly Arrow* Luke explained the situation to Peter. "Martin wriggled his way through the port hole and swam away, presumably not far out of Scarborough. Whether he is still alive or not, I do not know. I am certain he was not murdered or accidently killed by his abductors. They would not have needed to remove his clothes. They could have tossed a dead body overboard from a number of places. And the master was genuinely surprised that Moore had gone."

"Do we return to Scarborough and search?"

"No, return to your station off Nith. I will report to Jane and Felicity that as of this morning, Martin was still alive."

Mid-morning on that same day a naked man had come ashore on a small beach on the edge of Scarborough where moralistic locals arrested him and confined him in a small prison administered by the harbor master. The harbor master remembering Luke's visit listened to Martin's story and accepted it. He provided some clothing and put him aboard the first boat heading for Whitby from which Martin claimed he could find his way back to Nith Island.

Next day not long after Luke had reported to Felicity and Jane the saga of Martin Moore, the dowager Marchioness received a knock on her concealed door leading from the secret passages. She ascertained who was knocking and let her visitor in.

It was Martin Moore, wearing clothing several sizes too large for the trim athletic man.

Jane rebuked him for stealing the family gems, which she informed him had been found by Luke. He defended himself on the grounds that Felix's major purpose in having them hidden was to prevent their wanton disposal by his successor. He had no intention of a wholesale sale of the gems. He was only selling a few trinkets to earn enough for immediate survival until it was safe enough to return to Nith. He always intended to return the bulk of jewels to the dowager Marchioness.

Noting Jane's doubts about this outcome he confessed. "That's not quite true. I intended to keep the jewels until Harry died. After all, if Harry and Ralph die without heirs, the marquisate and its jewels could descend to the Moores."

"A pipe dream Martin! Harry is out to produce an heir as soon as his annulment comes through, and he is free to marry again. I am sure Felicity and Ralph have not given up the possibility of a child. In any case the Moore claim to succeed to the marquisate is so fraught with problems that should the Bohms die without heirs, the King will declare the line defunct, and reallocate the title and the lands to one of his loyal supporters. But why are you still in hiding?"

"Harry will not see my confiscation of the family jewels as leniently as you do—should he become aware of it. Secondly, I am convinced that Jerome Tighe is still alive and determined to carry out two further murders, Harry and myself, for deeds allegedly committed twenty years ago."

"Most unlikely! There has been no sign of him since he jumped overboard weeks ago," said Jane

"No, very likely. No corpse has washed ashore. I know the currents around this island better than anybody. From where he jumped overboard a dead body would have washed up along the south coast within two days. I was here then, and regularly searching the beach. There was never a body."

36

Jane informed Luke of Martin's arrival. "He has no desire to meet you. He is paranoid. He believes that Jerome Tighe is out to kill him, as is Harry for activities from their mutual past, or should he become aware of it, for Martin's theft of the family jewels. He also fears that you might exact an extra-legal punishment on him."

"Has his mind deteriorated?"

"He is certainly not his old self."

"What does he intend to do?"

"Hide on the island until he is absolutely convinced that Jerome Tighe is dead, and that the Marquess and yourself are not in a position to harm him. He is now a harmless old man who has been through a lot. Don't persecute him!" pleaded Jane.

Harry's re-organization of the island, and the adoption of his ideas and programs proceeded rapidly. His changes at the top required his sister-in-law the Baroness Felicity to play the role of acting Marchioness, whenever he required a female partner to carry out his official functions.

Felicity was outwardly compliant but explained to Luke and Jane her underlying concern. "This womanizing leopard has not changed his spots. He will certainly use the occasions we are together to advance his attempts to sleep with me. He has already slept numerous times with his older brother's wife, he will now attempt to do so with his younger brother's spouse. Harry will order Ralph to London on many unnecessary occasions to help achieve this end."

"What will you do, if he does make an attempt on your virtue?" asked Jane.

"For your future reference, Luke, if you find Harry stabbed it will be that I acted to stop being raped, if you find him poisoned, and I am an expert in that field, it will be revenge for an attack I could not prevent."

"Harry would not be that stupid," remarked Luke.

Jane disagreed, "The one thing I learnt about Harry over the past two decades is that what he wanted, he took—without any consideration of the consequences. And now that he is the Marquess, he believes that he can do what he likes. It is only the presence of your troops on the island that forces him to act temporarily with some degree of reason. Quite frankly when you leave the island Luke, I will leave also."

"And if things go the way I predict, Ralph and I will also be forced to depart," added Felicity.

"This island seems to breed malevolence," commented Luke. "Given the way Harry has behaved throughout his life, culminating with pretending to be Michael and living with the latter's wife, I now doubt the accuracy of our official version of Michael's death. Harry could easily have given his brother a push, simply to gain access to his wife," commented a pensive Jane.

'I am afraid you ladies may have to leave Nith sooner rather than later. My mission is coming to a close as we have solved most of the tasks that confronted us. Michael's death is one issue that I will never solve. All the evidence points to an accidental fall, but who can be certain."

"Do not give up on that. Martin's evidence from his fishing boat clears Harry of pushing Michael—but is it true. That may be why Martin fears Harry. Martin lied for his pretend friend of two decades ago and now threatens to tell the truth. Harry is ruthless enough to remove him before he can change his evidence. The same applies to James Denholm who says there was no one else in the area. With Harry taking away the control of the old smuggling ring from him, just as he assumed a position of power, will he stick to that story?" asked Jane.

"What you are suggesting Jane? That Harry's excesses as a womanizer and as an autocratic marquess may loosen a few tongues?"

"Exactly," added Jane squeezing Luke's hand.

"Watch what you are doing Jane, if your old friend Lord Stokey is to be believed this man has a reputation far worse than Harry's," commented Felicity, teasing her two friends.

While Luke was discussing these issues with Felicity and Jane, Martin was setting himself up for a life in hiding. He had opened up part of the network of caves and tunnels that had been unused for decades, but still provided easy access. Jane supplied a dark wig to conceal his telltale white locks should he venture abroad in daylight, and a variety of clothes to help in his disguise. Arrangements were made for Ellen to deliver urgent supplies of food to an agreed location.

Martin faced a new dilemma. He could take the pressure off himself and put it on another. He could give Luke another murder to solve—but for the moment he could not find the body that he knew existed.

But others did.

Three days later, Tom Kitchin and George Denholm were roaming the cliff tops along the eastern edge of the island shooting shearwaters and gannets to be consumed in the form of Isabel Denholm's renowned seabird pies.

Tom decided that a useful addition to the catch were common scoters, the sea ducks that were swimming in the rockpools that emerged at the base of the cliff at low tide. While George gathered the fallen shearwaters and gannets, Tom waded into the pools to catch the slow-moving ducks. As he clambered over the first rocky outcrops he turned to talk to George and uttered a half-muffled cry. "My god, is that a body under the cliff face?"

"Report it to the Marquess," said George whose mind was still on the birds.

"No, it is a matter for the constable. You stay here and I will get Mr. Corby."

"Perhaps on second thoughts the King's men might be more appropriate. The clothes the body is wearing are not those of we gentle folk," added George.

"It could be a false alarm, and the apparent body simply the clothes of some aristocrat that have fallen from a ship and washed ashore below. I will see. If it is only clothes, they may bring a few pence on resale," said Tom.

"The body or the clothes are not going to move in the near future. Let's collect all the birds first!" George began filling the bag that was tied around his waist with the birds they had shot. "You may be more interested in what lies in the sand ahead of us, but mother would be delighted with this catch of birds." George began to salivate in anticipation of his mother's culinary delights. Her seabird pie was an island icon.

Eventually the two men approached the object on a small area of sand between the rocks with caution. There was no doubt that it was a body lying face down in the sand. Tom and George rolled the body over. It was incredibly heavy, given the water-soaked mass of clothing that it wore. There was a gasp of horror. The body had no face. Time in the water and attacks from various sea creatures, large and small had eaten into the visage.

George vomited.

"I'll stay with the body. Go straight to Sir Luke. Tell nobody else! said Tom.

Mark and Luke were with Jane when George burst in, "My lady and gentlemen, Tom Kitchin and I have found the body of an aristocratic woman in Tyson Cove."

"Who is she?"

"Her face has been eaten away."

It was Jane who fighting a wave of nausea asked, "How do you know it was an aristocrat?"

"The clothing is fine, and obviously very expensive."

Luke turned to Mark, "Rally the men and bring a stretcher. We must recover the corpse."

"I am coming with you," announced Jane.

"I do not think it is a sight for your ladyship," said George.

"I agree. Why do you wish to come?" asked Mark.

"If there is no face, I might recognize the clothing. If the victim is a local, I can probably tell you who she is. Even the very wealthy have a limited amount of clothes."

Luke asked, "Had she fallen to her death where she was found?"

"Possibly, but she had been in water for some time. She could have died anywhere, and the tides pushed her ashore," answered George. He then excused himself.

He had to get the bag of birds to his mother as soon as possible.

Luke, Mark, Jane and half a dozen soldiers made their way to Tyson Cove. As they approached the body, Jane wailed and began to sob.

"You should not have come in the first place. It is not a pretty sight, my lady," said Luke sympathetically.

"It is not the missing face Luke; it is the sequence of petticoats and emerald green bodice. I know who this is—and the news will destroy our community."

Jane kissed her own fingers, and gently transferred the kiss to the corpse and solemnly announced, "This is my stepdaughter, Lady Alice Bohm. Carry her body to my quarters!"

"This discovery must remain a secret. It raises so many problems that the least people who know about it for the moment the better," added Luke.

Mark turned to Luke and expressed the obvious, "The new Marquess has a lot of explaining to do."

"Let's not jump to conclusions!" was Luke's cautious response.

Luke, Mark, Jane and Felicity, who had been apprised of the situation, met to discuss strategy. The women and their servants had just completed dressing the corpse for burial. Felicity asked, "When will Harry be told?"

"Hopefully, not until he has dug a hole deep enough for us to bury him in," said Mark vindictively.

"Who told you that Alice had gone to stay with relatives in the West Country?" asked Luke.

"The first we heard of it was when Felix announced it publicly," replied Jane."

"He was probably only repeating what Harry had told him," declared Luke.

Luke and six soldiers accosted Harry in his library. "What is the meaning of this Sir Luke? These soldiers are an affront to my status. It smacks of the regime we have just destroyed. We are no longer a military dictatorship."

"I am sorry your lordship, but there have been developments which require the military to act," replied Luke diplomatically.

Then he lied. "I have had a request from the Court for the details of Lady Alice's current location. Some of the returning courtiers are her friends, and they would like to meet up with her."

"I can't give you her address, but I can give you the name and address of her cousin whom she was to meet in London."

"Did you accompany her off the island?"

"Yes, I took her to Whitby and saw her board a ship for London, where she would meet her cousin, who was to take her to somewhere in the West Country."

"Is that so?" asked Mark emphatically.

"Checkmate!" was Luke's silent thought.

37

"How did you get her to Whitby? Did Tom Kitchin sail you there?" Luke asked.

"No, Tom was not available, nor was the island's official craft which James Denholm had taken to the mainland that morning. Martin Moore took us. He will confirm it."

"Did anything unusual or catastrophic happen on the journey to the mainland?"

"No, it was dark, the sea was calm, and Martin is a very able oarsman."

"Lies, all lies, my lord. The body of Lady Alice was found in Tyson Cove yesterday morning. She had been in the water for a day or so. She probably fell out of, or was pushed from Martin's boat," suggested Mark.

"Ridiculous! If Lady Alice's body was washed up, she must have jumped overboard on her way to London. She was not very happy, and clearly suicidal," was Harry unsympathetic response.

This clever reply by Harry completely derailed Luke and Mark's reconstruction of what happened. To Luke, Harry had pushed or thrown Alice into the sea. Harry's suggestion that as her London bound ship passed near Nith Island, she had thrown herself overboard, made it almost impossible to prove otherwise. His only hope was to check Harry's story with Martin. This may be another reason that Martin feared for his life. With Martin dead, no one could challenge Harry's highly suspicious version of events.

Luke tried to regain some ground. "What was the name of the London bound ship that Lady Alice boarded?"

"I don't know. Martin took her on board."

Luke bowed to the Marquess and left the room.

Later that day he met again with Mark, Jane and Felicity.

"I made a fool of myself. Harry's simple explanation completely demolished my theory, and he knew it," admitted Luke.

"I will get a message to Martin. If he confirms Harry's story then we may have completely misjudged the man," said Jane.

There was a knock on the door and a servant admitted the ship's surgeon whom Luke had asked to examine the body. Luke was jubilant at his news. "Lady Alice did not drown. She was the victim of a severe beating by heavy implements, or she had fallen from a great height onto rocks. The first scenario is murder, and second one, you have a choice of murder, accident or suicide."

The news for Luke was to get even better.

A servant entered the room and approached Jane. "We are in the process of washing the clothing of Lady Alice. Sewn to one of her petticoats was a waterproof leather container inside of which was this book."

She handed it to Jane, who opened it. "A godsend Luke, this is Alice's diary."

"Do not build up my hopes! Are there entries for her last few days on this island?" responded Luke.

"There are, but they are too good to be true. Alice states that Harry wants her to leave immediately before Tremayne gets too nosey. She refused but has agreed to meet him later that night for an urgent discussion of their situation. She concludes by saying if she does not return, Harry has probably pushed her off the cliff as he had done to her late husband," quoted Jane.

"What do you mean 'too good to be true'?"

"Alice was a very bitter woman. Harry's womanizing behavior had cost her the status of Baroness and made impossible her ever becoming Marchioness. Her life had been ripped apart. This entry sounds like a suicidal woman setting up her persecutor. Her claim that Harry murdered Michael would not hold up in court," said Jane.

"I agree with Jane. This diary could have been written by you Luke to discredit Harry. That is how a good defense lawyer would see it," added Felicity.

As Luke and Mark walked back to their apartment the former expressed his disappointment at the reaction of the women to Alice's diary.

"I am not surprised at all. Both Jane and Felicity hated Alice, probably more than they despise Harry," replied Mark.

"Are they right concerning the diary?"

"It's a possibility we cannot neglect, but we can certainly push Harry further having caught him out on more lies."

Next morning Luke confronted Harry alone. "What no military escort today Sir Luke?"

"No, because what I have to say is not to your benefit and should be heard by the least possible people."

"What further lies have you concocted?"

Luke decided to mix lies with facts. "Martin Moore did not take you and Lady Alice to Whitby."

"How do you know that?"

"Martin is alive and well and has spoken to us."

"It is Martin's word against mine—a Marquess against a defrocked and degenerate priest who is pursuing a vendetta against me. And even if what I told you was a lie, it does not in any way implicate me in the Alice's death."

"But Alice's diary does."

"Alice kept a diary! Where did you find it?" Or is this another of your falsehoods to unsettle me?

"On her body?" was Luke's factual response.

"It can't prove that I had anything to do with Alice's death, unless her ghost wrote the last entry. You may have many theories Tremayne, but no evidence."

"What evidence we have, shows that you have lied constantly regarding her departure from the island. She did not consent to leave. She was determined to stay. The two of you met on the night she disappeared. No doubt a last-ditch attempt by you to change her mind. She did not go to Whitby. And she was not drowned. The doctor believes she fell to her death. I believe you met on that night, probably well away from Nith Hall. An argument ensued and as Alice refused to submit to your will, you threw her over a cliff, and she was smashed to death on the rocks below—in the same fashion as her husband Michael had met his death. Her smashed bones indicated a fall from a great height. Her diary also claims you murdered Michael. In all I believe I have sufficient evidence to indict your lordship for the murder of Lady Alice Bohm and of her husband the then Baron of Nith, Michael Bohm."

"The second charge will not stick. You know full well that the evidence of dead people will not be accepted by the courts without verification from a third party."

Ignoring the comment Luke noted, "I and my men will return at noon to take you to York Castle."

"Luke, if you think that giving me a few hours to reflect on my sins, and then as a gentleman I will be so overcome with guilt that I will shoot myself may work in the army, but not in the world I inhabit. My response given two hours, is how to escape before you return."

"I will leave my men on all the exits, including the one into the secret passage, to ensure that that is not an option, my lord."

"It is a pity Luke that you have begun your career with the King so badly—arresting a peer of the realm for a murder he did not commit. I will be presenting an alternate explanation for what happened, and I can guarantee no jury would find me guilty of murder, especially a jury of my fellow peers"

"And what is this alternate scenario?"

"I am the victim of a vindictive woman who blames me for destroying her life. Yes, I did meet Alice on that last evening. She suggested we walk to the cliff where her husband Michael had died. As it was her last night on the island, promising to leave in the morning, she thought this was an appropriate farewell. I was suspicious. Knowing the bitterness Alice now bore towards me, I half expected she would attempt to push me over the cliff, to suffer the same fate as her husband, whose accidental slip she had never fully accepted. It was the brightest moonlit night for some time."

"And did she try to push you over?"

"No, but I became very anxious when she led me to the very spot where Michael had fallen which is marked by a small stone. Then she began a sudden outpouring of poison directed against me, blaming me for ruining her life. She had nothing to look forward to. I was now the Marquess and when the annulment of my marriage came through, I could remarry and start a dynasty. She would remain a barren failure, guilty in the eyes of the world of adultery with her husband's brother. She looked me in the eye and proclaimed that I would not live that long because within days the King's officers would arrest me for her murder. With that she turned and threw herself over the cliff."

"I don't believe it, but others might. Both your stepmother and sister-in-law have suggested to me something very similar."

"Listen to them, before you make a fool of yourself. There is a witness to what happened."

"If you have a witness that can turn your farrago of lies into the truth, bring him or her forth!" demanded a slightly shaken Luke.

"After I turned away from the cliff top having seen Alice fall to her death, I am sure I saw a figure against a neighboring wall. I called out after the shadow, but he or she had disappeared. If you are interested in justice find that witness, and in the meantime, release me!"

"No, my lord, I still intend to arrest you for the murder of Lady Alice Bohm."

Luke then arranged to transport the Marquess to York Castle. The *Deadly Arrow* would collect him and sail to Hull, from which he would be taken overland to York. The commander of the guard would carry the documentation of Harry's crime for the information of the governor, and the next meeting of the Quarter Sessions of the county where Luke hoped they would refer Henry Bohm to the Assizes to be tried by a judge alone.

Mark advised caution. "Luke, delay the arrest! Try to find this missing witness. Frankly I do not hold out any hope for a conviction. As a peer of the realm Harry will ask to be tried by the House of Lords, and an indictment originated by a former Cromwellian general is not likely to be viewed by people your Republic removed from power, with any great favor."

"In that case Mark, attach your name to the indictment rather than mine."

Luke was privately hurt by the refusal of Jane, Felicity and Mark to enthusiastically accept his assessment of the situation. He began to feel that this was a matter of status. The aristocrats were defending their own. Luke returned at noon, and Harry was waiting for him. They walked together through the tunnels and caves that led to the main entrance to the island. The *Deadly Arrow's* long boat was already there, and Luke gave his final instructions to the commander of his guard.

The sailors were about to push off when a voice was heard resonating through the cavern. It was Jane. "Stop Luke, we have proof of Harry's innocence!"

Luke turned around to see Jane accompanied by a lithe, agile figure with short black hair and an outfit in forest green that reminded him of both drawings of Robin Hood and an Irish leprechaun.

"Is this your evidence?" Luke asked, pointing at the ridiculous figure in green. The figure in green removed his hat and his black wig.

It was Martin Moore.

Harry was surprised. "You are alive. I thought that news was part of Tremayne's lies. Why are you wearing that stupid outfit?"

"To save your life, although you don't deserve it. I was the witness to Lady Alice's vindictive abuse of you on the cliff face. She then jumped. You did not touch her in any way. You did not murder her."

38

Harry was confused. "Why have you come forward? In recent years we have been in constant conflict, and I believed your disappearance was to escape my attention."

"I want you to suffer for crimes you have committed—not for a thin case of circumstantial evidence, which would have no chance of success"

Luke winced at the comment. Martin continued. "But you may not thank me for saving you from York Castle. You would have been safer there than on this island."

"Are you threatening me?"

"Of course, not my lord," was Martin's sarcastic response.

"Then why am I in danger here?"

"I just received a message from Red. He put a man in his thirties ashore two nights ago. The man told him he was born on the island and was forced to leave in 1642. He was returning to right serious wrongs. It can only be Jerome. After he jumped overboard from the *Deadly Arrow*, he obviously found his way to the mainland. No wonder there has been no sign of him on the island for weeks."

"And he intends to put things to right by killing Lord Harry and yourself?" asked Luke.

"Wasn't that the impression you received from him before his jump to freedom?" asked Martin.

"He was certainly determined to take revenge against those from 1642 whom he believed were responsible for his exile," confessed Luke.

Harry was freed and the longboat headed back to the *Deadly Arrow* without a prisoner. Luke indicated that Martin should stay with Lady

Jane, and Harry return immediately to his apartment. He would place additional guards both outside and inside their premises until the suspect was captured.

Luke and Mark wondered how long it would be before Jerome would strike.

It was immediate.

Jerome was very active. John Corby reported a sudden increase in thefts which were attributed to him. Loaves of bread, rounds of cheese, cooked chickens, containers of beer and much clothing disappeared across the island. Luke was intrigued by the theft of clothing—male and female.

Mark suggested that perhaps the clothes were not the work of Jerome. Luke strongly disagreed. "No, Mark, Jerome will become the master of disguise. I expect that he will make his first attempts dressed as a woman. He will seek to catch us off our guard."

Luke was soon proved correct. A plain looking, buxom woman waddled up to Lady Jane's apartment, and left a basket of Isabel Denholm's seabird pies for Mr. Moore. The donor insisted that the covering over the pies be removed only by Mr Moore himself, so that he could inhale the delightful aromas of Isabel's cooking.

Martin's weakness for these seabird pies were well known. Before he went into hiding, he would shoot the birds himself, and seek Isabel's skill to convert them into such irresistible pastry. Unfortunately, when the woman delivered the pies, Jane was not at home. She would have approached the basket of pies with caution.

Not so, Martin. He removed the towel covering the pies and thrust his hand into the basket to make his selection. His hand missed an adder that had being aroused into some activity by the heat of the pies.

When informed, Luke was puzzled. Why had Jerome tried such a half-hearted attempt to injure Martin? The adder was not lively and preferred to coil itself around the warm pies than attack anybody. Even if it had been more active, the chances of a successful bite were minimal.

Martin was furious—not with the clumsy attempt on his life, but the degradation of pies which given that they had been cuddled by a snake lost their appeal to him. Not so Luke's men, who having disposed of the snake, shared the pies amongst themselves.

Jerome's next attempt was even more nonsensical. The same plain looking, buxom woman paid a group of young women to flirt with the guards outside of Lord Harry's complex. While the guards' attention was diverted, she slipped through the door into his apartment. She carried with her a bottle of French brandy, identical with that normally consumed by the Marquess.

She was surprised that there were three soldiers in the room and perhaps in a panic, gave the bottle to one of the soldiers, claiming it was a present to Lord Harry from Lady Jane. She left the room immediately. The soldier handed the bottle to Luke, who in turn gave it to Felicity to test for poison. Luke assumed the initial aim was to place it in Lord Harry's cabinet along with his other bottles. There were so many things that had to go right for such an attempt to succeed.

Luke and Mark discussed the situation. Mark commented, "If Jerome is such an incompetent, Harry and Martin have little to fear."

"I can't agree. Jerome is playing us for fools. He is setting us up. He never intended those attempts to work."

"Then why did he do what he did?"

"To confuse us. He hopes that we will be focusing on a plump, plain looking woman. It may give him, in another disguise, those extra seconds he may need to carry out his task."

The first real attack was completely unexpected, and Luke had provided no defense against it. Just after dark there was a tremendous explosion, followed by an intense fire. It was Lord Harry's apartment. The whole island was quickly organized into a bucket brigade, determined to stop the fire spreading to the rest of Nith Hall.

It was with trepidation that Luke and his men broke down the door which had been jammed by the explosion. His heart sank. The twisted and broken bodies of four of his men lay dead across various parts of the room. He moved on into the adjacent anteroom. Harry was lying on the floor.

A quick examination revealed that he was alive, and no serious wounds were evident. Returning to the main room Luke concluded that one or more grenades had been thrown through a window. Red had not told Martin if the passenger he had unloaded had brought any luggage with him. He probably floated a small raft of potential weapons and ammunition behind him as he waded ashore. With Jerome in possession of grenades the situation was more serious than it first appeared.

Luke redeployed his men. He reduced the number of those within and just outside the apartments of Harry and Jane and increased the number of regular patrols—one to traverse the length of the secret passages in Nith Hall, another to circumnavigate the outside of the building. He sought re-enforcements by commandeering the six soldiers seconded to the *Deadly Arrow*. They replaced the men who were killed in the grenade attack.

For the time-being, Luke instituted what amounted to military rule. He had his men inspect and lock securely every exit from the secret passages and ordered the inhabitants of rooms that had access to those secret passages not to admit anybody, even if they thought that person was a friend. He persuaded Peter Hutton to free up a dozen armed sailors who would land their long boat at the eastern set of caves and search them. Jerome must be hiding somewhere in that vast system.

Luke and Mark were in two minds on how to treat Harry's survival. Would they inform the island that Harry had survived—inviting Jerome to have another attempt. On the other hand, they could falsely inform everybody that Harry had died. This would allow them to concentrate their defenses entirely on Martin and be a better legal justification for the imposition of military law. In the end they left the decision to Harry.

Predictably he sought the limelight. His escape would be emphasized, and he publicly announced that he would continue to live in his apartment, as only one of his rooms was critically damaged.

John Corby set traps throughout the island with men lying in wait at places where the suspect might attempt to steal food and clothing. Jerome could not last much longer without replenishing his supplies. He did this in a way that had not been anticipated. A sheep was taken from the fields and was killed and butchered on the spot. Nith Island had never needed shepherds as the island itself provided the most effective hurdle.

A stalemate had been reached. Luke felt that with his increased patrols and more strategic redeployment of his troops and sailors from the *Deadly Arrow*, Jerome's movements and ability to strike against Harry and Martin had been seriously reduced.

Jerome thought the same.

He would have to break the deadlock.

Harry received a note pushed under the locked door from the secret passage. It read, "My Lord, Tremayne has not succeeded in dealing with Tighe. You and I need to take the situation into our own hands. Meet me in the entrance to the tunnel next to my old cottage at midnight. You know how to avoid the guards, Martin."

Martin received a similar note signed Harry.

Martin's note was discovered by Jane who read the contents and immediately contacted Luke.

"Will Martin accept Harry's invitation?"

"Yes, something like this fits the personality of both men. They must be masters of their own destiny, rather than leave themselves in hands of people like yourself," Jane replied.

"Don't they see that it is a trap. The invitation has not come from Lord Harry, but from Tighe. He gets the two men in that small blocked up tunnel and eliminates them both."

"What are you going to do? Put an end to it by asking Harry if he sent the letter and letting Martin know that you are aware of his intended breach of your protective circle?" asked Jane.

"No, if I did that this stalemate could continue for weeks. If it is a trap, then we can put ourselves in a position to trap the trapper. Harry and Martin unknowingly will help capture their would-be killer."

Jane expressed her disquiet. "You will risk the life of both these men to capture a known murderer?"

"Let us not forget my lady that neither man is an innocent. Their life is in danger because one of their victims is seeking perhaps a justified revenge."

"That attitude is hardly legal."

"But it is justice," replied a serious Luke.

Jane was not convinced. She admitted to Martin that she had read the letter. Could this not be a trap set by Tighe. She offered to visit Harry and ask if he had written the letter.

Martin was touched by Jane's attitude but remained adamant. "Even if it is a Tighe trap I will be more than a match for that effeminate pipsqueak. I will be well armed and alert."

Harry was having quite different thoughts. He did not even consider that it was a Tighe trap. He was more concerned that it was a potential

Martin Moore ambush. He knew Martin felt that he had contributed to the murder of Ann by his gift of the pendant, which was a final straw for Samuel Kitchen. Moore was taking advantage of the situation created by Tighe to get his revenge for an assortment of past crimes, true or otherwise.

Moore was a good marksman but had little expertise with sword or dagger. If Moore was out to kill him, he would probably shoot him from a distance as he approached the meeting place. Harry would play it safe and move to the location through a circuitous route.

Tighe was no simpleton. He foresaw that one or both of the men might see it as a trap, and that one of the letters may have been passed on to the authorities. He had to be prepared for well-armed suspicious opponents, and a force of Tremayne's men.

He was. He had a trump card that none of his opponents would use. He was ready to die to achieve his ends. On the other hand, he would not throw away his life needlessly. He would take basic steps to avoid being trapped himself.

Martin arrived at the designated site first. He hid in the shadows cast by a bright full moon against the retaining wall that had hidden the cave entrance.

Within minutes Harry emerged from nowhere. "Well Martin, is this some sort of trick. Did you hope to get me on my own, and shoot me as I approached the entrance?"

"I do not know what you are talking about. You sent me a letter, almost demanding that I meet you here."

"I did no such thing. I am responding to a letter of yours suggesting we take the capture of Jerome Tighe into our own hands."

"It was no letter of mine. Lady Jane was right. She suggested that it was a trap set by Tighe to get us together so that he could kill two birds with the one stone. The minute we enter the cave he will strike, so let's move away!"

Suddenly both men heard a clear but distant voice that was carried through the clear night air. It was Jerome.

"Welcome gentlemen! I am glad you both accepted my invitation. I am about to administer God's justice for the evil you committed two decades ago, and from what I hear, both of you continued to commit ever since."

Harry whispered to Martin, "Where is he? He sounds too far away to harm us. Let's run for it. He is not a great marksman." Martin replied, "He is above us somewhere amongst the rocks of Big Head and the Three Trolls."

Luke's men were in strategic places around the entrance to the cave, but not as far up the incline as to be near the stones. Luke had assessed that the stones were too far away from the cave entrance to provide a base for the murderous Jerome. He was desperately trying to assess where exactly Tighe had placed himself.

Luke sent his men up the incline, but a single shot hit the leading soldier—fatally. Tighe was willing to kill anybody who moved towards him.

Before Luke could reconsider his strategy there was a tremendous explosion, followed a minute later by a second, equally pronounced. These were simultaneously complemented by a low rumble which grew louder as the ground began to shake. A third explosion followed, and this time small rocks were catapulted into the air in the direction of Martin and Harry—and Luke and his men.

Martin turned to Harry, "Quick inside the cave! He has dislodged Big Head and the Trolls. Huge boulders are sliding down the hill at increasing speed. Our only protection is inside the cave."

Luke likewise ordered his men back up the opposite incline to that down which Luke could see rocks as big as a small cottage, sliding rather than rolling down the slope. Luke looked up to where the stone monoliths had stood. The heads of all the figures had gone and the larger stones that made up the bodies of the trolls had also disappeared.

Watching until they had ceased sliding on a sea of smaller stones and rubble, Luke exclaimed in horror, "My God, where are Martin and Harry? Have they been crushed to death, or did they climb away in time?"

"They entered the cave," said Mark.

Moving to the cave, Luke was appalled to find that a gigantic stone, impossible for a dozen or more men to move had finished up blocking the entrance, and a number of smaller rocks had finished up on top of it. Unless Martin and Harry could dig their way out along the passages that led down to the sea, they were entombed.

Luke ordered Mark to take half a dozen of men and make their way up from the blocked entrance from the sea. They would have to remove much of the ceiling that had fallen in, not far from where the men were trapped.

Luke took another detachment of men to climb the incline to inspect the remains of the stone figures. Beyond all expectation not far from a standing base stone they found the body of Jerome Tighe.

Luke approached the body cautiously with his pistol primed. The body moved slightly. "Do not be alarmed Sir Luke! My musket is on the ground over there, and I am in no position to injure you. I am blinded in both eyes."

"The wrong amount of gunpowder?" asked Luke more interested in the technical aspects of the explosion than Tighe's dire situation.

"Not at all. I assessed that it needed three explosions to dislodge the larger rocks even though for the last few days I have been digging around the base of the four figures. I knew that I had to ignite three explosions in the short time available and would probably not have time to move back into a safe position."

"Unfortunately, your self-sacrifice is in vain. My men are at this moment approaching the sealed cave from the other end and will be able to reach Lord Harry and Martin Moore and free them."

"I am no fool Luke. I would not willingly sacrifice my own life, if the chances of my success could be so easily destroyed. I have spent the last few days exploding devices along most of the passage that leads from one of the big caverns to the small cave where the two monsters are entombed. It will take your men weeks to remove the debris and dig a new passage to the small cave. I am avenged, as have all the other victims of these two evil men. I die at peace with myself and my God."

Jerome was seconds from death and was now struggling to speak. He whispered, "Twenty years ago when we were both abused, Martin's niece Ann comforted me and told me that she was pregnant. I asked her was it anybody present at the party that night. She said no, it was the result of a consensual act with her then new brother-in-law, James Denholm. I am sure that now she would want her daughter to know who her father is?"

There was a series of gurgles.

Jerome was dead.

Half an hour later Mark returned. He verified what the dead man had said. There was no way entry could be had to the cave where Martin and Harry were entombed from the now completely blocked passage to the sea.

Luke was not one to give up. He sent men across the island demanding that every able-bodied man report immediately to the site with spades, picks and shovels. If Luke could not gain entry from either end of the cave, he could enter from the roof. He would dig a shaft into it.

A storm erupted over the disposal of Tighe's body that Luke wanted to be immediately buried.

John Corby refused permission to bury it in the parish churchyard and Vince Keddy objected to Luke's first suggestion that he be buried where he lay in an area where the Quakers worshipped.

Mark suggested he just be thrown over the cliff into the sea.

Luke expressed his deep personal thoughts on this to Jane.

"Jerome Tighe was an avenging angel who administered justice in a way that the King could not."

"And saved you from having to undertake a similar solution to the problem," whispered Jane as she squeezed his hand.

"He deserves a proper funeral. He served his country loyally under the previous regime."

"And how are you to arrange that?"

"As he was an active naval officer, I will ask his captain Peter Hutton to conduct a brief service and we will bury him at sea. I will bury Lieutenant Philip Bates not Jerome Tighe."

Next day, Luke, but unaccompanied by anyone from Nith, boarded the *Deadly Arrow* where he participated in a service, and then after the ship had travelled deep into the North Sea, personally pushed the shrouded body into the ocean.

He gave the falling corpse a final salute.

Meanwhile the attempt to rescue Harry and Martin quickly failed.

The diggers discovered that just below a few inches of soil was solid rock. The experts declared that it was at least five feet of solid rock that needed to be dug out. Even multiple containers of Jerome's gunpowder that were found on the site would hardly have any effect.

It was slow work and with rotating teams of pick wielders an ever-increasing hole was created. A fortnight later access was finally gained to the cave, but it was too late.

Both Martin and Harry were dead. The cave had been effectively sealed and they would have run out of air not long after their entombment.

The new marquess, Ralph, reversed his brother's policies. He placed control of the family's land transactions into the hands of the new Marchioness, his wife Felicity, who immediately returned the properties bought from fleeing Royalists at the price they received when they fled. He also discovered the missing phials of arsenic hidden in Harry's apartment. He would not become involved in the islands importing business which was reorganized under the control of James Denholm and Ellen Bentley, who would soon become Ellen Kitchin.

That arrangement created an awkward situation for Luke. He considered whether Jerome's dying confession of what he had been told by the then Ann Moore should be relayed to Ellen. Was it better to let sleeping dogs lie?

Mark suggested Luke leave it up to Ellen. Luke went to Jane's apartment where the door was opened by Ellen. "Her ladyship is not at home, Luke."

"It is you I have come to see on a very personal matter. I know the identity of your birth father. I understand why your mother did not wish to reveal his name, as it would cause hurt to a number of people. My advice is that you refrain from discovering this basic fact in your life to prevent discord on the island. What I can tell you, which will delight you is that Samuel Kitchen was not your father. You and Tom can have a normal relationship."

"Does my real father know that I am his daughter?"

"I doubt it."

"Is he married?"

"Yes."

"Does he have children?"

"Yes."

"So, I have a half sibling?"

"Yes, more than one."

"And father is not Sam Kitchen?"

"Correct."

Ellen gave Luke a big hug. "I will compromise. I need to know the name of my father, but I will not confront him with the knowledge."

"Are you sure you want to know?"

"Yes, this issue has obsessed me for the last few years. I must know."

"Your real father is your uncle by marriage, James Denholm."

Ellen was silent for some time. With tears in her eyes she finally responded, "My mother was not a nice woman. Fancy sleeping with her sister's husband. No wonder she wanted to keep it a secret. Uncle James has no idea that I am his daughter?"

"I believe so."

"Does Aunt Isabel know?"

"No, given your mother's subsequent obsession with Sam Kitchen most of your family assumed that he was the father. And Sam certainly believed that he was."

At that moment Jane returned, "You have come to say farewell?"

"Yes," lied Luke. "What are you going to do in the immediate future?"

"With my friend Felicity as the new Marchioness, and she is being given considerable responsibility in the running of the estates by Ralph, I will stay here and help her. It will be a much happier place now. Ralph has taken steps to have a new rector appointed, and I have acted on behalf of the Catholic community to have an eminent Catholic layman with the authority to conduct services, short of mass, to visit the island shortly. You will stay for their arrival as their first task will be the funeral services for Lord Harry and Martin Moore."

"No, I will leave in a day or two."

Two days later Luke, Mark and Jane had a farewell supper.

Jane commented, "Gentlemen, your mission to Nith certainly had its ups and downs, but I imagine the King will be mightily pleased. You legitimized the smuggling ring which will bring some income for his

Majesty and persuaded the family to sell back the lands of exiled Royalists at cost price, which will enable His Majesty to please many more of his loyal subjects."

"Felix prevented us saving him from a murderous female by dying before the date he created to enhance his predictive reputation, and I can find no evidence to prove that Michael's death was anything but accidental," concluded Luke.

"You did solve the murders of Ann Bentley, Richard Banks, and William Perry, and the manslaughter of Tobias," continued the buoyant Jane.

"Some of it was circumstantial, only confirmed by two confessions— Sam Kitchen confessed to the murder of Ann, and apparently told his son that he had shot at Richard Banks thinking it was Martin Moore.

Jerome confessed to the murder of William Perry and we all witnessed his revenge on Martin and Harry."

"And I can fill in a missing piece of the jigsaw. Martin confessed just before he left for his own death, that he had fired the shot at the vessel bringing you to the island—and that his target was Tobias. He believed that Tobias was becoming simpler by the hour, and he wanted to relieve his niece of this lifetime burden that she had endured from her youth," added Jane.

"And what are you about to do, Luke?" she continued.

"I will not stay for the funerals. I received a letter from my wife a week ago and her time is fast approaching. The *Deadly Arrow* will take me to Whitby tomorrow, and I should be home in time for the birth of my first child."

A tear rang down Jane's face. "I will miss you Luke. In different circumstances we could have become very close." She leaned across the table and squeezed his hand.

The following day Luke was landed at Whitby. Mark stayed on Nith with six men to wind up the operation. The *Deadly Arrow* left Whitby with the majority of Luke's troops who would disembark at Hull, and then march on to their garrison in York. The frigate continued south to rejoin its squadron based at Harwich, ready to join the fleet escorting the King from the Netherlands.

Luke immediately headed off across the moors. He was anxious to rejoin his wife, Matilda—but he would not forget Jane.